"WE HAVE UNFINISHED BUSINESS, YOU AND I.

"You remember what we were doing when we were interrupted," James continued.

Honoria paled, but her voice was steady and sarcastic when she said, "I have a vague recollection of some minor activity we were engaged in."

James twined his fingers with hers beneath the dinner table; her hand was icy cold. "In the garden," he whispered seductively. "Remember? The birds sang."

"The birds were caged."

"The fountain played."

"The base was cracked. It leaked," she sniffed.

"There were jasmine and roses."

She gave the slightest of haughty nods. "I do recall studying the garden in some detail."

"You were flat on your back on a bed of flowers." James ran his thumb slowly across the back of her hand. "We will finish what we started."

Other **AVON ROMANCES**

THE ABDUCTION OF JULIA *by Karen Hawkins*
BRIT'S LADY *by Kit Dee*
DONOVAN'S BED *by Debra Mullins*
THE MACKENZIES: JOSH *by Ana Leigh*
THE RENEGADES: NICK *by Genell Dellin*
A ROGUE'S EMBRACE *by Margaret Moore*
WITH THIS RING: REFORMING A RAKE *by Suzanne Enoch*

Coming Soon

THE DEFIANT ONE *by Danelle Harmon*
MY LADY'S GUARDIAN *by Gayle Callen*

And Don't Miss These
ROMANTIC TREASURES
from Avon Books

THE DANGEROUS LORD *by Sabrina Jeffries*
THE MAIDEN BRIDE *by Linda Needham*
A TASTE OF SIN *by Connie Mason*

SUSAN SIZEMORE

On A Long Ago Night

AVON BOOKS
An Imprint of HarperCollins*Publishers*

This is a work of fiction. Names, characters, places, and incidents are products of the author's imagination or are used fictitiously and are not to be construed as real. Any resemblance to actual events, locales, organizations, or persons, living or dead, is entirely coincidental.

AVON BOOKS, INC.
An Imprint of HarperCollins*Publishers*
10 East 53rd Street
New York, New York 10022-5299

Inside cover author photo by Glamour Shots
Library of Congress Catalog Card Number: 99-96453
ISBN: 0-380-80419-0
www.avonromance.com

First Avon Books paperback printing: May 2000

Printed in the U. S. A.

WCD 10 9 8 7 6 5 4 3 2 1

For my sister, Mary Buso.
Take care of yourself.
Love, Susan G.

Chapter 1

London, 1838

"I should *not* put up with this, Father. Not for a moment."

"Honoria."

She balled her fists at her side. "I am going to stamp my foot now. I tell you, since you cannot see it for the width of my skirts."

The Duke of Pyneham smiled.

He was an indulgent father. She was a loving daughter. Their disagreements were few, and her tendency since the death of her mother had shattered him eight years ago had been to give in to whatever he wished of her. There had been entire weeks back then when he'd stayed in his room with the curtains shut. She'd nursed him and coddled him and whispered and tiptoed and done whatever else she could to bring him out of his grief. Gradually, he'd returned to the world.

Honoria realized that what had been necessary for his well-being back then had now become habit for both of them. Still, she hadn't expected this when he'd asked for a private word with her in the library of their London townhouse—though she supposed she should have. Eight years in the country among her books and correspondence must have dulled her wits.

She looked into his smiling face and added, "You are trying to manipulate me."

He crossed his arms. "I've been manipulating you from the first. Of course I was planning your marriage when I asked you to come to London to act as my hostess for the Coronation season, instead of your cousin Kate. I'm surprised you've just now realized it, a clever lass like you."

"I am no lass. More of a Scottish milkmaid tricked out in a silly dress." She glanced down at her gown, a frothy creation of palest foam green and creamy lace, and grimaced. Why she had allowed her dressmaker to talk her into such an unbecoming gown, she had no idea. A moment of feminine weakness, perhaps? Here she was, a strapping, freckle-faced redhead wearing spectacles and standing nearly six foot tall, tricked out in an outfit far more suitable for a delicate young miss's come out. She'd come out, and gone back in, quite some time ago. What she wore might be all the rage, but it was most definitely not her. "Mutton dressed as spring lamb," she scoffed. "I'm twenty-six years old."

"All the more reason for you to do as I bid. Every eligible man in Britain is waiting in the ballroom upstairs for you. And you look lovely."

"As cows go."

"You're beautiful, my dear."

"You are looking through the eyes of love, sir." She laughed bitterly. "And all those eligible men will tell me I'm beautiful because they're looking through the eyes of greed."

She was the rarest of rarities, a woman who was heiress to a ducal title and fortune in her own right. She'd have ignored them tonight as she always did, but her father had just informed her that she must choose a husband. They'd been arguing about it for nearly half an hour now, late for their own ball.

"I trust you to know the men who are fools and liars and cheats from the one who will truly mean it."

"I didn't before," she reminded him.

"You were young. You are not so young now," he went on relentlessly. "And I want grandchildren."

She simply was not ready to deal with this subject—would never be able to deal with it.

She had left her heart somewhere in North Africa—well, it had been broken, anyway—and her freedom was all she had left. Now her father was demanding she give that up.

She had been betrothed once and betrayed twice. She wanted no man in her life. No husband. Children would have been a blessing, but she was willing to settle for supporting large numbers of orphans rather than enduring the physical act required for begetting progeny. It was not that she loathed the idea of a man in her bed. Her problem was exactly the opposite, in fact. Passion was her downfall, one she would not allow in her life ever again.

"If you wish to dandle something on your knee, I don't see why I have to be involved in the process." Honoria took a deep breath. "You are not so old, sir. Any woman in Britain would be lucky to have you as a husband."

She had expected the hurt look that came into his eyes. She had not expected his fist to come down forcefully on the polished alabaster top of the table next to him. She took an involuntary step back.

Her father's face, as red as a beet for a moment, returned to normal and he crossed his arms. "I will not wed again, my dear. You know that very well," he said reasonably. "There are many reasons I want grandchildren, but among the most important is that I want something of your mother to survive. You are so like her, in looks and in temperament." He put his hands on her shoulders. "I want you to have children and grandchildren of your own. You are my and your mother's legacy."

Honoria's throat tightened with emotion.

"Therefore," he added sternly, "you will wed. Soon, my dearest Lady Alexandra Margaret Frances Honoria Pyne. I command it."

And he had the right to command her, as head of the family. He very rarely did. He was a man who asked nicely, or suggested, or merely hinted—and not very often, or for very much. She was used to doing pretty much as she pleased most of the time, and liked it that way. But it was his right to command her obedience, as his daughter and his heir. She could see the stubbornness in his eyes and in the set of his jaw. She'd often seen similar stubbornness looking back at her out of a mirror, and knew how hard it was to get around a Pyne who'd made up his mind.

"I vowed never to marry after Derrick broke off our engagement," she told him. "Perhaps I have never mentioned that to you before, but I did make the vow."

"You were young and heartsore. Your heart has had time to mend. It is time for you to go back out into the world." He smiled fondly, though he looked no less adamant. "Go out and conquer it."

"Ah," she said. "You want me to heave some

likely lad over my shoulder and haul him home for stud service, is that it?"

"No. I want some likely lad to be strong enough to conquer you." He waved a hand in the general direction of the world beyond the library. "Unfortunately, we have to start the search among the peers of the realm. It's not milquetoast you need, my girl, but a real man. We'll start with every eligible bachelor of noble birth in Britain, and move on from there if we have to. I'd as soon see you married to an innkeeper, if the man made you happy."

"We?" She canted an eyebrow at him. "I want no part of this manhunt."

"The hunt is on, whether you like it or not." He offered her his arm. "And now it's time to meet our guests."

Blast! Well, there was really no use in prolonging the argument. All she had to do was go off and be her usual prickly self, and the suitors would scurry off to find more accommodating game. She smiled just a little at that thought. Then she plucked off her spectacles, which she never wore in public, and gave her father her arm.

"Lead on, sir," she told him. "And we'll let all those would-be St. Georges have a turn at the dragon."

"It's about time your father asked me to take you in hand," Cousin Kate whispered, none too quietly, as she stood beside Honoria in the receiving line by the doorway. Most of the guests had finally arrived, and the duke was now making his effusive way around the knots of gathered people. Honoria lingered by the entrance, in the formal role she preferred. She could speak a polite word or merely nod and send people on their way as propriety demanded. Here she was in control while behaving in a manner that was utterly correct for her position in society.

"I have plans, indeed I do," Kate added. "There hasn't been a wedding in the family in too long a time."

Lady Kate Kilgrew was a widow in her fifties, a second cousin of the duke's on his mother's side. The late General Kilgrew had served honorably under Wellington, and rumor had it that Lady Kate had as well. She never denied having been anyone's mistress, though she never claimed to have been, either. She said that gave her an air of mystery, though in these sadly moralistic times it was better to come down on the side of discretion, if a choice had to be made. She was as fond of society as Honoria was of privacy, and quite the most opinionated person Honoria had ever met, save herself, of course. Lady Kate was a short thing, as round and pink as a ripe peach.

"I've married off four children of my own," Lady Kate reminded Honoria, tapping her on the arm with her folded fan when Honoria persisted in ignoring her. "So it isn't as if I'm not experienced in these matters. You look ridiculous in pastels, by the way," she added.

"I know," Honoria agreed. She knew Kate had been expecting an argument and was pleased to have confounded her. "I've already ordered gowns more to my taste, so you needn't bother foisting your dressmaker on me." She plucked at the satin bell of her skirt. "This was an experiment."

"A failed one," Cousin Kate added. "You used to have a sense of style. It was society's loss when you ran off to hide in the country."

"Yes," Honoria drawled cynically. "Society lost a scandal to gossip about."

"Derrick Russell was a fool to throw you over, after what you'd been through. You should have defended yourself, you know."

"Father needed me more." Besides, no one really knew what she'd been through. She had needed to escape, as much as her father had needed her to care for him. "I don't intend to discuss the past," she added with steel in her voice, "and I do not wish to hear Captain Russell's name mentioned ever again."

Lady Kate drew herself up indignantly, but the nearby footman stepped forward before she could speak. He took a folded parchment invitation from the hand of a guest who had just entered, and Honoria gratefully turned her attention back to her duties as hostess. She had not expected to have so many old wounds opened this evening, nor had she expected the pain to still be so fresh and sharp after so many years. She was happy for any diversion.

"The Viscount of Brislay and the Honorable James Marbury," the footman announced.

Honoria turned her weak-eyed scrutiny on the newcomers.

Though the men who came toward her were both tall, one was slender, while the other's broad shoulders were set off to perfection by an expertly tailored black frock coat. Even with all the stirred-up pain coursing through Honoria, the larger man riveted her attention instantly. Something in the graceful way he moved and the confident tilt of his head sent a strange sensation through her. His hair was dark brown and wavy and his complexion sun-kissed, glowing bronze beneath the blaze of candles in the chandeliers. He had heavy arched brows, a wide, full-lipped mouth, and a strong, stubborn jaw.

She could make out no more details without her spectacles, yet she could imagine his eyes. She had had a necklace of amber once. She remembered the clear, golden glow of the beads as she held the strand up in the intense Mediterranean light, how warm they'd felt as they'd played through her fingers, how beautiful and sparkling. His eyes should be like that: captured sunlight.

"Brislay brought his bastard, I see," Lady Kate whispered, using her fan to cover her words.

Honoria turned a swift, shocked look on her cousin. "A bastard? At my father's ball?"

"And a fine bull of a lad he's turned out to be. My son tells me he's taken the sporting clubs by storm with his boxing and riding and fencing skills. That crowd's taken him up as the latest fashion, but the viscount was wise to introduce the boy to society here. Wise, if not discreet," she added, as she seemed to notice finally that Honoria was appalled.

Honoria's thoughts tumbled in shocked outrage. A bastard! It was not proper. She would not have it—not in her father's house! She didn't care how close her father and the Viscount of Brislay were, nor did she care if Brislay chose to be kind to his byblows. Admirable behavior had nothing to do with correct behavior. Queen Victoria was very different in the matter of morals and propriety than the unscrupulous, lackadaisical uncles who had held the throne before her. If word got back to her and her high stickler of a companion, Baroness Lehzen, that Lady Alexandra Pyneham had allowed herself to be introduced to someone's illegitimate son, the duke's standing at court and in the political arena would be damaged. And Honoria took the idea of reform very seriously. She could not walk into the House of Lords, but her father could. So as usual, she must take it upon herself to protect him.

For decorum's sake, she could hold her tongue and offer her hand. For propriety and politics' sake, there was but one thing she could do. People would gossip either way, but disapproval would fall on the unfortunate young man who should not be here, rather than on the good name of the Duke of Pyneham.

Honoria turned her back before the men reached her. Head held high, spine as stiff as a board, she walked away from them. If Lady Katherine greeted the viscount and his bastard, that was fine. If her father should choose to speak to the men when they approached him, that was his choice; it would not be the same as actually being formally received. Upholding the family's position, Honoria fled at a dignified pace toward the back of the room. Stares and whispers followed her, as she knew they would. But she did not look back—not even when she heard *his* voice.

Because, of course, it could not be *him* at all.

"Was it something I said?"

James Marbury was well aware of just having been insulted, but for his father's sake, he lightened the moment with a joke.

"Hardly, James." His father put a long-fingered aristocratic hand on his arm. His right arm, James noticed; his sword arm. Edward Marbury, Viscount of Brislay, looked beyond the little woman who had put herself between them and the tall, proud creature everyone was watching walk away. "I believe the lady of the house must suddenly be indisposed."

That was clearly nonsense, but James nodded his agreement. The Cut Direct had just been issued to him by the hostess of the ball. He almost laughed, as he was used to a direct cut hurting a great deal more than his pride. "It is not so serious, sir," he said with quiet reassurance, "if there is no blood involved." He received an understanding smile in response. It was good to see how the deep lines around his father's mouth and eyes lightened when he showed pleasure.

Though James was furious with the woman who had dared insult his father, he had learned long ago when not to let his true feelings show. The scars on his back twinged a little beneath the fine linen and wool clothing, reminding him of the days when keeping his feelings masked was necessary to staying alive. *I might have liked her,* he thought. Now she was his enemy. He wondered if he should show her how dangerous it was to be his enemy. He did not recall her face, for he had been caught by the sight of her flame-red hair. He had a weakness for red-haired women.

It was that weakness that drew him on, as much as his temper, more than any need for revenge. He kissed the hand of a handsome older woman who looked him over boldly and told him to call her Lady Kate. Then he excused himself. He knew it was not wise, but could not help but follow the very tall red-haired woman.

James stalked her as carefully as a hunting cat through the crowded rooms. Heads turned to follow his progress. Many had seen the duke's daughter's behavior, and word of it spread in a wave to those who had not. Yet he ignored everything but his chosen prey. He spotted her standing amidst a group of hired musicians, staring at a huge portrait of a horse. The musicians watched her warily as they attempted to set up their instruments. She was in their way, he thought, and too arrogant and thoughtless to care. James approached with caution, and a smile that spoke clearly to anyone who cared to note it that he was intent on conquest. The whispers about propriety would change to speculations of seduction soon enough. He had nothing to lose, but the haughty, disdainful woman would have to live with what she had started.

What the devil is the matter with me? What have I done to that poor young man? Honoria thought, as she discovered she'd come to a halt in front of the place where the musicians were setting up to play for the ball. She returned to her senses with an abrupt rush of mortification. She'd let fear of scandal cause her to act like a fool. She stared at the painting of her grandfather's favorite hunting horse as her thoughts whirled. Such unkindness was not usually part of her normal behavior. She'd been cruel to a man who'd had the misfortune of being born out of wedlock—hardly something a Pyne should take offense at.

She would have liked to blame her unconscionable behavior on her father for his scheming, or Lady Kate for her bluntness. She did think that if Lady Kate hadn't mentioned the man, that with one exception, Honoria loathed above all others, she might have handled meeting the Honorable James Marbury with her usual aplomb.

For the footman had announced Marbury by a title that would belong to the Viscount of Brislay's heir. She couldn't recall ever hearing that her father's friend was married, but he would not be likely to name a bastard his heir. Lady Kate's gossip must be wrong. She should not have paid attention to her cousin's tattling.

"Oh, no." She sighed. "My behavior was not only utterly reprehensible; it was totally groundless," she whispered to her grandfather's horse. "And where did this peculiar inclination to talk to paintings come from?"

Aware of a violinist eyeing her nervously, she stepped back—into a solid, living wall. Before she could whirl around, a voice whispered in her ear, "Perhaps you're afraid to speak to a real, living man."

Honoria lifted her head defiantly. "I'm not afraid of you," she announced to the man who wasn't there as his finger slowly traced down the side of her throat. Her pulse raced in the wake of that invisible touch.

"Perhaps you'll learn to be." His other hand touched her waist. She was drawn subtly, slowly, ever closer against him.

She was trembling and her knees had gone weak, but she attributed this reaction to the fact that she had gone completely mad. She refused to faint when a large, warm hand came to rest on her shoulder, but it was a near thing. The room whirled around her, her already faded view of her surroundings worsened as darkness threatened on the edge of her vision. A sound like the buzzing of angry bees filled her ears.

His hands were not touching her, of course—nor did she really feel the warm, solid body she knew too well for her own good pressed against her back. This was some sort of fever dream, a hallucination. Perhaps she was sick in bed, fighting for her life with a high fever, her presence at the ball just a nightmare brought on by illness. She longed for that to be true.

But then—she *was* mad . . . or she wouldn't be hearing his voice. She had never, in all these years, imagined hearing his voice. She'd remembered it, of course—every deceptive or cruel word. But never before had he come into her dreams and said something new. He had always stayed safely in her past. Well, not safely. Nothing about him was safe—not even the memories.

"Turn around and look at me."

She shook her head, which did nothing to help the dizziness. "Go away. I don't want you here. Leave me alone, you bastard."

"My parents are married, *señorita duquesa.*"

Of course. They'd had this conversation before.

"My parents were married," he insisted. "So you should not call me that." He paced back and forth, his large presence filling the small but opulent bedroom. He wore a heavy brocade robe of scarlet and black with nothing on beneath it. It was loosely tied, so it showed off his broad chest and the occasional flash of strong, sturdy thigh as he moved. She curled her bare legs beneath her on the end of the bed and watched as he restlessly crossed from one side of the Oriental rug to the other. A flame flickered behind the colored glass shade of the lamp on the table beside her, throwing rainbows among the shadows on the wall, and on her naked skin. The breeze that came in through the latticed window brought the scents of jasmine from the garden and of the sea beyond the walls of the city. "Mamacita has a ring with a jewel in it," he went on. "A ruby. She wears it around

her neck because it was not safe to wear jewels where we lived. I pray she still has it," he added.

"I was referring to your character, not your birthright," she said now, as she had said then—and turned around to face the thing she feared. "Hello, Diego," she said, and slapped the Honorable James Marbury in the face with all the strength that was in her.

She did not wait for his or anyone else's reaction. She picked up her heavy skirts and ran toward a side door and out of the room.

Chapter 2

"Get out."

The gaggle of females gathered around a cozy fire in her suite's sitting room turned toward her as one. Honoria couldn't make out their faces, between weak eyes and a flood of tears, but their united gasp was loud on the air. She pointed at an exit. Her maid, her maid's assistant, her secretary, her hairdresser, and her mistress of the wardrobe were wise enough to scatter, at least after Huseby rounded them up with a look. Huseby had survived twenty years of being Honoria's personal servant by knowing when to fight and when to flee Honoria's temper.

Once they were gone, Honoria barricaded every entrance to her apartments with the heaviest furniture she could manage to drag in front of the doors. If she'd had a weapon available, she would have taken it in hand.

Her father soon stormed along to demand an explanation, but the most he could do was bang on the hall door while Honoria buried her head under a pillow and ignored the racket. His rage soon turned to worried parental imploring about her well-being. Eventually he called out that they'd speak in the morning, and went away.

After her fit of hysterics had passed, Honoria felt weary but much calmer. She had to have been mistaken about his being Diego, of course. And now the gossip would already be flying, when all she'd wanted was to avoid any breath of scandal.

She supposed the one good that would come of it was that now no one would think to offer for her hand in marriage. She even managed to smile a little at the thought. Father would be disappointed and hurt, but the damage was done. She couldn't go back and undo it; she could only wait for morning before offering him her apologies and begging to be allowed to return to the country.

Once the emotional storm was past, she wished she could fall into a dead sleep, not to wake for at least twenty years. But sleep, like every other form of peace, eluded her. So she rose from her ornate gilded bed and proceeded literally to rip off the green pastel satin gown she'd looked ridiculous in.

"It's not as if I could ever do anything right,"

she muttered, once she was standing in a puddle of seafoam-colored rags. She did not find reminders of the sea pleasant, so she kicked the remains of the dress aside and went to work on unlacing and tugging off her corset and chemise. Then she wearily dragged herself off to discover where her nightgowns were kept.

The problem with being pampered and provided for by an army of servants, Honoria concluded, after a search of the dressing room finally yielded up a drawer full of embroidered linen nightgowns, was that she really had far less control over her life than she thought. If there was one thing she hated, it was lack of control. If she wanted a cup of tea, for example, she had but to order it and it would be brought in a china cup on a silver tray. But how to make tea, or what merchant provided it, or even where the kitchen of this house was located, she hadn't a clue.

"Now, I ask you," she murmured, as she walked back into the bedroom, "what kind of control is that?"

For all her wealth she had no independence, no true freedom. Her servants had more dominion over her life, at least here in London, than she did. Her life was as narrow and proscribed as that of any harem woman locked away in the bagnios of the east . . . not that she knew all that much about the indolent, luxurious life of a harem girl. Oh, no, not Honoria Pyne.

I do, however, know how to brew a fine cup of Turkish coffee. It was one of several lessons she'd learned in how to please a man, she recalled bitterly, as she claimed her spectacles from the damascene coffer on her writing table. Once she had them perched on her nose she could see clearly again, though her jaded view of the world remained as dark as ever. Honoria absently ran her fingers over the top of the desk while her thoughts drifted in odd unconnected circles.

Coffee making was one of her few domestic accomplishments, she thought, remembering the dark color of the beans, the deep aroma of the steaming brew, the thick, grainy taste of the sweetened liquid on her tongue. Not that she had done it in years, for questions would be asked as to how she'd come to have the skill. She had not tasted Turkish coffee, either, for fear the very taste would set off all the wildness that would destroy her. She drank tea; led a quiet, controlled, proper life; and kept all her secret desires to herself.

Honoria did not embroider through her quiet days at the family's country estate; neither did she garden. Nor did she practice music or drawing. Ladylike pursuits had always eluded her interest, though she'd been provided with the finest teachers in the world. Books were the only true love in her life, a skill in reading languages her only natural talent. Other than a sizable inheritance, she'd never possessed any of the artifices or skills likely to attract the attentions of a suitor.

Yet she'd believed in the devoted love of one man, once. Oh, yes, she had . . .

Honoria tried to divert her thoughts from going down yet another rocky, thorny road. It didn't help that when she grasped the stack of correspondence off the desk to divert her thoughts that the envelope on top was written in a familiar hand. It held the signature of Captain Derrick Russell.

She flung the letters from her and grasped her hands nervously before her.

"Oh, God, Derrick!"

Her fiancé patted her shoulder and said in a distracted way, "There, there. Buck up." His steely glance turned out to sea as the shore of Majorca receded in the distance.

Honoria wiped a tear away and held down the black skirts of her dress against the assault of the wind. News of her mother's death had come with the docking of one of her father's merchant ships, the Manticore, *and they were now on board the same ship, returning to England as swiftly as possible.*

"It's wonderful of you to leave your own ship to travel with me," she told the Navy captain who now stood with her on the deck of the merchant ship. He

looked restless, and she didn't blame him. His own vessel had taken damage in a fight with a band of ragtag Barbary pirates and put in to Majorca for repairs. She knew he was anxious to return to fighting in the joint effort with the French navy to finally rid the Mediterranean of the outlaws who had plagued these waters for centuries. Derrick had earned the title of Scourge of Algiers from his enemies. She was so proud of him.

Honoria watched him with open admiration from beneath the wide rim of her black bonnet, her eyes shining as much with devotion for him as with tears at her loss. She could only pray that her mother would understand the mix of grief and love that filled her right now. She had accepted Derrick's proposal only two days before. Her joy had seemed so complete, before the Manticore *had arrived with the awful news of her mother's untimely death.*

Before she had left England, Derrick had asked her to marry him in a letter posted from Naples, and had asked her to meet him. Father had told her that since her happiness meant everything to him, he would give his consent to the match. So she'd left to visit relations on Majorca, in the hope that she would be able to spend time with the Naval hero when his ship put into port on the Mediterranean island. Her mother had already been ill, and Honoria wished now that she'd stayed home to help nurse her. Regrets gnawed at her, but Derrick's presence was a steadfast comfort. She knew her father would be pleased that Derrick was accompanying her back to

England, even if her servants and the ship's crew might not be considered appropriate chaperones by the highest of sticklers. What did it matter? They were to be married, after all.

Father had spoken of reservations about the young man's suit, and had said that his permission for the match with a mere Naval captain was given reluctantly. But Honoria knew the duke's hesitation had nothing to do with any fault her father found in Derrick Russell. Derrick was perfect. He was solicitous, kind, brave, chivalrous, and thoughtful. He loved her for herself, and not the estate to which she was heir. Honoria knew that the Duke of Pyneham was merely concerned that his heir make the best match possible for the continuation of the family name and fortune. Derrick's father was but a baronet, and Derrick was not even the baronet's eldest son. His prospects were tied to his Naval career—not that Honoria cared a fig about that. It was Derrick she adored, since the moment their gazes met at her very first ball. In his dashing uniform he had glittered like a bright jewel among a flock of crows. His gold head stood out in the crowd, as did the healthy glow of skin kissed by the wind and sun of the Mediterranean. She did not feel so overgrown next to the tall, slender man. She'd danced her first waltz with Derrick, and prayed that she would dance her last one with him, as well. She prayed she would be as good a wife to him as her mother had been to her father.

"I so want to make you a good wife," she told him

now. "To be with you wherever in the world you happen to sail."

Derrick patted her hand and graced her with his wise smile. "Darling, where I'll need you to be is safe and sound at home. I need you there protecting my interests—our interests, my darling." He touched her uptilted nose.

She found it hard to see his dear face through her tears. Derrick had taken off her spectacles when they came aboard the Manticore, *reminding her that wearing them in public was unladylike and unbecoming. His advice was always for the best. She vowed to follow it always. "We will make a wonderful team, Derrick. I know it."*

"Indeed, my dear little wife-to-be. Where I lead, you will follow, and all will be well."

Honoria now put her hand on her stomach as a wave of nausea shuddered through her. "Fool." The word was a low, dangerous snarl, though she wasn't sure who her fury was aimed at. What a sick, naïve, besotted thing she had been. "And Derrick wasn't even the worst of it."

How dared they reappear—both of them in one night! Why the devil didn't her ghosts have the decency to stay in their much-deserved crypts? If she could live in limbo, why couldn't they? *How dared they?*

She shook her head and looked about her, trying to bring herself back to this room, to this time, and to push the past back into the dark abyss where it belonged. She found that she was seated behind the desk. While memory had played its evil trick on her, her hands had broken the seal on the letter. She'd crushed the dried wax, and it had mixed with damp sweat of fevered memory so that her fingers were stained red with it. The pristine linen of her nightgown was also marked with the color, red on white. Like blood on a bandage.

She held her hands up before her. She knew she was staring at sealing wax—tinted and scented beeswax, and no more. But she saw the blood, and the scent in her nostrils was of gunpowder.

"I'm shot!"

Though Derrick's lips were close to her ear, she barely heard his words over the pounding bellow of cannon fire. Not that she needed words to know the truth; she held him in her arms and his blood was on her hands. All around, people screamed and shouted and ran. Swords clashed and guns roared. Clouds of stinking gunsmoke hung in the air, choking her, further dimming Honoria's frail vision. It was all so confusing, so frightening. Three pirate galleys had come up on the Manticore *with surprising speed. Though the* Manticore *was equipped with modern cannon, it was no war ship. Its crew was outnumbered by the sailors who manned the banks of oars on the corsair galleys. Barbary pirates normally preferred to just threaten European merchant ships and collect bribes for safe passage through Mediterranean waters, but these outlaws had attacked without warning instead.*

"Desperate men," she'd heard Derrick say to the captain as the attack began. "Looking for booty and slaves. Taking what they can while they can."

"Desperate because of your efforts, sir," the master of the Manticore *had replied. "If they know the Scourge of Algiers is aboard, they'll kill you for sure!"*

Derrick laughed recklessly. "Then we'd best see that they don't get the chance to board your ship, sir."

After that the fighting began in earnest. Honoria was sent to hide in her cabin, but after a while she could take it no longer and ventured onto the deck to see if the Algerian scum had been driven off yet. But instead of the victory she expected, the ship was being overrun with boarding parties from the three galleys.

She frantically made her way to Derrick's side, and he took a bullet in the shoulder just as she reached him. He collapsed to the deck in her embrace and Honoria forced her own terror aside as she concentrated on the man she loved.

"I'm shot," he repeated, his tone disbelieving. He grasped her hand so tightly she thought her fingers would break. "Tell them nothing!" he warned. "No matter what they do to you, don't let them know who I am or I will surely die." He gasped in pain,

but went on bravely despite it. His gaze burned fervently into hers. "They know I courted a duke's daughter. Keep my secret, girl. Do you hear me?"

She understood, and her heart sank even further at the knowledge. She nodded. But before she could make her promise to the brave man she loved, a hand grabbed her arm and hauled her roughly to her feet.

"What are you doing on the deck, woman? Do you want to die?"

The voice shouted in Arabic and she answered in kind as she was whirled to face her captor. "What does it matter where I am when you kill me, you filthy animal?"

He wasn't filthy. The big man who held her was dressed in sparkling white. He held a cutlass in one hand, her in the other. His hair was hidden by the folds of a turban, his lower face covered in a neatly trimmed brown beard.

Without her glasses, the world around her was mostly a blur, but her captor's face was crystal clear to her in all the chaos. Cannon roared and guns continued to fire, men shouted and swore and screamed, but around Honoria the world went suddenly silent. Energy prickled along her skin, arced like lightning between her and the pirate. He smiled, bright teeth flashing in a wide, sensuous mouth. It was not a kind smile, yet it sent a shiver of response through her. His eyes were vivid and beautiful, the color of amber and warm honey, the lashes long and thick. And they were full of wild fury. They told her that reviling him was a deep, dark mistake on her part.

When he threw back his head and laughed, she knew that she would pay dearly for the words she had spoken.

"This is intolerable," Honoria announced. "Insufferable." She would not think about any of it, or either of them. She most certainly would not think about *him*. Diego Moresco held no power over her now. So why was it she could close her eyes and still feel his hands on her flesh? Why was it that ashes that should have been long cold still burned deep inside her? "Because you're a fool!" she angrily answered her own questions. And to distract herself from thinking about one of the males she hated, she opened the letter from the other man who had betrayed her.

"It was her?"

It was not right, it was not fair. It could not be. And of course, she had run away. What more proof did he need, James wondered bitterly. "Yes, sir."

"Lady Alexandra? Pyneham's daughter? Impossible."

Diego—James, as he tried to remember to think of himself—dropped his head into his hands. His elbows rested on the polished wood of the writing table in the viscount's study. He had spent many nights in this quiet, book-lined room since journeying to London with his father. It was his favorite place in the townhouse. His father thought it an unpretentious place for a man of his social standing to dwell, but Diego—James—thought the place quite grand, though he'd had larger gardens at the houses he'd called his own. His soul loved gardens, fountains . . . small, private places of beauty surrounded with walls so the outside world could not see—

"La señorita duquesa," he said. He lifted his head and looked toward the study window. The heavy red drapes were drawn, of course, against the mild chill of the English night. He longed to escape into that night. Gas lights and candles and the hearthfire did too good a job of lighting the room. There were places he could go with shadows enough to hide him, and oblivion could be bought for a few hours, places where he could be alone of his own free will instead of abandoned by another's. But the window was too small for James's wide shoulders to fit through, and his father took care to stand before the door. There was no other exit. He could leave if he truly wanted, but then he would have to face his father's disappointment when he finally crawled home hung over and battered from brawling. Because he *would* come back eventually. Having a home and someone who wanted him meant too much to him, despite his lapses. Better not to have lapses at all,

he'd learned. James had found out the hard way in Malaga that he would rather face death, or even *Mamacita's* wrath and heavy hand, than his newfound father's hurt look.

"I want," he said now, "to run away." To abandon her before she abandoned him, perhaps? To end the game before it started? He sighed. He'd made a vow; honor dictated he at least try to fulfill it.

Edward Marbury put his hands behind his back. His voice was calm and uncompromising. "No doubt you do."

"I thought I was prepared." There was a plan in place; he knew his role, knew exactly what to do. His world was in fragile order, but he had believed he was beginning to make some sense of it, to find a path out of the dark toward a high, honorable goal. James shook his head again.

"You're sure it's the same girl?"

His father's suspicions rankled, but he understood them. He looked up to meet the older man's worried gaze. They had the same eyes, he and his father. Cat's eyes, she had called them, and other things after they made love that first time. He could still smell the jasmine on her skin. James sighed, too confused to be angry.

"I was sober, sir," he reminded his father. "Taken by surprise, yes, but I made no mistake." Besides, what other woman in all the world had such height and hair? And he remembered all too well the sweet curves of her body. His mouth almost watered at the memory of that amazing body. Frustrated, he ran his hands through his neatly trimmed hair, then tiredly down the sides of his now beardless face. Oh, he had made mistakes, all right. Many of them. The worst mistake of all, eight years before.

Don't be a fool, *Diego told himself, as he laughed and angrily pulled the tall woman closer. She fitted perfectly against him, hip to hip, with the buxom, lush body of a real woman beneath the concealing layers of heavy clothing. She was dressed all in black, as he was all in white. Her hair was loose about her shoulders, a tangled mass whipped by the wind, blazing in the sunlight. It should have been modestly covered. Her eyes blazed as well. Without a veil to cover her emotions, her face showed the world that she was utterly without fear, full of brave passion. It was obvious that no one had ever commanded this woman, that she didn't think anyone could.*

Ibrahim Rais will call it your mistake if anything happens to a valuable hostage, *he reminded himself, as a bullet slammed into the deck near where they stood.* You'll pay the price if she gets herself killed. *The woman, with her fiery temper and hair to match, provoked him, with her words, with the wild anger she turned on him. It wasn't only his temper she aroused, either. In the midst of a battle when he had far more necessary things to do, he came upon this milk-skinned black-clad bundle of fury, and—*

"You speak Arabic!"

"Get your hands off me, pig."

When he responded to this insult with a few very rude words in Spanish, her cheeks flushed bright red, and she slapped his face. Diego laughed again, though his cheek stung fiercely—but not as fiercely as the joy that flooded him. "A scholar." He pulled her even closer, putting his lips close to her ear. He whispered, "Tell me, fox-hair, can you read?"

She struggled in his embrace. "Let me go! I have to help Der—my fiancé."

"I should have let him die," James murmured. "That was my worst mistake. Pity the wound wasn't deep enough to do the job."

"Your temper, James . . ." His father paused, and then he laughed. "All right, son, I won't try to talk you out of that particular urge for revenge." The viscount crossed to a side table and came back with snifters holding a small amount of brandy for each of them. He handed James one, then took a seat in a nearby chair. "I think we need to revise our strategy, don't you?"

James tasted the powerful spirit, then answered, "None of this makes sense to me, sir."

"Quite understandable. Or rather, quite confusing." The viscount put his untouched glass down on the desk. He looked intensely curious as he leaned forward and said, "I hate to harp on this subject, because I'm sure you trust your perceptions, but how is it that the Lady Alexandra is the woman you're looking for?"

A thought struck James. "How is it that *you* did not know they were the same woman? You told me that you've known the duke since you were boys."

"I have, though we've lost touch occasionally since we were at school. I don't see how my old friend and your Honoria could be connected."

She did not belong to him, but she did not know that. He'd had her brought to his cabin. She didn't know it was the safest place on the corsair galley for her to be. Her eyes were large blue pools in a face that was pale in the lamplight. Freckles stood out starkly against her fine white skin. Diego fought the urge to trace the line of them across her nose and cheeks. Her full mouth was drawn into a hard, brave line. He wondered if he could tease a smile from those lips somehow. But he stuck to business, standing tall and menacing before her. He wore fresh white robes and had bathed after the battle, while the proud girl wore the chains of a captive.

He took a step closer to her. "What's your name, fox-hair?"

"But you *know* the girl," James insisted. He half-suspected that he was the victim of a cruel joke. The suspicion caused him a twinge of guilt, but learning to trust a man who claimed to have his best interests at heart was something that came hard to him.

"I truly had no suspicion your mysterious merchant's daughter and the duke could be related. Pyneham's quite proud of his girl, but that's what he calls her: 'my girl,' or 'my daughter.' The last time I saw her was at her christening. Oddly enough, I can recall the church and the service quite well." He closed his eyes briefly and ticked the names off on his fingers as he spoke them. "Alexandra Margaret Frances . . . Honoria . . ." His eyes opened. "Ah. I remember now." The viscount raised a hand to his forehead. "I know the duke of Pyneham's titles, and the nicknames we gave him at school. But I haven't heard the family name in years, and as I said, I thought your Honoria was a merchant's daughter."

A sense of darkness threatened to overwhelm James. At the same time his temper stirred, telling him that this woman had made a fool of him—not just this evening, but for years. He stood slowly, and carefully set the brandy snifter down rather than hurl it angrily into the fireplace. He didn't show his building fury, but spoke with all the careful neutrality covering his emotions he'd learned from years serving Ibrahim Rais. "My quest is over, at least."

"On the contrary, I would say that it has barely begun," his father responded.

James made a small negating gesture. "I found her. She clearly wants nothing to do with me. She has the power and freedom to do whatever she wishes, and she will not wish to be with me."

The viscount rose to face him. "Can you let that matter, James? You are on a quest, a mission. Nothing has changed."

"Everything has changed." James just managed not to howl the words in anguish. He cursed himself, and her, and the letter that had brought them together in the first place.

His English father steadfastly refused to acknowledge either his defeat, or any sense of drama. "Nonsense." He put a restrained hand on James's arm. "You came to England to marry Honoria Pyne, and that is exactly what you are going to do."

Chapter 3

"Read this!" Honoria's voice was shrill above the gentle sound of morning rain pattering against the library windows.

The duke came around from behind his desk to meet her. His face was gray with strain and he did not look as if he had slept any better than she had. "Honoria, about last night. I am most disturbed—"

Honoria waved the letter in front of her father's face, too perturbed to have her usual care for his feelings. "The devil with last night, sir. Read this."

"Your correspondence does not concern me, young lady. It is your reprehensible behavior that does." He drew himself up to his full height and declared, "You are spoiled and willful and—"

* * *

"Spoiled and willful you may be," the Spanish corsair told her. "But you belong to the Bey of Algiers now."

"Do I indeed?" The words were meant to be spoken with arrogant defiance, but somehow they seemed to come out closer to a sultry purr as she looked up at his blurred form through lowered lids. She did not understand why she spoke as she did, or why she shivered instead of bristled when a wide flash of smile briefly crossed the Spaniard's bearded face. She had no idea why he'd had her brought to his quarters, away from Derrick's side in the hold of the galley. She was determined to defy him no matter what he wanted from her. She stood up straight and glared. "I belong to no one, Spaniard."

She didn't know why she assumed he was Spanish, other than that it was the language in which he had addressed her. The aged Oxford scholar who had taught her Hebrew, Turkish, and Arabic in the staid surroundings of a country house library had seemed more of an Ottoman to her than the man who now held her captive. Except for his Arabic robes, the scimitar in his sash, and his command of one of the corsair galleys, she did not find him exotic. She did find him dangerous.

He put his strong, broad-palmed seaman's hands on her shoulders.

She didn't flinch, but her legs grew shaky, a shudder passed through her, and a wild, heart-quickening heat spread through her. She could tell that he registered her reaction by the way his honey gold eyes lit with amusement. Despite humiliation she refused to drop her gaze from his. "You seem to be touching me, again, pig," she told him.

"Indeed, I am," he replied. "It is most pleasant. However . . ." He took a step back and turned to a nearby table. When he turned back he held something in his hands.

She gasped and stepped back fearfully as he approached. She didn't have time to turn her head when he lifted his hands, but she closed her eyes. "Don't—!"

"Better?" he asked, and stepped back again.

She blinked, recognizing the familiar weight resting on her cheeks and her ears. When she opened her eyes she could see her adversary clearly.

"They were found when your cabin was searched," he told her.

"Oh." She blinked again as the details that had been a blur before came into vivid clarity. Good gracious, but the smirking fiend was handsome! She lifted her head to as haughty an angle as she could manage, but still couldn't stop herself from saying, "Thank you." She added, "Captain," for courtesy and formality's sake.

He nodded at her acknowledging his authority at least in this small way. "I would be tempted to bite, too, if I were half-blind. Now, let us begin where we left off on your ship, before I was called away to finish the battle. Tell me your name, fox-hair. Where will we be sending the ransom request? For your sake I hope your father is a wealthy merchant."

If he meant to frighten her, he certainly succeeded. His chilling words also reminded her of the danger her beloved was in if these Barbary animals learned who he truly was. That her father could indeed pay a king's ransom—or at least a duke's—for her return would do nothing to help Derrick. The corsairs had spies in the ports of the Mediterranean; it would be known that the Scourge of Algiers was betrothed to the daughter of the Duke of Pyneham. If she admitted her identity, they would know who Derrick was. He would be tortured and killed. She could not think of her own comfort and safety, when the man she loved was in such grave danger.

So she answered the corsair's question with the truth, but not a truth that would save her. She did it for Derrick.

"I should have let them execute him," she muttered now, as she held the letter out toward her father. How could anyone be so young and romantically foolish as she'd been in those days? "Will you please stop pacing and talk to me, Father?" she asked. "This is important."

He pointed an accusing finger at her. "If I am agitated, whose fault is that?"

"Mine," she answered promptly. She shook the paper at him. "Will you please read this?"

"I didn't send for you to read any excuses you might have jotted down, mistress scholar. The viscount and I have been friends for years. I cannot believe that you would insult him and his son in such a cruel fashion. You, Honoria. You of all people, who know what it is like to be whispered about and falsely accused. After the debacle with Captain Russell—"

"That's what I'm talking about," Honoria persisted. She waved the much-wrinkled paper before him again. "Derrick." She nearly choked from making herself speak the name, that was how much it still hurt. "Captain Russell." The formality came easier—of course. Formality and propriety were the only armor she had. She wrapped herself in her defense now and went on with precise clarity. "Captain Russell wrote me this letter, Your Grace."

Her father finally snatched the letter from her. Honoria stepped back and breathed a sigh of relief as he quickly read the paper. Everything would be all right now. Her papa would deal with everything. She could go back to the country and forget all about—

The Duke of Pyneham lifted his head and gazed on her with a bright, benign smile. "This is wonderful news, my dear!"

Honoria sat down. That there was no chair nearby had no effect on her action. She could not stand, therefore she sat, landing with a hard thud on the Turkey carpet before the desk. She could not draw breath and lights danced before her eyes. "Wha-wha-wha . . . ?"

Her father helped her up and to a seat near the hearth. "Good gracious, child," he asked worriedly. "What's gotten into you in the last twenty-four hours?"

She did not know what had gotten into her, either. She was behaving most uncharacteristically. She had shown her emotions in public, put on a display of temper, and cried and raged and shouted. And for what? A pair of worthless men. It had to stop, and it would. Right now.

Honoria put her hand over her heart and drew in a deep breath. She would be calm. She would not allow the man—any man—to rob her of her self-control! No, and no, not ever again. She was poised, self-possessed, cool, and impervious, above such petty, foolish things as emotions. Upset? Her? Never.

"I think, sir," she told him, "that I should ring for tea." But when she rose from her chair, it was not to summon the butler as she'd intended. She walked first to the desk, then to the hearth, where she tossed the letter onto the fire.

Honoria gave a small shake of her head. "Oh, dear," she murmured very softly. "Another dramatic gesture." She blushed hotly at the memory of slapping poor Mr. Marbury, and told herself the warmth that burned through her was from being so close to the fire. She did not want to think about Mr. Marbury. Not about what they had done last night; certainly not about what they had done—

"That was another man, another place." She took another one of those deep, calming breaths, which did not help steady her racing pulse at all. She tried to make herself believe that Marbury and Moresco were not one and the same, because it was illogical to believe otherwise. Logic dictated that she deny the sensory information of her response to his voice, his size, his eyes, his bold touch. There was an obvious superficial resemblance between two men of mixed Spanish and English heritage, and no more. Some odd flight of her imagination had supplied other resemblances that did not exist in reality. "Imagination is so inconvenient."

"What did you say, my dear?" Her father sounded calm, rational. Good.

"Tea," she said, and turned from the fire. This time she was able to accomplish the sensible, undramatic task she set for herself. Once the butler left to fetch refreshments she took her seat once more, folded her hands primly in her lap, and looked calmly at her father. "Surely I was mistaken in what I thought Your Grace said about Captain Russell. It seemed to me that you were happy to learn that I had received a communication from someone you once referred to as the 'scum of the earth' and 'that base, vile maggot.' " Honoria took a certain amount of pleasure in speaking the insults, though they were mild compared to her thoughts on Derrick Russell's antecedents, habits, and place in the order of creation.

"My opinion of the man is colored by your

feelings toward him, my dear," he responded with equal calm. He leaned forward in his chair, gazing on her with earnest, loving concern. "I know what the man meant to you once. What you sacrificed—"

"Do you?" she interrupted. "I sincerely doubt that, Father." *I pray you do not, Father,* she whispered to herself.

She clasped Derrick's hand tightly as she knelt beside him. His flesh was hot with fever. He did not appear to be awake, but he turned his head toward her and called out, "Honoria!"

She was thankful that he called her by her pet name. She had never much liked Alexandra as a first name. Honoria was for intimate friends and family; it was the name he called her when they were in private long enough for him to steal a quick kiss. Strangely, a thought of what it would be like if the Spaniard were to kiss her flitted through her mind. Repulsive, no doubt. Never mind that he was attractive; there was nothing civilized about his features. His was the beauty of a wild, dangerous animal. Still, her lips tingled as she pushed away unwanted speculation.

She put her lips close to Derrick's ear and whispered, "Your name is Derrick Lacey. Do you understand?" Lacey House was the name of the Pyneham family seat, and the best alias she could come up with on short notice. She prayed that he understood through the pain and the fever. She glanced up and met the worried gaze of her maid, who knelt on Derrick's other side. She'd left Huseby to tend to her beloved when she'd been taken to the captain's quarters.

"That took a while," Huseby observed. She looked Honoria over suspiciously. "What did the corsair want with you, my lady? Did he do anything—"

She cut Huseby off with a gesture. "No titles! You serve Honoria Pyne and her betrothed, Mr. Lacey," Honoria whispered. As for Huseby's questions . . . well, she had no intention of answering them. Simply having been alone with the Spaniard sullied her reputation, never mind that he had put his hands on her. Or that she had found his touch curiously . . . energizing.

"But, my la—"

"Miss Pyne. Please, *Huseby." Huseby was seven years older than Honoria, one of many children of a family that had always served the Pyneham line. Honoria often thought of Maggie Huseby as an older sister. Huseby was intelligent, incisive, and very intuitive. Honoria trusted and loved her, but now she exerted her will on the reluctant maid. "The disguise is necessary. For Der—Mr. Lacey's sake."*

Huseby's rebellious look turned thoughtful as she looked down at Derrick. Slowly her expression soured as she recognized that their chance of being easily ransomed was being compromised. She did not argue, but sighed reluctantly. "I serve you . . . Miss Pyne."

Honoria reached across Derrick's poor prone body

and squeezed Huseby's hand. "Thank you, Maggie. Nothing ill will come of this. I promise you." She turned her attention to Derrick, and wiped beads of sweat off his brow. His eyes were closed, his breathing light and rapid. "You will recover, my love. Nothing will happen to you. Could you fetch more water for him, Huseby?"

Honoria shifted to put Derrick's head in her lap as Huseby moved away, muttering. Honoria glanced furtively around the hold once she was settled. While she was heartsore at what had befallen the crew and passengers of the ship, for Derrick's safety she was glad that the captives had been divided up by the pirates. She did not think anyone else aboard the Spaniard's galley knew their true identities. Derrick had not worn his uniform aboard the Manticore. *The common sailors were still aboard the* Manticore, *which was being sailed to Algiers by a pirate crew. The officers and passengers were being held as prizes to be ransomed by the various corsair captains. The* Manticore's *captain had been killed in the battle. She and Derrick, Maggie Huseby, and a few others had been brought to this ship by the Spaniard.*

There was very little light in the space where the prisoners were being kept, and there were few amenities. The manacles she'd worn earlier had been removed when she was brought back to the hold. Derrick had at least been provided with a pallet. They were in the shadows enough to hide the impropriety of the intimate way she held her beloved's head in her lap. No one saw her run her fingers lovingly through his silken hair as she gazed into the distance. After a while she scarcely noticed where she was or what she did. Honoria's senses read back to her every look, gesture and word that had passed between herself and the Spaniard during this long, hard day.

The man was so, so—

Honoria gave a start when the sick man suddenly rasped out, "What did you say to him? Did he ask about me?"

It took her a moment to catch her breath. Huseby came back before she could speak, so Honoria took another moment to resume a more appropriate position and to get her thoughts in order.

Derrick's intense gaze burned into her when she looked at him again. He raised himself with great difficulty to a half-sitting position. It hurt her to see the effort it took such a strong man to move. She cursed the Spaniard for causing this good, fine man such pain. His voice was a barely audible anguished rasp. "What did you tell him?" Honoria quickly whispered back the names she had given, and Derrick nodded in satisfaction. "What a good girl you are. What a clever child." He settled back down on the pallet. "He likes you, the infidel swine. I could see it when they boarded the ship and he grabbed you. That's good."

Is it? she wondered. Why?

"Promise me," he whispered. "That you'll please

him. Do whatever you must for my sake. Promise me, as you love me."

She had promised as her maid came back with the water. Huseby had gasped, then taken her aside and explained exactly what she had vowed. Honoria had neither understood nor believed her, though it had been the first time she'd heard Derrick Russell referred to in any but the most glowing, heroic terms. The earthy Huseby had done a great deal to increase Honoria's already considerable vocabulary that night, but Honoria didn't actually learn anything from what her friend had to say. All the bitter, painful knowledge of passion and betrayal was something that came later, and Diego Moresco had done the teaching.

The butler brought in a heavy tray and discreet silence reigned while they were served. Honoria took a cup of tea and sipped it decorously. She chewed and swallowed a bite of spicy cake. She was neither hungry nor thirsty, but these were ordinary, proper actions, so she dutifully did them, though she tasted nothing. It was the action that mattered.

After the servant withdrew, Honoria's father said, "You have pined for Derrick Russell for the last seven years."

Honoria had scraped together enough control not to drop the cup in shock. She placed it on the table beside her and clasped her hands tightly in her lap. She said, calmly and clearly, "I do not pine, Your Grace. For anyone."

"You try not to show it, but my dear, I am far from blind. Do you think I don't know why you've hidden yourself away in the country? Why you fret at the notion of marrying? You loved and lost."

"True," she agreed reluctantly, though Derrick didn't have anything to do with all that. Her father knew nothing about her relations with Diego.

"Derrick Russell meant the world to you once."

"Once," she acknowledged with the slightest of nods. "Briefly, and to my cost. I am long over that infatuation."

"I think not." Her father was intent on not listening to her. It seemed she had inherited her overactive imagination from him. He made an expansive gesture, and continued his scenario. "You loved him the way I loved your mother, and have waited for him to realize that you are indeed the woman for him. And now he wishes to reconcile. Your patience and fidelity have been rewarded. I call that delightful news."

"I call that a load of sentimental hogwash."

He merely smiled benignly, obviously not believing her protestations. It was his urge to make her happy that blinded him, she supposed.

Honoria allowed her gaze to drift to the rain-pattered windows and the soaked garden beyond, while her thoughts ranged in a hundred different places, each of them leading to a dead end. What to say? What to do? She was trapped in a maze: trapped by her father's love and the demands of society, trapped by the past, most of all. It was best to deal with the present.

"Am I to understand that your sudden fondness for Derrick Russell has something to do with your desire for grandchildren, sir?"

"Yes, my dear, it does. It has even more to do with wanting you to be happy. If Derrick Russell is what you need, well, then, I'll welcome him with open arms."

Honoria rose. "But I will not."

"There's no need to be stubborn about it, child." Her father got to his feet as well. "If it were up to me, I'd have the man tossed out on his ear if he dared to approach my door, but for your sake I'll welcome him to my home."

"Toss away, sir. I'm all for it."

He frowned mightily, and went on. "I'm going to invite Russell to the dinner we're hosting on Friday. You may pretend you don't want him for the sake of your pride, but once you see him again, you'll rush into his arms and all will be well."

Despite everything, Honoria couldn't suppress an ironic smile. "Or you'll know the reason why?"

He smiled back. "Exactly."

Derrick. At her dinner table. She glanced around the packed library shelves. Surely there were some books on poisoning somewhere in the room. It was a pleasant thought. Perhaps she'd find out where the kitchen was located, after all.

She put aside this fantasy and spoke to her father. "I have an apology to write to Viscount Brislay and Mr. Marbury, sir. So, if you will excuse me—"

"Marbury!" Her father's annoyance returned. "That's what I called you here to discuss. I demand you apologize, Honoria!"

"Yes, Father," she responded. She didn't remind him that she had already mentioned apologizing. "You are absolutely right. I behaved abominably. Completely uncalled for."

"You'll apologize in person to Mr. Marbury."

"But—"

"He's a fine young man. In fact, if Derrick Russell wasn't back in the picture, I could see you making a match with my old friend's newfound son."

"But—"

"In person, Honoria. In public. At dinner this Friday."

"But—"

"You humiliated the lad in public; making it up the same way is only fair."

Honoria gulped, and accepted her medicine. "Fine. Of course. As you wish, Father." She told herself it didn't matter as she walked to the library door. Surely dealing with Marbury was a minor irritation compared with facing Derrick Russell after all these years. Never mind that James Marbury strongly resembled the unlaid ghost of Diego Moresco. Confronting Derrick would certainly be easier than meeting Diego Moresco in the flesh once again.

Fortunately, that wasn't likely to happen in this life. *"I'll see you in hell, sweatheart," he'd said, just before he'd drawn her into one last rough and desperate kiss.*

"So you will," she murmured now, and touched her aching lips. "But in what circle, I wonder?"

Chapter 4

A few hours of deep, dreamless sleep helped. The strong, sweet coffee his servant Malik brought him as soon as he woke helped even more. A hot bath, a shave, and fresh clothes all proved refreshing. James was almost ready to face another round of life as a peer of the realm when he came downstairs to join his father in the dining room. The meal laid out on the sideboard for them was dinner, not breakfast, but James didn't mind that he'd slept all day. He doubted he'd missed anything more important than a visit to his tailor, or a boxing match or fencing match at his sporting club. While he knew such functions were necessary for appearance's sake, the whole process of being part of respectable society was deadly dull. He could remember too well when he'd possessed no more than the clothes on his back, and when that back and all the rest of him had been owned by another man. He hadn't used a sword or his fists as a form of exercise, either, but to defend his life.

But he'd fought his way up in the world, making something of himself, using his brains and cunning as much as his fighting skills.

"You look as if your thoughts are a million miles away, James."

His father's voice brought James's attention back to the dining room. He had to pass his hand in front of his face as though lifting a veil before he actually saw the dark shining wood of the furniture, the gleam of silver serving dishes, the yellow and blue pattern of the dishes, the cream and burgundy striped wallpaper, the botanical paintings in their heavy gilded frames, and the slender man sitting at the head of the table, watching him with quiet patience.

He realized that he had paused inside the doorway, and moved to the sideboard to pick up a plate. "Not a million miles, sir," he said. "Only a few hundred." The rich aroma of roast pork in wine sauce assailed him, but he passed over the heaping platter to take a serving of whole grilled fish. "But in a completely different world," he admitted. There was a certain familiarity in the spicy scent of a dish of poached pears. The rich scents of nutmeg and cinnamon and cumin spoke to him of the bazaars of Algiers. He heaped on a double helping of the warm fruit.

His father sighed as James brought his plate and took a seat across from him. "It's a hard world to escape, isn't it?"

James ate in thoughtful silence for a while, finished off a fresh cup of coffee, then finally replied, "Escape was all I could think of for eight years."

This time it would work—he knew it. It had to, because time was running out. He could almost hear his fate racing close behind him. It carried a sword, or a gun, or a hangman's rope. That was how the French and English punished pirates, wasn't it? By hanging them? He almost asked the Englishwoman he'd had brought to his quarters for a second meeting. Almost, but he was so used to keeping discreetly silent that the impulse was caught in time. That he had an impulse to talk to a woman at all amazed and confused him. Diego told himself that all his impulses concerning her were because she was so important to his plans. He needed to know about her; that was why he had her brought to him again.

He should have settled matters when he'd talked to her the day before, but something had held him back then. He'd gotten her name from her, but had given her no explanation of what she must do to save herself. She was too wildly concerned about the wounded man to respond rationally. Diego had seen the Englishman's shoulder wound and thought it no grave matter, but had not offered her any reassurance. In fact, he'd been annoyed that the man she kept referring to as "Dear Derrick" was all that occupied her mind when he'd wanted her full attention. He'd sent her away after brief questioning.

Today he had sent for her again. He'd spent the night thinking about her, and not just because she was crucial to his plan. Some madness from his old life must have invaded his thoughts, now that he'd formed an escape plan, some fever of the mind that whispered that he could have what he wanted. That was the only explanation he could think of for the compelling attraction he felt toward the tall, red-maned Englishwoman who'd haunted him in his empty bed. She was not the sort of woman he was used to at all, with her proud carriage and bold eyes behind the horn-rimmed lenses of her spectacles. It was a pity that her pride would be broken before all this was over.

You have no time for pity, fool, *he reminded himself.*

"Welcome," he greeted her, and waved her to a seat with the same courtesy he would show a guest in his home. She stood just within the doorway after the guard thrust her inside Diego's cabin and lifted her hands, the silent gesture graceful and eloquent. "My apologies," he told her in Arabic, "but you must wear restraints whenever you are not locked in your quarters."

Her head tilted sideways and she raised an eyebrow, small, economical gestures that spoke volumes to Diego. "Why?" she answered him, in Arabic.

The chains were not necessary, except as a tool of humiliation. It was a way to break the pride and will of wealthy captives. Instilling fear was important in those who were used to power and freedom. Fear was very effective in coercing the largest possible ransom to be delivered in the shortest possible time. If fear and humiliation proved ineffective, there were other ways.

"It is as Ibrahim Rais wishes." He spoke in Turkish this time. He was not proficient in the language of the Ottomans, but could manage that much.

"I do not think I like your Ibrahim Rais," she responded, in far better Turkish than Diego's.

Her facility with languages had him practically dancing with delight, but he showed nothing. He switched back to Spanish. After all these years among the Barbary corsairs it was still the tongue he was most comfortable with, the one he thought and dreamed in. The one he prayed in, and now those prayers were close to being answered. If he moved with caution.

"Believe me, lady," he informed her, "when I tell you that you will know worse punishment than being chained if you cross Ibrahim Rais. Those who cross my master suffer for their mistakes." He laughed, a soft, dangerous sound. "If you cross me I will make the punishment very personal. Am I understood?"

It was the standard speech given to get prisoners to cooperate. It was also the truth. He should have gained satisfaction when the girl's already pale complexion blanched a dead white with fear and she swayed forward in reaction. Instead he rushed to her side, lifted her off her feet before she could fall, and set her down gently in his own deep-cushioned seat.

"I'm not afraid for myself." She seemed to be reassuring herself as she whispered the words in her native language. He gave no clue that he understood English. Instead, he poured her a cup of water in a blue porcelain cup, held it to her lips, and made her drink it down, knowing how refreshing it would be after the brackish ration Ibrahim Rais allowed to be doled out to prisoners.

He touched her moistened lips once he'd put the cup down, and found that he was kneeling in front of her. He touched her cheek with the back of his hand, then pushed a fall of bright hair from her face. Her skin was so soft, as were the silky curls that clung to his fingers. She took no notice of these liberties but stared past his shoulder, perhaps at the illusion of freedom offered by the blue sky and sunlit sea framed by the cabin's small window. His impulse was to kiss her, to taste her lips to see if that would get her attention.

He smiled. Oh, yes, if he touched her in the ways he knew how to pleasure a woman, she would certainly be aware of him. She might even forget the fear she told herself was for another. He could make her feel for herself. He could make her forget her beloved Derrick, and he would take great pleasure in it.

He took her face gently between his hands. His thumbs slowly stroked a long, sensuous line down her throat. He felt her shiver, and waited until her gaze shifted to his face and her lips parted before he leaned forward.

Only to drop his hands to his sides as he shot abruptly to his feet. "What I want from you is not mine to take." He turned his back on her as he spoke. The words came out a low, rasped whisper that he prayed she didn't hear. The need he felt for this woman was strong and basic, a sudden storm that threatened to overwhelm his careful planning. Diego scrubbed his hands over his face, fought to banish the fire from his blood, and made himself think of Malaga, of the woman he hoped waited there, and what he must do to get safely home to her. Duty came first, not desire.

He stared out the window, at the sea and the sky, and shared the Englishwoman's yearning for freedom, multiplied by eight. "It has been so many years." He heard the faint jingle of chains and the rustle of fine fabric as she stood. He turned back to her. "Too many years." Her cheeks flamed a bright pink; she would never be able to hide her emotions with such tender, fair skin. Her bright eyes were full of many conflicting feelings, and Diego could read them all. "You'll find veils useful," he told her and stepped behind the cabin's scarred writing table. "Come here, Honoria Pyne."

She stood tensely in the center of the cabin for a few moments, swaying easily with the movement of the ship. The galley cut swiftly through the calm southern Mediterranean, the rowers obeying the steady drumbeat that set the time of their strokes. To Diego the drum was as familiar as his heartbeat. He perceived it now only because he noticed the subtle way her body moved to the primitive rhythm. It was not the sound that quickened his pulse, but the sensual sway of the woman's beautifully rounded hips and breasts.

He couldn't help but wonder what it would be like to see her dance.

"Why are you smiling like that, James?"

James looked at his father's puzzled face, then tilted back his head and laughed. "Some things," he said, "a man cannot discuss with his father."

"Things of a delicate nature, I presume?" James expected his father to look disapproving, but instead saw fond amusement in his pale blue eyes. "It's a blessing that you're still attracted to the young lady." He tilted his head to one side. "You were thinking of Lady Alexandra, I trust?"

The question struck James like a blow. His first thought was, *Who?* He stared at the fish on his plate, which stared blankly back, because he could not face his father's discerning gaze as he replied, "Of course."

Lady Alexandra. Who the devil *was* Lady Alexandra? Haughty, he recalled, stiff as a board, and proud beyond bearing. There had been no life in her cold eyes, nothing but disdain in her demeanor. She was a duke's daughter, too good for the likes of him, and she knew it. She was also Honoria Pyne. The two were one and the same, and nothing alike. A rush of pain and anger went through him with the knowledge that his Honoria had lied to him. Every word she spoke, every deed, every look and touch, all the passion, from the moment they met, had been a lie.

His. Oh, yes. She had been his, in every way a woman could belong to a man. His lips lifted in a grim smile as he remembered how alike he and the duke's daughter were on some basic, primeval level. It wasn't just in how their bodies fitted so perfectly together; there was a matching of souls between the duchess and the pirate. After all, everything he had done was a lie, as well.

"You should save your smiles for the lady herself," Edward Marbury said, and tossed a pile of envelopes across the table. James looked up questioningly as the fine, heavy stack of paper landed beside his plate.

"What's this?" He rifled through the pile.

"Invitations, of course," Edward Marbury answered. "And a few letters."

Letters. James fought the surges of both bitterness and irony. Everything between them had begun because of a letter.

* * *

"What is this?" Honoria asked, as the pirate thrust several pieces of paper across the table at her.

A bright smile flashed across his bearded face. "We should have done this yesterday. How is your sick friend?"

"My betrothed," she corrected swiftly. It shamed her to admit that she reminded herself of the sacred relationship she shared with Derrick as much as she did the corsair whose touch . . . "Derrick and I will wed," she reminded the Spaniard.

"If you make it home."

His tone was a dangerous, frightening purr. Honoria swallowed her fear. "If?" she asked coolly. "It is my understanding that there is an unofficial agreement about the return of captives between His Majesty's government and the Bey of Algiers."

"Understanding?" He laughed softly. "Sweetheart, you understand nothing."

She understood that he was large and dangerous and frightening. She understood that she was in chains, that the man she was to marry and her best friend were locked in the hold of a corsair galley. She understood that she was powerless, and that her captor was looking at her in a bold way that she could only define as covetous. It sent unnatural heat through her that shook her resolve even more than the fear.

That disturbing glitter in his expressive, honey-colored eyes changed to hard determination when he said, "You will do as I say."

She eyed the blank pages, and noticed the inkwell

and quill pen, and the man's bright eyes. "What do you want from me?"

"You can write, can't you? And read?"

She bridled at the hint of suspicion in the Spaniard's tone. Lifting her chin proudly, she replied with a tart, "Of course. In several languages."

"He *laughed*," she said. "The—bastard—laughed." How well she remembered his laugh—lusty, boisterous, *alive.* And so full of triumph, brimming and bubbling with wild glee when he laughed at her that afternoon in his cabin. "The faithless, lying, scheming—!"

"Who, my lady?"

Huseby's voice brought Honoria back to the present, where she sat at the writing desk in her suite with a great stack of correspondence laid out before her. She blinked, adjusted the spectacles on her nose, and frowned up at her maid. "Have I been talking to myself very much, Maggie?"

At the use of her first name, the neutral expression on Huseby's face softened considerably, becoming more friend than servant. They were alone in the room as afternoon wore into evening. Honoria vaguely recalled sending her secretary off to her favorite bookseller with a long list some time ago. She'd gone through tiring hours of fittings with her dressmaker in the morning. The woman and her assistants were still pouting because of losing the battle over their employer's own taste versus the *artiste*'s longing to try her hand at all the latest styles. She was more comfortable setting fashion than trying to be fashionable, and was not going to pretend to try to fit in again. People her size didn't fit in, they stood out, and might as well enjoy the unavoidable.

A housemaid had left a pot of tea and a plate of sandwiches on a corner of the desk a while ago. The tea was cooling, and Honoria had no appetite. Another maid had made up the fire against the evening chill and drawn heavy velvet curtains, muffling the sound of rain pattering against the window glass. The room was full of shadows despite the gas lights glowing in wall sconces. The brightest spot in the room was around her desk, where a tall branch of fragrant beeswax candles behind her head added both light and warmth to the area. A footman had delivered yet another stack of correspondence a half hour or so ago, but there was a lull in the household traffic for the moment.

"Alone at last," Honoria said. She took the opportunity to stretch her arms tiredly over her head and out to her sides. She finally brought her hands to rest, folded demurely, on top of a letter she'd been reading over and over while her thoughts ranged wildly into her misspent, misguided past.

Maggie Huseby moved a pile of fabric

swatches Cousin Kate had left and sat down in the chair nearest Honoria's desk. "You've been talking to yourself quite a bit since yesterday, my lady," Huseby answered Honoria's question. "It's a habit I'd thought you'd outgrown."

"So had I," Honoria confessed. She sighed. There she was, feeling sorry for herself—another bad habit she'd tried to eschew. She eyed the fabric swatches that Huseby had put on the desk. The colors and materials were rich: velvets and brocades in emerald green, royal blue, peacock, cream, champagne, old gold, turquoise, silver gray, and midnight.

"You've gotten us quite worried, those of us who're up from Lacey House," Huseby went on. "We're used to you sometimes going for days without speaking a word. Do you recall those two new chambermaids at Lacey House who thought you were mute?"

Honoria smiled slightly, recalling the incident a few months before. "I didn't mean to frighten those poor girls, but I was rather annoyed when they accidentally set fire to the bedroom. I didn't yell at them until I'd gotten them to safety, though."

"That's true, my lady. But they swore it was a miracle that restored your voice."

"The miracle was that I didn't sack them."

"You shouted at them like a fishwife."

"I have never met a fishwife, but I will take

your word for it. Of course I shouted. They very nearly burned down my home."

Huseby smiled. "Wouldn't want that to happen, my lady. We Husebys and Pynes have lived there nearly two hundred years. Fine old families—and their retainers—need their places."

"I want to go home." Honoria sighed. "I am so heartsick, Maggie. Homesick!" she hastened to correct herself. She had surged to her feet, and now sat back down, her bottom hitting the chair with a firmness that was almost painful. This caused her to twitch in a most indecorous fashion. She swore.

Huseby watched her calmly through all this. "Homesick," she said with an understanding nod. "Yes. Of course."

Honoria was annoyed at the woman's mild tone, but then, everything had annoyed her since she'd come up to London. She sat back in her chair and folded her hands on the desktop once more. She sounded as calm as usual when she said, "Everything is simpler at home."

She kept busy at home. She kept to herself. She occupied her mind with books. She had enough physical exercise so that she got a good, honest night's sleep when she took to her bed from sheer exhaustion. Her days were orderly, her pursuits intellectual; she occupied time with good works and charity rather than frivolous social engagements. She rarely even thought of

Derrick Russell. If Moresco's dark presence was harder to banish from her soul, at least she didn't go about mistaking every devilishly handsome, tall, broad-shouldered man with wavy brown hair and amber eyes she encountered for a Spanish corsair who'd no doubt been hanged eight years ago.

Hanged. Without realizing it, a hand went to Honoria's throat. A fist squeezed her heart, and she couldn't breathe for a moment.

"Simpler." Huseby nodded. "Your life is simpler when you've got everything under your control, you mean."

Honoria took a deep breath. She didn't *know* he'd been hanged. He was clever enough to have escaped. "Precisely. Which is just as it should be." She managed to smile despite the fact that she really wanted to cry. She hated that tears had been threatening for hours and hours. Come to think of it, how often, even in London society, did she encounter devilishly handsome, tall, broad-shouldered men with wavy brown hair, eyes like warm honey, and . . . *his* voice?

"James Marbury," she said, surprising herself. "What do you know about him?"

Servants knew everything. Huseby didn't try to deny it. "The butler says he heard that . . ."

Chapter 5

Overhead the sun blazed down out of a perfect sky. The whitewashed walls of the Casbah rose above the sparkling bay, gleaming like a pearl against the forested mountains behind the ancient town of Al-Jaz'ir. Diego moved from the deck of the moored galley onto the gangplank, dressed in fresh white robes and a twisted scarlet and black turban. His clothes proclaimed him to be a renegade westerner, a corsair under the patronage of the Bey of the city and the Sultan of the Ottoman Empire. He glanced up to read the time in the way the shadow of a minaret slashed across the blue tiled dome of a nearby mosque. Al-Jaz'ir—or Algiers in his native Western tongue—did not feel like home to him, and never had, but for once he was happy to have made it back to the corsairs' last safe haven. Their small fleet had had to dodge French war ships, and Diego guessed they were massing to mount an attack on the ancient stronghold within the next few weeks.

They all knew it wouldn't be a safe haven much longer. That world was ending, but in the meantime, it was still a noisy, busy place, full of merchants and commerce. Pack donkeys jockeyed for position with porters, stevedores, sailors, and slaves on the crowded stone jetties. The wharves smelled of rotting fish and a dozen kinds of dung. Or perhaps, Diego thought, the choking scent that clogged his nostrils came from the man who approached him through the bustling, jostling crowd.

"My son!" Ibrahim Rais called, as he strode toward the gangplank. The corsair leader was accompanied by bodyguards, servants, and the captain of the third vessel left in what had once been a mighty pirate fleet, but the tall old man was obviously the commander of all he surveyed. At the moment Diego was the focus of his intense interest, and Diego had long ago learned to look the old bastard in the eye and pretend respect and affection.

"Admiral!" Diego called out, and hurried to reach Ibrahim Rais's side. He was careful to bow elegantly when he did so. Many beatings in his youth had taught him excellent manners.

Ibrahim Rais held his arms out wide as Diego straightened. The old man's full white beard gleamed in the mid-morning sunlight; his red, purple, and yellow striped robes stood out even in the hubbub of the busy port. Ibraham Rais was never one who would be ignored, no matter how noisy or crowded a place he might be in. His garish wardrobe and the sharp scimitar and pistols in his sash assured that he caught the eye. To be called a cutthroat's cutthroat was a high compliment to the ruthless corsair.

"Those captives had better be worth the risk we took," Ibrahim Rais declared, as he motioned for Diego to walk with him. He glanced across the harbor to the stolen merchantman they'd sailed back to Algiers. "That ship alone was probably worth the risk." His eyes narrowed as he returned his attention to Diego. "But what of the survivors you took on board? Are they wealthy enough to buy their way out of the bagnio?" He put a hand on Diego's shoulder when he wasn't answered immediately. "Do we sell them or ransom them, my boy?"

Diego did not glance back at his ship. He could not see the copper-bright head of Honoria Pyne turned away from him in disgust. He could not see her brave demeanor, or the hurt in her eyes. Though she was locked in the ship's hold with her dear Derrick, Diego felt her accusing look cut through him. Or was it a twinge of guilt? He almost smiled bitterly—what pierced him was no mere twinge. But it could not be helped. It truly could not. The very touch of Ibrahim's hand on his shoulder burned Diego like a brand, and he had firsthand knowledge of just what a brand felt like. His hatred for the corsair admiral choked his spirit, and left a taste of bile in his soul. He had risen high in the ranks by using violence when he must, and cunning constantly. Diego knew himself to be a dangerous man; he must be ruthless and heartless, for Ibrahim Rais was just that *much more dangerous than he was.*

He would use Honoria Pyne because he had to. He cared nothing for her. Besides, she cared only for her beloved Derrick.

"You hesitate, lad," Ibrahim cut into his thoughts. The tough old man laughed, revealing a healthy set of sharp teeth. There was a lewd twinkle in his eyes as he went on, "I'm told there was a red-haired woman among the ferengi*. Is she worth more than a ransom to you?"*

Far more than Ibrahim could know. Diego gave a casual shake of his head. He had already considered asking for Honoria Pyne as his share of the booty, and rejected the idea. To show any interest in the fox-haired captive would draw Ibrahim's attention to her. Ibrahim Rais's suspicions were easily aroused, and he had many spies. "No woman is worth more than a ransom, lord."

"Some fetch a good price," Ibraham Rais observed. "Depends on market value, I've found."

"As you say, lord."

"What of the woman you brought aboard?"

"There were two women," Diego was quick to clarify. "And a wounded merchant."

The truth was, Diego possessed letters he had had Honoria write to the British trade representative in the city—letters that would ensure an easy captivity and quick freedom for her and her companions if he were to hand them over to Ibrahim Rais for delivery. He would see that two of those letters were delivered; he could do that much for her. She had not questioned his asking for three separate letters, though she had thought asking for Greek and Latin as well as English was peculiar. He had told her that he was testing her since she was so proud of knowing languages. That, at least, had not been a lie.

"Two of the captives I hold will go to the cells in the Citadel, lord," he told Ibrahim. He handed two folded letters to Ibrahim's clerk. "We will transfer the red-haired woman from my ship to the bagnio cells," he informed another of the servants. "She can at least earn our master a commission on her sale."

"I cannot go in there," James said as he stood before the clean white Georgian face of the Pynehams' townhouse. *I cannot face her. Not after what I did to her.* He looked at his father in utter panic. The cool blue gaze the viscount turned on him was pitiless. "You do not comprehend, sir." The viscount said not a word, but kept a stern, steady gaze on his son. James was well aware of the man's own years' long search. "It does not compare," James told him as a trio of familiar women, dressed as gaily as butterflies, emerged from the next carriage in the line crowding the street before the Pyneham residence.

The women crowded up behind them, leaving James no chance to back away and run for his life. He took a deep breath, reminded himself that he had faced hell itself a few times, and this could hardly be very much worse. Duty and honor required this of him, though the strange woman who awaited him inside would care not a fig for the requirements of his conscience. The girl he had known in Algiers— He sighed. That girl was gone forever. She had been glad to go, though sometimes he pretended otherwise. He had seen her face and form at the ball, and discovered his craving at least was no pretense. But he had seen no sign of his Honoria's personality within the stiff, stern, but altogether glorious shell of the duke's daughter.

Perhaps he could remember the scent of his Honoria's skin with vivid longing, and the feel of her legs wrapped around him when they cradled him inside her, but that was only memory and imagination. The woman he intended to claim was a stranger, and clearly counted herself his enemy. There was battle waiting inside, not reunion.

The relish of the challenge stirred to cunning life. He smiled with wicked anticipation. Honoria, dried up and manhating or not, had the same memories of his bedchamber as he. And he'd had eight years more practice at making love. The woman who'd snubbed him the other night was a bluestocking spinster, but she had wildness running deep inside her that he knew very well.

Rumor and gossip proclaimed the duke's heir to be beyond any interest in men, but she had been his wanton lover once. Was the wildness dead? Had he killed her passion? There were heavy bets laid in the clubs against the duke's heir taking a groom despite the dowry and her father's open attempt to find her a husband. He had heard those rumors without knowing the cruel jests were aimed not at a stranger, but at a woman he'd known with delicious intimacy. There were bets about who would take her and her huge dowry.

James didn't want the dowry. He didn't want to win the wagers. But, he decided as he stood on the steps, he would see that no one else won the bets, either.

Then the women behind them were on the stairs. James found himself suddenly immersed in the scent of perfume and the sound of breathless laughter as his father made a witty comment to Mrs. Ashby and her daughters. In this crowd, James marched forward bravely into the lair of the Pynehams.

There were no odd looks from the Ashby women, no comments on the embarrassing incident in this very house a few nights ago. There was a certain amount of sympathetic cooing and a pat on the arm from Mrs. Ashby, but whatever they thought, nothing was said. Buoyed by their presence, James took a deep breath, filling his lungs with the scent of lavender and ambergris, and stepped into the front hallway of his quarry's home.

His moment of trepidation was over. He was

prepared to hunt. In this mood, it mattered not at all to him that his entrance was greeted with sudden, stark silence.

All eyes were on him, but his gaze flashed instantly to the fox-haired woman in a royal blue gown. Honoria stood tall and proud at the bottom of the stairs, where the rules of etiquette dictated her guests must come to her. She had no expression on her fine-skinned face at all, not even boredom as she spoke to a tall blond man in a Naval uniform. Her indifference sparked James's touchy temper, the temper he no longer had to carefully hide. Honoria Pyne had lied to him, had brought him trouble. He had not profited by their encounter. It would serve her right for him to bring her trouble in repayment. His smile blossomed into a full blown wicked grin at his Lady Fox Hair. The woman had always been infuriating; something definitely needed to be done about it.

His father leaned close and whispered in alarm, "You look like the very devil himself has entered you."

"I am the devil," James whispered back. He pulled away from his father's touch on his arm and walked forward, his gaze riveted on Honoria. "The devil indeed," he murmured. "As you will remember soon enough."

"Hello, Honoria."

"Captain Russell." It was not a greeting, simply an acknowledgment of the existence of the man before her. The descriptive words that came to her lips after she spoke the name, she kept to herself.

Honoria looked the tall man standing before her in the eye without any outward show of emotion. In fact, other than exasperated annoyance, she *had* no emotional response to him. She was quite pleased about that. That his features were fuzzy without the aid of her spectacles did not help at all. He looked older, but no less handsome. Time had refined Derrick Russell, but had not been as unkind to him as she would have hoped. A pity. There was a familiar arrogant boldness about him. His use of her familiar name was galling and presumptuous, but she gave no sign of offense. She let him lift her limp hand to his lips and plant a kiss, and made a mental note to have the glove burned.

Huseby stood discreetly behind her, a few steps up, but would move aside if Honoria chose to cut and run. She straightened her spine even more instead, and lifted her chin even more proudly. *She* wasn't going anywhere but in to dinner on her father's arm after the guests had all been greeted. Despite the escape route behind her she was trapped by the benign gaze of her father beside her, and by the crowd's awareness of her wretched behavior a few nights before.

She would do nothing to cause any further

comment. She carried the blood of a famous actress in her veins, so she could act the perfect hostess and paragon of virtue for a one-night performance, surely? She wanted the reviews to be spectacular, to replace everyone's memory of her last poor performance. Sometimes it seemed that life had become nothing *but* performance, but with nothing else to live for, she was going to do it well. Even though that performance now consisted of facing this man she despised.

She was nearsighted, but not so blind that she couldn't tell that the handsome guest's gaze lingered on her a moment too long before propriety dictated that he move on to pay his respects to the duke. "I hope we can talk later," he said, and took the necessary step away from her. She did not let her gaze follow him as he moved away. She smiled a slight, stiff acknowledgment at the next person who approached, and said something appropriate—though she didn't see them and had no idea what she said. Her thoughts were much too far away for that.

"You can't be separating us!" Derrick protested to the guard. "I can't go to the Citadel. It's a prison. I've heard what happens to foreigners there. Who'll take care of me there? Honoria, help me!"

"No one will harm you," she promised, burying her own fear under a briskly confident façade. Derrick had regaled a drawing room full of fascinated listeners with tales of wicked corsair practices on

their last evening in Majorca, so she knew how prisoners languished in the dungeons and cells of the Citadel while they awaited ransom. Those with no hope of ransom were claimed as property of the Bey—forced into work gangs, or auctioned off for the Bey's profit. Derrick had passed over the details of the dire fates of women prisoners, and Honoria refused to dwell on the things he had only hinted at. Derrick needed her, and that was all that mattered.

"Hush, my dear." She ran a hand through his hair. "All will be well. Let the man help you to stand. I'll help to hold you up."

"He can stand on his own. He is a man, isn't he, fox-hair?"

Honoria had not been aware that the Spaniard had followed his guards into the crowded hold. She gave up trying to cope with the feverish Derrick as he flailed ineffectually at the man who was attempting to help him stand. Indignation boiled out of her at the Spaniard's callous words. She rounded on the true source of their troubles, spinning so quickly that her spectacles were knocked askew.

"Leave him alone!" she demanded of their captor. "Can't you see he's ill?"

The corsair took a moment to straighten her glasses on her nose. "He'll live."

She'd been shocked by the effrontery of the gesture, but more than shock raced through her when he took her arm. Reaction blinded her to everything but his tactile presence; her universe spun around and around, and she and he were the only things in that universe for a moment.

"Honoria!" Derrick called, casting out a lifeline with his voice. "I need you to care for me!"

"But who will care for you, fox-hair?"

She fought to ignore the Spaniard's sarcasm and concentrate on the voice that reminded her of duty, of truth, and of pure unselfish love. She was surprised at how hard it was to drag her attention from the threatening sensuality of Diego Moresco.

"Coming, my love!" she called, but she could not look away from the Spaniard. "Take your hands off me, swine!" The words were spoken with indignation, but no great conviction. Did he hear it? Did he know how her pulse was racing? Was that amusement glittering in his honey-colored eyes, along with a banked fire of temper?

"Hand," he corrected. "And I'm barely touching you."

"But the point is, you are *touching me."*

"Perhaps you should get used to being touched."

Honoria bridled with indignation; it hid a shiver of fearful anticipation. "By you?"

He tilted his head to one side. "By men in general." He gave a slight shrug. "A slave goes with who she is told."

She tore her arm out of his clasp and faced him with her hands on her hips. "What are you talking about?" she demanded angrily. Her knees were shaking and she feared she would sink to the deck in terror, but she did not show it, would not show it.

Not to this creature who was the dregs of the dregs of the Mediterranean. "We are to be ransomed. I wrote the letters you wanted. You'll be paid the price you demanded within a fortnight."

He shrugged again. Suddenly she could read nothing in his face. His eyes became blank, hard amber. He jerked a thumb at Derrick and at Huseby, who had come to stand by Honoria's side. "They go to the Citadel. You are to be sold."

"Help me," Derrick said, lunging away from his guard to clasp Honoria's hands. "Don't let them take me to the Citadel. You promised you would help me."

Honoria looked at her hands. They felt as cold and numb in the stuffy warmth of the hall as they had that horrible moment in Algiers when she'd been informed of her fate by the faithless, lying Spanish renegade.

"What are you thinking, my dear?" her father's genial voice asked, close to her ear, but sounding very far away.

"Just that I really must have these gloves burned, sir," she replied, in a voice that sounded surprisingly normal.

"They don't look soiled to me."

Of course not—nor would he ever see how soiled his only child was. He often told her how much she was like her mother, and a part of him had died with that virtuous, spotless woman. She feared his learning the truth about the wicked things she'd done would kill him in fact as well as in spirit. He told her once that he endured the loss of her mother because she was as much his angel on earth as her mother was now in heaven. Her father was prone to ardent sentimentality on this subject. He spoiled and protected her, and she made it her life's work to do the same for him. She always did whatever was necessary to protect the ones she loved.

This finally brought the thought that should have been in her mind from the moment she first saw Derrick Russell's letter. What the devil was the man doing here? She knew what his letter said, but why had he written her, really? Had she not learned the hard way that no man's word was to be taken at face value?

Frantic worry crawled suddenly along her nerves as she recalled the duke's welcome to Captain Russell when Derrick had turned from greeting her. It had sounded far too pleasant, as though he was welcoming back an old friend. She knew her father was being affable for her sake, because he'd taken it into his head that languishing over Derrick was the reason for her retirement from the world. Those who recalled that she had once been courted by Captain Russell no doubt took note of both her and the Duke's acknowledgment of him. Well, nothing had passed between them that would cause any adverse gossip. That was one hurdle over with; she would deal with Derrick soon enough, and in private. Now all she had to do was correct the faux pas with Marbury. Surely he had arrived by now. Though she did not let herself seek him out among the blurred mass of people, she was somehow aware that he had entered the room. She concentrated on protocol and the performance of her life as she made out the approaching figures of Viscount Brislay and his broad-shouldered, half-Spanish son.

She'd told herself that she was preparing to kill two birds with one stone by facing both men at once when she prepared herself methodically, wholeheartedly, and with a vengeance for the evening. She'd chosen the armor of sophistication, wearing a rich blue satin evening gown that showed a bit of shoulder and had short sleeves and not a speck of lace. The hairdresser had been forbidden from doing Honoria's hair in any à la mode style, but had wrestled her thick natural curls into an upswept hairdo. She had not dressed for fashion, but with style. As she looked in the mirror when the maids and dressers were done with her, she found herself wondering what James Marbury would think of this version of the duke's daughter.

What Derrick Russell thought of her mattered not at all, which was curious, considering what they'd once been to each other. Marbury must be more on her mind because she truly did owe him reparation for insulting him. She owed Derrick nothing. Well, perhaps a bullet or sword thrust in the heart. What a pity women weren't allowed to duel.

She'd been thinking about the Spaniard—no, she would not call him that—for days. Probably to keep her mind off Derrick, because what other reason could there be? Well, there were nerves, and guilt. Blast, how she wanted to get this evening over with! Why didn't the man get over here, make a leg, and let her do a bit of groveling?

As the frustrated thought sprang to mind, the Honorable James Marbury strode forward with a swift, brisk assurance, all grace and fire. Even if she had not caused such a scandal with him a few nights before, Honoria believed all eyes would have turned his way simply because he was in the room. It was not fair that he could look his fill at her while she was limited to shadows and outlines, though Lord knew the man was drawn on a large enough canvas for even her to make out some detail. It was very tempting, however, to lean close when the big man gracefully took both her hands in his—and temptation was something she hadn't felt for a long time.

"Stop that," she said, when his lips brushed across the back of first one hand and then the other. Her words were spoken barely aloud and with little conviction. She added with more aplomb, "Or is that how it is done in Spain?"

"I don't know," he answered, his rich voice a low Arabic purr. "I never kissed a duchess in Spain."

There was something in his tone that said he intended to do more than kiss her gloved hands. The intimation sent a shiver of anticipation through Honoria that she fought down. His assured, arrogant attitude did serve to reassure her that she had not imagined the way he had touched her at the ball, or the sensual way he had whispered in her ear when their bodies were so close together.

He had spoken to her in Arabic.

Marbury stood very close to her once more when he straightened, as if he had a right, or even a need, to be near her. He was so close that she had no trouble making out his boldly drawn features. Not that she needed any assistance in knowing exactly what he looked like. How well she recalled that characteristic tilt of his head, the strong jaw, the heavy arched brows, the wide, full lips and thick, dark lashes surrounding large, honey-amber eyes. She'd hoped—all right, pretended—she had been mistaken at the ball. She had told herself she was deranged, since that made more sense. But here he was, larger than she remembered, more arrogant. Alive. Here.

"Diego."

"Please call me James," he said with rote politeness, as he switched back to lightly accented English. He calmly stepped back to an appropriate distance for a man and woman together in public. If he was aware of the attention swirling around them, he gave no sign. "Though I suppose 'Mr. Marbury' and 'Lady Alexandra' are the proper forms of address for two people who have such a short acquaintance." He smiled as he looked around, showing that he was conscious that they were being watched. Honoria was aware of a flash of bright white teeth. She recalled how devastating that smile could be when set off by a dark beard. "I have had etiquette lessons," he said, playing to that crowd.

She could not see the charming twinkle in his eyes, but she heard it in his voice, felt it in the response from the onlookers. He could make them like him, believe him. Want him. When they laughed, it made her want to scream.

Somehow, she smiled instead. "The deportment lessons seemed to have taken—Mr. Marbury. I'm not sure the same can be said for mine." She was speaking! Actually coherently speaking!

"Untrue, Lady Alexandra." He touched his cheek with the tip of a finger. "The note you sent me was a masterpiece of propriety. And you have such lovely handwriting."

"I don't imagine you had any trouble making it out." Was his smile as frozen as hers? She couldn't tell. "Does your facility for languages extend to being able to read them as well? Arabic? Turkish? Latin and Greek?" *Fool!* she shouted to herself. *This is not the time or place!* But she had to know.

"Alas, no, Lady Alexandra. Until recently I could make out only a bit of Spanish. I was never a very good student, though I am told my comprehension of English is progressing nicely. I haven't had the advantage of your classical education."

"How odd," she said in Arabic, "I thought you took advantage of it quite thoroughly." He could always be lying. He probably *was* lying. It had not clawed at her soul for years, and it didn't matter, anyway.

Diego tilted his head appealingly and shrugged slightly. She wanted to kick him. "You always had me at a disadvantage. Led me around by my—"

"Greed," she interrupted hastily.

He smirked. "You could call it greed." His gaze swept boldly over her. She took an angry step toward him.

"What did you say, my dear?" her father asked, before either she or Diego could do anything. "And what was it you replied, Mr. Marbury? How nice to see that you and my daughter have something in common."

Was that a hint of speculation in her father's voice? Oh, no—was he sizing up another candidate for her marriage bed? She leaned closer to her father as her gaze flew to his face. Yes, there was definitely a hint of benign but crafty conjecture in his features. This did not bode well from a man who wanted grandchildren. She squinted past him, trying to make out if Cousin Kate, standing on the other side of the duke, was looking as smug as Honoria suspected. There was tension in the air, as though everyone in the room was poised for the very dishonorable Honorable James Marbury's response.

"Yes," he answered. "I am sure your daughter and I have much in common, Your Grace." Diego's voice sounded rich as cream, and as smug as that of a cat who'd gotten into that cream. "I look forward to many opportunities to explore our common interests, and to develop new ones with her."

"Well spoken, young man." Her father clapped the scum from Algiers on the shoulder. "I look forward to it as well."

Honoria very nearly choked; her racing heart made an attempt to leap from her chest; but all she could do was curl her hands into tight fists at her side. She caught the flash of smiles on faces she couldn't make out, and there were too many nearby faces. Someone in the crowd giggled. Giggled—how galling! How appalling. Didn't these people have anything better to do than stand about eavesdropping on a private conversation? The level of interest in her encounter with Diego was much higher, more titillated, than when she'd spoken to Derrick.

Huseby had posted herself at the top of the stairs. Now she came to stand like a guard at Honoria's back. "My lady?" she whispered, in a voice full of the naked fury Honoria could not show.

"Thank you, Maggie," she heard herself say in the most ordinary way possible. "You may go now."

To the world she sounded as if she were dismissing her servant; only she and Maggie Huseby knew that she was sending away her only friend and ally. She turned her head to meet Huseby's frantically worried gaze. "Please wait up for me," she added. She gave Huseby the briefest of nods, the lightest brush of her hand on the woman's arm, urging her to go. Derrick was an irritant; Diego was disaster incarnate. But she would face him alone, because, of course, she had no other choice.

She'd been made to wear a voluminous robe over her clothes and a heavy veil that covered her hair and face for the journey through the city. The coarse wool smelled of dust and someone else's sweat, and the veiling had been terribly hot. Underneath the concealing clothing she'd worn chains. The city was noisy, noisome, and strange. She'd been too terrified, too bereft and confused to understand much of what she'd seen. She would have welcomed even the Spaniard's company, but she was not granted even that much mercy. The guard who took her from the ship was an indifferent stranger; the slave dealers he left her with showed only a certain commercial interest in her. A woman examined her intimately and declared her to be a virgin. They looked at her teeth with the same interest. The only response she received when she protested was someone making a note that she spoke their language. Apparently this added to her value as property.

She was shaking and sick when they finally locked her in a small room with stone walls and floor in a place called the Bagnio. It was stiflingly hot inside the narrow room, without even so much as a pallet to lie down on. There was a slop bucket, and she was grateful to have that to throw up in. When she was under control once more she noticed that there was only one small window in her cell, up near the ceiling. It let in little light and little air. She tried jumping to get a view of outside, but the window was too high up.

After a while the silence and the solitude began to prey fiercely on her nerves. She could not remember a time when she had ever been alone. For the first time in her eighteen years, she realized that she had never been alone.

Honoria paced the small cell, solitary but for her thoughts and a smattering of rats. The rats were easier to deal with than her wild imagination, for, bold as they were, she could scare them away. Her thoughts refused to scurry off. She was trapped, lost, alone. No one would ever know what had happened to her. She would never see her parents again.

"Oh, God!" she whimpered, and covered her face with her hands, consumed by grief and guilt. Her mother was dead! Now her poor father had lost her, as well. She could do nothing to help Derrick or Huseby. She could not even help herself.

"Why are you doing this to me?" she raged, her face turned up to the ceiling as she shook her fist. It was not God she railed at, but the Spaniard. She was going to be sold into slavery. She was alone—and no one cared. And the Spaniard was to blame.

Chapter 6

The Spaniard was also seated next to her at the dinner table. For the first time in years she did not feel alone in a crowd, and the sensation was most disturbing. Her father was seated at the head of the long table, she at the seat to his right. Normally she would have taken the hostess's place at the opposite end of the table, but Cousin Kate had agreed to preside tonight. Honoria had wanted to be near her father while sharing a meal with Captain Derrick Russell. The plan had been to demonstrate to the duke that she carried no secret tender feelings for the man she had once been engaged to.

James Marbury had not figured into her plans for the evening—not past a show of reasonable politeness to the man she had offended. Assigning him the place of honor to her right had seemed like a perfectly rational idea when the object of the exercise had been to make up for her rudeness.

So, here she was, surrounded by the last men on earth she wanted to be with, and there was no way to escape them. Ignoring them was her only course. In Derrick's case this was easy enough, as her vision, the width of the table, and a large silver centerpiece effectively kept his golden countenance out of her sight. Derrick was easy to forget about with the Spaniard by her side. The Spaniard—Diego—James—the Honorable Mr. Marbury—was a large, living, potent reality. She knew, to her disgust, that she would be totally aware of James Marbury's vibrant presence if he were seated across the table, across the room, possibly if he were seated in a dining room in an entirely different house. Now that she knew that he was alive and well and—

James watched as Honoria took a deep breath that told him she was forcing her emotions to stay under control. She'd been taking quite a few deep breaths since they had come face to face earlier in the evening. The movement was subtle, but he knew what to look for. Besides, he thoroughly enjoyed watching the swell of her magnificent bosom. The deep blue of her dress accentuated her fine skin and the cut of the gown showed off her womanly curves far better than the dress she'd worn a few nights ago. He took great pleasure in studying those curves. At least she had not slapped him, not yet, nor had she run from him as she had in the ballroom. She was tempted, he could tell, by the faint flush of her cheeks and the heightened color on her throat that brought out the faint line of freckles across her collarbone. She wore them like a necklace, those pretty freckles—much prettier to him than the cold stones of the necklace she wore. One could covet diamonds and sapphires, but a man couldn't kiss them.

Did she remember his kisses? Perhaps the temptation she fought was of a different sort. Perhaps she was fighting against throwing herself into his arms rather than against clawing his eyes out. He smiled at the thought. He was tempted as well, and not to run. His moment of weakness was past. What he wanted now was privacy. Perhaps he should suggest to her that they leave.

Conversation around them was loud. The blond man directly across from Honoria was glaring at them—James recognized the scoundrel but paid him no mind. If the English swine had behaved like something that walked on two legs—not even necessarily a man, but something above serpent in the order of creation—in Algiers . . . well, the Englishman was no man. He should be fed with the curs rather than allowed to sit at a dinner table. James did not know why "Dear Derrick" was a guest, but at least Honoria was ignoring her "Darling Derrick" as conspicuously as she was him. That was good, but not good enough.

James leaned toward Honoria, and watched her stiffen. He could almost hear her heart racing like a frightened rabbit's. Ha! Furious lioness was more like it. Whatever the reason for her reaction, he slipped his large hand reassuringly over hers where it rested in her lap. Beneath the din of conversation, he whispered in Arabic, "We have unfinished business, you and I."

Surprising him, she turned her head in his direction. While she did not look him in the eye, her haughty gaze settled somewhere around his chin. "Business?" she responded in the same language.

He couldn't keep the teasing smile from his lips. He continued the conversation in what amounted to a secret language between them. "You remember what we were doing when we were interrupted."

He expected bright color to rise on her cheeks and throat; she paled instead. She lifted her head sharply, exhibiting the sort of pride meant to quell her inferiors. It made James smile even wider, as the resentful tavern maid's son inside him accepted the aristocrat's dare to challenge her superiority. She had grown cold and hard since they had parted, become a woman of ice and pride. Both could be broken, but was it a shell or who she really was?

Her voice was quite steady and sarcastic when she said, "I have a vague recollection of some minor activity we were engaged in at the time."

He twined his fingers with hers beneath the table. Her hand was icy cold, like the hand of a marble statue. "In the garden," he whispered seductively. "Remember? The birds sang."

"The birds were caged."

"The fountain played."

"The base was cracked. It leaked."

"I sang to you."

"Was that what that caterwauling was?"

"There were jasmine and roses."

She gave the slightest of nods. "I do recall studying the garden in some detail."

"You were flat on your back on a bed of flowers." He ran his thumb slowly across the back of her hand, and received no reaction. So he said, "We will finish what we started."

The gaze she turned up to meet his sparked with hot anger, and equally hot memory. "Why?" she asked, tart and tense. "Haven't you managed to get your member to relax after all these years?"

James threw back his head and laughed, uncaring of the attention it brought from everyone who had been openly and surreptitiously watching them. The man on the other side of the table, who had been making no secret of trying to eavesdrop, leaned even further forward across the table. James noticed the snarl on his pale English face, and seeing that the cuff of Russell's coat rested on a slice of mutton added to his amusement. Having Russell jealous of him for once brought a certain amount of satisfaction. It was almost a pity that Captain Russell did not know who he was. Russell had always been blinded by his vanity and self-involvement, far less aware of the world around him than Honoria on a dark night without her spectacles. How odd that Honoria had been blind to Russell's true nature. Blinded by love. And how odd, James discovered, that it still hurt.

He slanted a warning look at his rival, which Russell didn't even notice. The man's angry gaze centered on Honoria. He looked for all the world as if he blamed her for speaking to another man. That Russell wanted Honoria was blatant, and infuriating, and it added a dangerous edge to James's humor. Were they to make a game of it, he and the English fool? Oh, that's right, he was English, too. He was as much of a fool as Russell: for he intended to win.

Honoria jerked her hand from his clasp, regaining his full attention. Twin spots of bright color burned in her cheeks. He was very tempted to kiss them. Would that serve to unleash the passionate fury she held so tightly under control? Even the blush faded quickly, leaving her expression as bland as before. Her eyes still sparkled with memory, with deep feelings, with fury. In a blink those feelings were gone, as well. Locked away, or had he imagined something he wanted to see in her look? Was there passion left inside her for him? Or for Russell?

He would have asked her outright, if the Duke of Pyneham had not chosen that moment to speak. "Whatever is so amusing, Mr. Marbury?" He smiled indulgently at his daughter. "Will you share your wit, my dear daughter? In your native tongue, perhaps?"

"Mr. Marbury and I were discussing gardens," she replied, prevaricating with an ease that brought a fresh smile to James's lips.

"An Islamic garden," he added, joining easily in her dissembling. "I was telling her of the one I had planted for my mother at our home in Malaga." The garden was the truth, at least. "When one speaks of Persian roses, blue-tiled fountains, and caged desert doves, it is best to discuss them in a language they understand." He looked apologetically at the people seated nearest him.

"How—fanciful," the duke said, rubbing his chin thoughtfully.

"How thoughtless on my part," James responded. "I was teasing Lady Alexandra a bit."

Honoria lifted an eyebrow at him. "Teasing?" Her expression was sardonic, but outrage underlined her one-word question. "And I remember now," she continued in Arabic. "We were finished in the garden. Finished for good, if you will recall."

"You were finished, perhaps," he responded, with more bitterness than he intended to show. "I was interrupted."

"A pity you did not achieve your heart's desire."

"I intend to rectify that."

"You'll not have my help this time."

"You gave me very little last time."

She picked up a glass of wine with her left hand. He thought for a moment that she was going to hurl it at him, but she took a sip and placed the crystal goblet back on the damask tablecloth with delicate precision. She then picked up a gold knife, and held it like a weapon instead of an eating utensil. Honoria, he recalled, was left-handed.

"Your father is very proud of you, James," the duke interjected."We talked a great deal about you when we met at our club yesterday. He told me that you had studied many languages, traveled the world."

"Did he?"

"Honoria likes that sort of thing. Girl's looking for a husband, you know."

"Father!"

"I'm sure she will make a wonderful wife. My father knows a great deal about your lovely daughter." He spoke to the duke, but his gaze was riveted on Honoria's.

He saw that she understood his meaning. The sudden fear in her eyes was like a dark bruise. "He does?"

"He tells me he was at your christening," James went on smoothly. "Please put down the knife," he added in Arabic. "You should never draw a weapon unless you plan to use it."

Honoria responded by slicing a piece of meat and eating it.

"That's true," the duke spoke up. "I remember it well."

James took quick note of the fond glance the duke bestowed on his daughter before he turned back to Honoria. "My father knows that you and I have much in common."

"It seems that you do," the duke said, before Honoria could recover from the sharp breath she took to answer. The thoughtful tone of his voice pleased James. It caused Honoria to drop the knife and turn her head swiftly toward her father, which was just as well. It hid James's smug smile from her. He and the Duke of Pyneham exchanged an understanding glance.

"Mr. Marbury and I have nothing in common," she insisted to her father. "Truly. Nothing."

"You speak the same language," her father said.

"Well, so do I," Russell spoke up suddenly.

"Why would anyone want to speak more than the Queen's English?" He was ignored.

"Our families have been friends for generations," James added, and the duke beamed.

"So have ours," Russell persisted.

Honoria squinted, peering at James's face for the first time in years. He was tempted to smooth away the frown line that formed between her eyes. "I don't want to think about it," she said. "That your family and mine—" She shook her head.

"Amazing, isn't it?" James asked. "It must be *kismet* that we met. Meant to be," he added, looking directly at her father. "Fate."

"Hmmm." The duke stroked his chin. "Yes. I think I see."

Honoria glared at her father. "No. You don't." Beneath the table, she kicked James in the ankle.

"*Kismet,*" Russell spoke up louder, drawing the attention of all the guests seated at this end of the long table. "That's a heathen concept, isn't it, Marbury? Foreign nonsense's bad enough, but where'd you pick up such heathen drivel, old man?" He added an edgy smile with his last words, to keep them from sounding too much like the insult he meant them as. He looked around as though he expected applause for having just said something endlessly witty.

James saw no reason to pay the man any mind. It was Honoria who replied, "The Moors ruled Spain for centuries. I'm sure Mr. Marbury has knowledge of Islamic philosophy from his own land."

He doubted Honoria was trying to protect his identity with her explanation. From her furtive glance toward her father, he guessed that the Duke of Pyneham was ignorant of her adventures, and that she intended him to stay that way. That would be useful. "And Malaga is a Mediterranean port," James added, to help her story. "We've had trade with the Barbary"—Honoria kicked him again—"cities for centuries."

"I know the town," Derrick Russell replied, with a sneer. "A none-too-savory place. Your mother's from there, is she?"

James ignored any implied insult. He ignored Russell. "The Moors were before my time," he said to the duke. "But I have some vague memories of the French occupying the city."

"Ah, yes, the French," the duke said. "Your father and I were both in Spain during the Napoleonic wars. We were young." He chuckled. "And your father was very much in love with the lovely Lady Graciela."

James and Honoria spoke as one.

"You met my mother?" James asked.

"Do you know his mother?" She looked back at James.

"I'm afraid I never had that honor."

"Any moment now I am going to discover

that Mr. Marbury and I are long lost cousins, aren't I?" Her voice was remarkably pleasant, though James recognized her blistering anger.

"No," he answered quietly, only for her to hear. "But we are long lost from one another." She jerked as if she'd received a hard blow. Her hand was cold in his. It was in that moment that James realized she hated him; hated him with her heart and soul. She must have hated him even while they were lovers, even on that last night. Her heart was cold as well. Only toward him? he wondered. He glared at Russell. Did she still want that fool? Why couldn't she need *him*? Perhaps she hated him, but he knew how to make her want him. He would take great pleasure and revenge in reminding her of that. Perhaps he would be the one to do the abandoning this time, vow or no vow.

Revenge did not matter, he reminded himself. Let her heart be cold; he would warm other parts of her soon enough, and it would achieve his purpose. A streak of pleased anticipation ran through him at the thought. Honoria must have felt it, too, because her skin warmed beneath his touch. "Soon," he said in Arabic, and stroked the back of her hand with his thumb once more. Honoria ignored him, speaking to her father instead.

James looked around him, hating the necessity of attending another pointless social function when he had in mind a far better way to spend the evening. The long dining room glittered, and so did everyone in it. The women's elaborate gowns sparked with jewels, and the chandeliers were of scintillating faceted crystal. The array of glasses before him were crystal as well, the china pattern was etched in gold. Flowers arranged in huge silver bowls marched down the center of the enormous table. The floor was of shining white marble, the painted ceiling portrayed a multitude of ancient gods and fantastical beasts feasting in a sunny garden. Footmen in bright blue coats moved around the table with exquisite precision, serving course after endless course of heavy English food.

James could hardly wait for the meal to be over—though there had been a time when he would have killed to be accepted as an English gentleman. Truth was, there was a time he *had* killed for the chance to return to the life of being a Spanish tavern maid's son. Killed, and worse.

She would be all right, Diego told himself as he accompanied Salah, the captain of Ibrahim Rais's third galley, through the arched doorway, moving from the midday heat of the courtyard into the cool interior of the house. Memory guided his silent steps through Ibrahim's mansion while his mind whirled with unaccustomed concern for the woman he'd sent to the slave market. He could not forget the fear in her eyes, or the moment when the pleading look she'd turned to him changed to anger. She'd finally given him one last glance full of utter contempt and turned away. She had still been shaking with terror, and he knew she hated that he realized how afraid she truly was. She did her best to put on a brave show. He understood and admired her behavior. All he could do to help her was send a bribe along to the bagnio guards to make sure Honoria was given a solitary cell. It would be better for her to be kept safely away from the crowded slave pens.

If he could do this differently—

But he could not. He must move cautiously. He should not be so worried about the Englishwoman. Many had been through worse. He *had been through worse—but he was not a gently reared young woman. He had taken her chance of easy rescue away out of his own desperate need, had put his bid for freedom above a foolish urge toward chivalry. And why not put his needs above a stranger's? Why should remorse claw at him just because of a piteous look in a pair of blue eyes?*

She would be all right. He must look to his own survival first. With that harsh reminder, Diego nodded to the guards on either side of the reception room doorway and walked into the watchful presence of Ibrahim Rais.

The quickest of glances served to show him that the silver scimitar was no longer hanging on the wall of the reception room. The place of honor it had occupied behind the pirate admiral's red velvet divan was bare. Diego was both disturbed and pleased to see that the precious thing was gone; the sight of it would no longer be a mocking reminder. But he would know where it was soon, or he would be dead. The scimitar meant everything to him, but he did not let his gaze return to the empty spot on the wall again. He did not have to see it to remember every detail, especially the warm, rich glow of the rubies, emeralds and sapphires that studded the hilt. There was a diamond in the hilt as well, only one, but it was the size of a dove's egg. Diego did not have to think too hard to imagine what a man could do with the fortune a diamond such as that could bring. But he did not let himself imagine anything about it here in Ibrahim Rais's presence. The old corsair had too uncanny an ability to read other men's intentions; to survive around him, one learned stillness and caution. Instead of looking at the bare spot on the wall, or the white bearded man seated on the divan until he was sure his hatred wouldn't show, he slowly looked around the rest of the large room. Diego's nerves tightened further as he saw that there were more guards present than usual—not a good sign. He kept his visage calm, his step light. He bowed respectfully toward the man seated on the divan and kept his hands away from any weapon, but his skin pricked a warning of danger.

He had not been in this room for months. It was large and beautiful and lofty, said to be as lovely as the bey's throne room. Having been in the Bey of Algiers' throne room once, Diego knew that the de-

scription was not quite true, but the luxury Ibrahim Rais bought with theft and peoples' lives was indeed impressive. Diego always had to fight hard not to spit on the finely glazed white and black tiled floors of his "benefactor's" house. He had lived in this house for years, knew every room and passage, knew all the slaves by name, and called most of them friend. He had thought once that commanding his own ship was all he wanted. Then he had added wanting a house of his own to his list of desires. Though both those desires had been fulfilled, he still felt hollow inside. Neither of those small steps toward freedom gave him more than a taste of what he really wanted.

He was not alone in the reception room with Ibrahim Rais, and he was glad of that. Salah was a big man, with a big, booming voice, and a bold, flamboyant presence, a man happy to be the center of attention. Diego admired the man's swaggering bravado and could match it if he must, but today he chose a more circumspect course. Salah seemed to take no notice of the guards' alert gazes as he strode up to where Ibrahim Rais was seated with a covered bronze dish on the floor by his feet. Diego kept a careful distance, waiting to be invited.

Ibrahim Rais's bearded chin lifted sharply, but Salah took no notice of the old man's annoyance at this breach of protocol. He planted himself before Ibrahim Rais and demanded, "Why did you send for me, old man? You know I'm setting sail for Alexandria. You're not going to stop me this time." Tense guards drew closer, but Salah went on as if he didn't notice. "I've served you well, but our time is over. I'm taking my spoils and going home to my wife."

"Leaving me," Ibrahim Rais said softly, regretfully. Diego flinched at the deceptive gentleness in the old man's tone. "To be with your wife." He gave the big Egyptian corsair an evil, deadly look. Diego's gaze went to the bronze bowl. He knew what was coming, and wanted desperately to look away.

"The French fleet will be here in a matter of weeks," Salah pointed out. "Time we all cut our losses and ran. I'd rather go home than run with you, Ibrahim."

"What if I sent for your wife?" Ibrahim Rais rose slowly to his feet.

Salah shook his head. "I'd rather go to her."

"Too bad. Your wife is already here." Ibrahim Rais kicked over the bronze container, and Salah screamed as the woman's head tumbled out. The guards closed in on him.

Diego backed away, sickened, disgusted, glad that he'd made more cautious plans for his own escape.

Chapter 7

After dinner, Honoria stood her ground by the piano near the open garden door. They were all looking at her, of course, behind their fans and beneath their demurely lowered eyelashes. She was well aware of how ladies could stare without seeming to do so. The men were still enjoying their after dinner brandy, but soon they would join the ladies in the music room, and Honoria's evening would only get worse. She doubted this awful evening would ever end.

She heard the women whispering in their little groups, by the door, on the settee, near the fireplace. She was not fool enough to pretend that the whispering wasn't about her; they would not be whispering otherwise. Whispering about her and Derrick Russell. She knew his reappearance would be of more interest than Mr. Marbury. As far as society was concerned, apologies had been tendered and accepted; the Marbury Affair was settled.

At least she had gotten through the meal with no one the wiser. The important thing was that her father suspected nothing. Her father had paid far too much attention to Diego—James—but it had been normal paternal attention. The Spaniard—the Honorable Mr. Marbury—had been at pains to show his charming side to the Duke of Pyneham. Her jaw clenched in fury as she remembered all too well just how charming he could be. She was still singed around the edges from having his warmth turned on her this evening. Knowing that it was a false warmth didn't lessen the effect any, it only served to make her wary. She was still frozen inside. He was responsible for the ice around her heart that would never melt, especially not in the light of his sunny smile.

What about the heat of his kisses? The fire from his touch?

Honoria pushed away the questions that rose unbidden, and the memories they brought with them. She reminded herself sternly that having been burned beyond healing once, she was not fool enough to risk a second exposure. Ice and fire, indeed, she added with a mental snort of derision. What fanciful nonsense!

Lady Asqwyth said something to Cousin Kate, who replied, and Honoria realized they'd been involved in a lively conversation for several minutes. Whether either of them had spoken to her in this time, she didn't know. All she knew was that the smile on her face was so fixed, she doubted her lips would ever return to their normal shape again.

Her attention kept turning to the open doors that led to a wide terrace and the back garden beyond. She very carefully did not look toward the hall door. The men would arrive whenever they chose, and this waiting would then seem like a pleasant purgatory compared to the hell of enduring *his* presence once more.

Yet she knew very well that she was waiting for the door to open and for him to come in.

She took a few deep breaths, hoping the fresh air would aid in calming the nervousness she ordered herself not to feel. The breeze was pleasant, scented by roses and air washed clean by rain earlier in the day. The garden beckoned her, dark and mysterious—as much as a neatly groomed walled lawn in the middle of a safe city neighborhood could be. The truth was, anywhere away from this crowd of brightly clad, avid-eyed females beckoned to her.

Why had she not taken the coward's way out, pleading a headache and fleeing to her room as soon as the meal was over? She had already done her duty to society and her father this evening. *Could it be,* a creeping snake of speculation whispered inside her, *that you want to see him*? Nonsense. The man was not the fruit of the knowledge of good and evil; he was not ripe and rich and tasty with sensuality. Well, he was—but the analogy to an apple certainly didn't suit. He was not sweet. His kisses were, she remembered. *Concealing bitter poison*, she argued back to the snake of memory.

He would not tempt her. Not again. She would keep control of her emotions and her life, perform the duties expected of her place in society, and bring no shame or criticism upon her father or family name. She had her books, her quiet place in the country. Those were rewards enough for leading an exemplary life. She'd put the past behind her; now all she had to do was get through the present.

"Only a few more hours," she murmured.

"What, my dear?" Cousin Kate asked, over the piano music.

That she was talking to herself again frightened Honoria. Any lack of control was disturbing, and now more than ever, with *him* to face. "It's been a long evening for me." She smiled and spoke pleasantly, as she looked from her cousin to Lady Asqwyth. "I am a country girl at heart, you know. I would be in bed by now if I were at home."

"You'd be up reading a book," Cousin Kate said, as though this was a nasty habit she intended to break her younger cousin of. "You're in London now, my girl." She gestured about the room with her fan. "At the height of the

Season, I might add. With Her Majesty's coronation and—ah!" Her voice lit with joy. "The gentlemen have joined us at last!"

Looking toward the hall door, Honoria was aware of large black lumps spilling into the room and spreading out across the floor like an overturned bucket of coal. The timbre of the women's voices changed, skirts rustled, the whoosh of fans stirred the air, and excitement lit the air brighter than gas lights or candle flames. With bitterness, Honoria realized that the past hour had been the lull in an ongoing hunt. The Season was a long, elaborate mating dance. Most of the women here were involved in that dance, either for themselves or for their daughters, or as avid observers and critics of the chase. Honoria was not one of the hunters, or allowed to observe with the aficionados; she was one of the observed. And a veritable prize among the prey animals, as well.

Honoria snarled angrily at the thought.

"Indigestion?" Cousin Kate questioned. "Or is it the sight of Captain Russell approaching that makes you look so sour?"

Honoria made out Derrick's form a moment after her cousin spoke. She caught a gleam of gold hair in the lamplight and a pale oval of face, a suggestion of broad shoulders. Was that a hint of desperation underlying his confident swagger as he moved closer?

She turned her back, ostensibly to speak to Lady Asqwyth.

This didn't stop him. "I must speak with you, Honoria. Alone."

The intensity of Derrick Russell's whispered entreaty when he came up behind her was more annoying than disturbing. He had bad breath as well. Too much wine, and not only from tonight's meal, she thought, was the cause of the sour stench that hung about him. Possibly it was an outward manifestation of his rotten soul.

Lady Asqwyth put her hand over her mouth and tittered at the sight of Derrick Russell standing so close behind Honoria. Lady Asqwyth, of course, knew that they had once been betrothed. Almost everyone else in the music room did as well. Everyone was watching. Was *he* in the room? Did he care who she was with or what she did? And did she care if he cared, or not? She decided that she did—if she could in any way hurt him. Such maliciousness was foolish, she supposed, since the man was heartless and soulless and had no personal interest in her at all. If she could manage to get even some small measure of revenge, would it be sweet? She had no way of knowing, having never even contemplated revenge before.

The thought that she might make him uncomfortable was a pleasant one. Of course, showing Derrick any attention might make

Marbury think he could still use Derrick against her. She would disabuse him of the notion, if necessary. Right now, it would be politic to disabuse Derrick of any notions he might have as well. She'd managed to fight her grimace into almost a smile when she turned to face Derrick.

"Alone?" she questioned, as coquettishly as she could manage. "That would hardly be proper, Captain Russell." That she could pronounce his name with anything approaching civility delighted her.

"We have a past relationship." He sounded as if he thought that what they had once meant to each other somehow granted him private privileges. "I hope to renew that relationship," he added for everyone nearby to hear.

He spoke with a sincerity that twisted in Honoria's guts. Her soul and heart might have been affected as well, if another apparition from her past were not occupying those hollow, aching spots.

"Derrick," she said quietly to her former fiancé, "you are such a nuisance." She sighed and stepped toward the garden door. "All right. Five minutes." He hesitated until she glanced over her shoulder upon reaching the glass door. Apparently Captain Russell had forgotten that she was as used to giving orders as he was.

Oh, that's right; he had *never* known that side of her. Her smile was quite genuine and sharp as a sword when she said, "Come along, Derrick. Cousin Kate," she added imperiously, "we need a chaperone."

She did not wait to see if they followed her as she went into the garden. She did hear a man's hearty laughter as she exited, but she refused to think who the man might be.

Cousin Kate wisely stayed on the terrace while Honoria marched to a bench in the middle of the garden. She was aware of roses and moonlight, but the scene was incongruous with her mood. When Derrick put his hands on her shoulders, she shook him off.

"Don't you dare," she snarled, so fiercely that the Scourge of Barbary took a startled step backward. Scourge, indeed. She had to force down a bitter laugh before she could go on. "How *dare* you come to my father's house?" she demanded.

He gestured dramatically. She could barely make the movement out in the dim light with her dim vision. "I was invited. Your father invited me himself." He sounded smug, pleased, sure.

Her voice was deadly calm. "And why do you think he invited you?"

"Because you need a husband. You have not wed, Honoria."

"That is in no way relevant to you, Captain. You requested in your letter that I forgive you," she went on, before he could make some false declaration of tender sentiment toward her.

"Very well, I forgive you. I didn't think it was possible, but having laid eyes on you again, I see that holding a grudge against such a pathetic twit as you is not worth the effort. It would be beneath me." No, she would save her hatred for the one who deserved it the most. She could spare some contempt for Derrick Russell, however.

"I have had my solicitor make inquiries about your current circumstances, Captain. Unfortunately, I was not able to present the results of those inquiries to my father in time for your invitation for tonight's function to be withdrawn. I assure you, there will be no further invitations."

Derrick stood very straight and tall. She supposed that he probably looked quite fierce—not that she cared.

"You love me," he announced.

"Irrelevant," she responded. She clasped her hands before her and added coldly, "Also, your tense is incorrect."

"Your father will accept my suit. We will be betrothed again."

"The information about your gambling debts will be on Father's desk in the morning, along with information of a less savory nature. I was unaware that there were any brothel keepers in London quite so foolish as to extend credit to their customers. You've run up quite a bill for services rendered."

"Honoria!"

She had no idea why the man sounded so horrified, but took delight in shocking him. "I realize a long, and unsuccessful, sea voyage can exacerbate certain tensions common to the male anatomy, but really, Captain Russell, such excess is hardly sensible for a man of your limited funds."

"How can you speak so, so—"

"Frankly?" she supplied. "Maidenly modesty is something I lost years ago. I hardly need to remind you of that, since it was at your suggestion."

"Honoria," he went on doggedly, as though reciting from a memorized scenario, "I have come to rescue you from a lonely spinsterhood. To offer you my hand in honorable marriage. And—and—"

"The pleasures of the flesh? The comfort of the marriage bed?" she asked with a sickly sweetness.

The smug satisfaction returned to his voice. "Precisely."

"I'd rather not risk the pox, thank you very much, Captain Russell."

"A maiden should not know about such things."

"I am not a maiden." Why did she have to keep reminding him of this indelicate fact?

He took a sly step closer. He lowered his voice conspiratorially. "But your father does not know that you were dishonored. The world does not know the truth."

She ignored the threat of blackmail, well aware that she could play the game better than he could. "You are a desperate man with a ruined career who wants my fortune and the place in society I can give you."

"Yes," he had the grace to admit, adding with a very poor show of sincerity, "but that is not all I want from you, Honoria. I was wrong. I have wronged you."

He sounded as if he had just played his winning card. Honoria could not hold back her laughter. "Oh, Derrick, go away."

"Go away?"

He came toward her again. She put a hand out to hold him at arm's length. "You lied to me when you told me you loved me."

"I do love you."

"You never loved me. You told me so yourself."

"That was the lie."

"Please. I have eaten a rich dinner; I cannot bear to pour such treacle on top of lobster."

"You always did like to eat."

"That's my Derrick: remind me that you think I'm a cow. A stupid, spotted bovine. No, you didn't call me bovine—I don't think you actually know any words with Latin roots. Cow is a good English word, and you used it quite plainly to describe me."

"I was ill. Delirious."

She responded with several short, rude words of Anglo-Saxon derivation that any sailor was sure to recognize. "Go away," she repeated. "Attempt to contact me again, or attempt to inform my father of your version of our shared past, and not only will my solicitor's report make its way to the Admiralty, but I will personally draft a letter detailing your abominable behavior in Algiers. I will send this letter not only to the Admiralty, but to the Prime Minister, the newspapers, the Queen. Dear old Lord Wellington might find it amusing to call you out as a coward, cad and traitor."

She felt light as a feather, happier than she'd been in years. The threat of revenge was proving to be quite delicious.

"You would not dare!"

"If my father is in any way hurt, I most certainly will."

"You could not bear the public humiliation any more than I could."

"Do you want to find out?" she asked. Her words were soft, but he seemed to hear the danger at last.

Derrick backed up a few steps. "You are distraught," he said in the mild, polite, insufferably superior tone a male used when a woman made any show of opposing him. "It has been many years since we have seen each other."

"Not enough."

"I will give you time to recall what we meant to each other. To reflect. To remember." He whispered the words, as though they would conjure up memories of sensual delight. "I'll leave you now. The Season is only beginning, Honoria," he went on relentlessly. "We're sure to see quite a bit of each other. Given time and association, you will realize that you still love me."

Fortunately, Derrick finally chose to make a strategic retreat before she called for footmen to eject him bodily from Pyneham property.

"That felt good, didn't it, fox-hair?" James murmured from the concealment of a topiary bush. He could tell by the tilt of her head and the spring in her step as she rejoined her *duenna* and went back inside. The conversation between Honoria and the fool had been intense, but not loud. He had had to get very close to overhear as much as he had. He and his father had made their farewells and left by the front door only moments after Honoria had marched the idiot outside. James had had to rush around to the back of the house, jump over the garden wall, and stealthily speed to his hiding place. He'd had a few moments of furious worry that he would arrive to find Honoria in her "dear Derrick's" arms and he was still tense and snarling, even though the kiss he'd imagined had not happened.

It's not jealousy, he told himself, despite the

tightness around his heart, the anger that clawed inside him, and the discovery that his fists were balled in tight knots. And all that only at the thought of the fool's touching Honoria.

James made himself assess the scene with a cooler head. He had not been forced to use the scheming, devious part of himself for some time, but that did not mean he had lost the capacity to study the weaknesses and strengths of others, or to know how to use those strengths and weaknesses to his own advantage.

She had made it clear she would not be blackmailed. James rubbed his chin thoughtfully. That was not good. Then again, she had also said that she would not let her father be hurt. Her father was her weakness—that was good.

Having Russell in the picture was most definitely not good. Russell seemed to think that he could charm his way back into Honoria's good graces. Who was to say that the fool was not right? She had thought she loved him once; they had a history together. They had their place in the British aristocracy in common. Russell was right about having many opportunities of seeing Honoria as the Coronation Season progressed. He would be there, at parties and balls and at the theater, in his dress uniform and medals, smiling and dancing attendance on the woman whom he had once tricked into thinking she loved him. Who was to say Russell would not be able to trick her again?

"Me," James Marbury said. He was not jealous, but Honoria belonged to him. "I paid good money for her," he added, and looked up at the upper stories of the duke's townhouse. He did not intend to give Russell time to be his rival, therefore direct methods were called for. Finding out which room was hers should not be at all difficult.

And breaking into that room would hold no challenge for the likes of Diego Moresco, now, would it?

Chapter 8

"My lady?"

"Hmm?"

"You're humming."

Honoria turned to Huseby. "So I was. I am always as good as my word, Maggie." She handed her maid her corset and took the nightgown Huseby handed her.

Huseby eyed her with worried suspicion. "Are you all right? You're flushed, and bright-eyed. You look like a cat that's been in the cream, and a bit feverish at the same time."

Honoria adjusted her spectacles on her nose. "I do not have a feverish nature."

"The devil you don't."

Honoria finally noticed that Huseby looked very, very worried, and her ebullient mood dimmed somewhat. "I was savoring a triumph. Now you're going to make me come back to the real world, aren't you?"

"That man, my lady." She looked around as if afraid they would be overheard here in Honoria's bedchamber, in the very heart of the house, with no one else in the room. "Please tell me I was mistaken about—"

"The Honorable James Marbury," Honoria supplied, "is half Spanish, as you already know." She took an emerald silk robe from Huseby and jerked the belt tight with one hard tug. Buoyed by a sudden burst of elation, she had no memory of what had occurred after she went back into the music room. No, she recalled her father informing her that Viscount Brislay and his son had left, and telling her she needn't look so relieved and that he wanted to talk to her after all the guests had gone. Yes, she remembered that, but how had she gotten from the music room to her bedroom, and when? She suspected she might have floated there. She *had* waited a long time to speak her mind to Derrick Russell; pity she hadn't had the opportunity sooner. And to think she'd almost been afraid to face the fool!

Well, however she'd gotten here, she was in her bedroom now and dressed for bed. She might as well go to sleep. Huseby's gaze on her was still anything but serene, though. "We will not be bothered by any further intrusion by Captain Russell," Honoria reassured her friend.

Huseby made an impatient gesture that dismissed Derrick Russell. "The Spaniard?"

Honoria reached up and ran her fingers through the loosened mass of her curly hair. The blasted stuff was altogether too thick and difficult to manage; it fell halfway down her back. "I suppose the Spaniard will have to be dealt with as well, Maggie."

"But how? What does he want? Why is he here? I thought you said he must have been killed in Algiers."

"I have no answers. I suppose I'll have to find out. Why can't those men leave me alone?"

Huseby glanced toward the bedroom door. "Your father sent word that—"

"I'll speak to him in the morning. Get some rest, Maggie."

Huseby eyed Honoria worriedly. "Are you sure you wouldn't like to have a tantrum now, my lady? You may not get another chance for a while."

Honoria gave a breathless laugh. "I had a tantrum after the ball. Another when I received Derrick's letter. I haven't had my secretary check my engagement book, but surely two tantrums within a week is more than the calendar can bear."

The closed cream-colored brocade curtains of the huge bed invited her to rest inside them. The heavy carved bed had been in this room for over a century. Though the bed might be antique, the feather mattress was soft and new, the blankets warm and comforting. "I'm going to sleep now, Maggie."

Huseby shook her head, then assumed the blank face of a well-trained servant and came forward.

Honoria waved her away. She grasped two handfuls of her heavy hair. "I can plait this myself, thank you. Goodnight." Huseby frowned, but she didn't argue. Honoria would have locked the door behind her maid, but there was no lock on the door. On any of the doors leading into and out of this room. "Foolish oversight on the architect's part, if you ask me," she murmured.

She turned toward the bed, then away from it again. She knew that sleep would not come just yet—or if it did, the dreams would no doubt be of nights spent in bed in Algiers. Those sorts of dreams were anything but restful. She had to calm down before she attempted to sleep, or her passionate nature would slip its leash and cavort with salacious memories of Diego Moresco while she slept.

She crossed the room but could not bring herself to sit down before the mirror when she reached the dressing table. She did not want to face herself. That was the point of avoiding closing her eyes. She could always take her spectacles off, but having clear vision was too precious a thing to lose so soon after an evening of confronting her worst enemies at such a great disadvantage. Or perhaps being unable to see their faces had made her less vulnerable to them. She didn't know.

She restlessly walked to the window and pulled back the heavy curtains. She looked outward, up at the moon, the stars that showed bravely but faintly above the sooty city lights. Oh, Lord, what a day! What a night!

She pressed her forehead against the cool glass. As much as she wanted to avoid it, her thoughts began repeating every word, gesture, nuance, and possible meaning of the last several hours.

"You could not bear the public humiliation."

She had sounded so confident in her reply to Derrick's threat. She laughed faintly, and pressed her hands against the glass, palms damp with remembered fear, sweat making them slippery on the smooth surface. Several shudders went through her, cold, then hot. "Could not bear . . . ?" She made some faint sound, something that was between laughter and a sob.

She was being looked at, but no one was actually looking at her. *She was being talked about, pointed at, touched, and examined—at least, her body was.* She *was in no way involved in what was happening to her. She was as much alone here, where the slave dealers exhibited their wares, as she had been in the bagnio cell. More alone, because the personality that made her who she was had no meaning here, no place. She was fully dressed in the black mourning dress she'd been wearing when she was captured, yet Honoria felt naked and exposed. She had walked up a few steps, been turned to face the front of the square, and lost all identity. They had taken off the veils and enveloping robes and she'd wished desperately to have their safe concealment back. They had unbound her hair, which was considered a good selling point. Her freckles were not. Someone had hefted her bosoms in his hands and pronounced them favorable, as well. Her hips had been equally squeezed and pronounced fit for childbearing. Her height was not going to help her price, the men agreed. Her pale complexion was something they couldn't agree on: one thought it interesting, another could not see why anyone would be interested in a European woman. He did think she might make a good enough domestic servant, maybe even a field hand. At least they had left her with her spectacles. Not because she needed them to see*—she *had no needs—but because one of the slave dealers thought the lenses might add to her value as a European curiosity. The dealers had agreed to snatch the spectacles off her face if someone didn't make a bid soon.*

She should have been grateful that the sparse crowd gathered in the barren square was so indifferent. The sun was too bright, hurting her eyes as it threw heat and light off the pale stones of the surrounding buildings. It had been dark inside her cell. It had also been hot, but she now thought of the isolated bare room as a cool haven. Dust stirred in a hot wind, and the dust stuck on her tear-damp face. Water vendors moved through the square shouting their wares with more effectiveness than the bored slave dealers up here on the platform.

Someone pushed her from behind, forcing her to stumble to the edge of the platform. A hand twisted in her hair and her head was yanked back. Something was said about her throat being long and beautiful. A hand stroked it as if proving the point. The dealer shouted out a price, lower than the last one he had suggested as an opening bid. Several people in the thin crowd glanced at each other. A few comments were made. Someone shrugged. No one cared.

Then, after a long, hot silence, someone in the back of the crowd finally called out a price.

James had always been able to move silently, though as he approached Honoria he knew he didn't have to. She was looking out at the stars, but he could tell from her reflection in the glass that her thoughts were turned inward. She looked vulnerable, all her formidable pride stripped away. He knew that she would not like to be caught this way, that she would not be forgiving of anyone who saw her without the shield of her sharp wit and intelligence. She wasn't likely to be forgiving of him, anyway, but why make things worse than they already were?

He smiled, though pain twisted his mouth into a grimace. Why was he here? Why was he bothering? Because of a promise made to his father?

Promises and honor were for fools. His father lived by a quaint notion of chivalry. So did his mother. What had it brought them but decades of anguish? Anguish they claimed had tempered and refined them like Toledo blades. Perhaps they did have the strength of steel, but James feared he was a creature of much cruder iron. His parents had been unwillingly separated because of fate. His and Honoria's separation had been a deliberate act of will. Still, he had made a vow. He had no more to lose now than he had eight years ago, and this time he was determined to claim and keep something that was his, whether she wanted it or not.

He paused halfway between the bed, where he had hidden behind the concealing damask curtains, and the woman who clutched a matching window curtain tightly in her hand. Tendons stood out starkly on those long fingers, the skin pale and bloodless. Was she holding onto a lifeline? Was she even aware when her hand had moved to grasp the sturdy material? He remembered her hands, soft and long-fingered and skilled. He shook his head a little, forcing memory to go back further. She had been clumsy and fumbling and shy once upon a night long ago. And furious. And proud.

The night had been so much warmer than this thin English summer. She hadn't needed a heavy nightdress or a quilted robe. He remembered the outline of her long, lush body in the glow of a colored glass lamp. She'd worn a gown of gossamer thin cotton, embroidered white on white. The gown revealed as much as it hid in shadows and curves, the effect mysterious and seductive. He recalled bare flesh in moonlight, hers and his, brown and pale limbs twined together. But for the long fall of her thick hair he barely recognized the woman in the shapeless satin robe and the nightgown buttoned up to her neck.

She hid too much. Time for it to stop. He moved silently forward again, crossing the physical gap between them.

The first thing he touched was her hair. It was spread out before him like a river of molten copper, heavy in his hands, scented with prosaic English lavender when he remembered sultry spice. The bright curling strands were softer against his fingers, and more clinging than memory, but then, his hands were not so hard now as they had been then. If he burned at the touch of copper hair, he told himself that it was a stirring of ashes, not some new spark in his blood. Still, he was the one who gasped as her gaze flashed up. Their gazes met as reflections in the window glass.

She said on a sigh, "You might have paid more than fourteen drachma for me, you know."

"I was not a wealthy man," he answered, and thought better of it instantly. Perhaps she wanted to hear that she was worth the moon and the stars to him. He stepped back, but she turned to face him before he could dramatically take her into his arms. He had lost the edge with this woman, the advantage that should have come with surprise and physical closeness. Now he would have to use his wits, and hope that hers were as out of practice as his were. He doubted that. No, he knew it, he'd heard her sharpening her tongue on the fool English captain in the garden. And she had not exactly been slow of tongue when they'd traded barbs over dinner.

James feared he was in for a long night. Penance, his father would call it. Was any woman worth this?

She looked past his shoulder and the frown that was already on her face deepened. "The bed curtains were closed. You were hiding in the bed?" Her eyes widened and her gaze flew back to his. "In my *bed*? How dare you? For how long?"

"I have been in your bed before."

"You have not," she corrected, her diction precise. "I've been in yours."

That was his Honoria, accurate and specific. He grinned confidently. "Frequently." The dark anger that filled her eyes looked like it came straight from her soul. He shrugged. "The bed was the only private place in your room. It was logical."

"Your logic was ever sloppy."

"I had to improvise."

"Also not your forte."

James put a hand thoughtfully on his chin. "Now, why did I come here? Certainly not to share a pleasant conversation with you."

"I am not a pleasant person," she snapped back. She doubted the Spaniard had sneaked into her room, her very bed, for the purpose of seducing her. Or had he? Why? How long had he been hiding behind the bed curtains? Long enough for his scent to remain on the sheets? Her stomach tightened at the thought, even as a tingling of excitement raced through her. "I shall have to have the bed linen burned, I suppose."

He looked indignant. "Do you suspect I have lice?"

"I don't dare to suspect where you might have been, or what filth you might have acquired along the way."

He gestured at his elegant clothing. "I have acquired the polish of an English gentleman."

"Stole it, more like." She saw how he bridled at this implied insult to his father. Good. That gave her a weapon to use against him. Perhaps not a good one, but—she sighed. "Go away. We'll fight another time, if you must have a fight. I'm tired now."

"You've had one confrontation too many today, Honoria." His words broke gently into her thoughts. "You want me to go away. You want me to never have been born," he added. "You don't want to argue, though you think hurting me would be nice if you could manage the energy."

She nodded slowly. "I would like those things, yes."

He took a step closer to her, catching her gaze with those warm golden eyes of his. He had such expressive eyes. Clear, perfect eyes. Everything about him was perfect. She couldn't help but note how a swath of dark brown hair fell in a graceful arc across his wide forehead, how his heavy brows arched emphatically over those so-expressive eyes with their long, long lashes, how his wide shoulders and muscular thighs were shown off by his well-tailored evening clothes. She'd always known he was perfection to gaze upon. What difference did it make? Derrick was a fine physical specimen, as well, yet he was the lowest type of lifeform. This man with the warm honey eyes was even lower in the great chain of creation, as low as the serpent in the Garden. He was the devil himself.

The difference, she knew as the air heated around her, was that Derrick no longer tempted her. Perhaps he never had. Diego—James—whoever he was and whatever he called himself—might be the spawn of Satan, but that didn't stop her from wanting to—

Honoria reached out her hand toward his cheek, the movement slow, unwilling, the ache to trace her fingers along the strong line of his jaw and trace his sensual full lips perverse and foolish. She was barely able to draw her hand back before it made contact. She was left furious with herself, and with only a years' old memory of the warm suppleness of his skin.

"You are evil incarnate!" she declared, thrusting her hands behind her back and clasping them tightly together. "I shall scream now," she added, standing stiffly erect before him. She refused to look into his eyes anymore. "I will call for help."

"Why?" he asked, in his familiar, teasing way, head tilted boyishly to one side.

"Because I need help." She shouldn't let herself be drawn into conversing with the devil; she should be screaming.

"Perhaps it is something I can help you with." He took another step toward her.

She took a step back, and her shoulders came up against the cool glass of the window. "Helping me is not a concept you are familiar with."

"I helped you," he reminded her. "For a price."

"It was always commerce with you," she snarled.

"I know." He did not look in the least

abashed or ashamed by this admission. He glanced around the bedroom. "Are you going to scream and compromise yourself when the household rushes to your rescue?" he asked mildly. "Or may I continue with what I have come here to do?"

She held a hand up between them. It was a very dramatic gesture, just the sort of theatrical thing she loathed. She put her hand down and faced him with proudly raised chin. "If you've come here to ravish me—"

"When did I ever have to ravish you?" He sounded genuinely affronted.

She had the strongest urge to stomp her foot. "Nobody *ever* wants to ravish me." The complaint came from the deepest part of her, unbidden, and terrifying in the dark anger it stirred in her. Her tone was sharp as glass shards when she snarled, "I know I'm an overgrown ugly cow, but why not pretend just for once that what you have on your mind is—" Honoria clamped her hands over her mouth. What was she saying? She didn't *want* to be ravished—that wasn't the bloody point!

He looked stunned. "Honoria—"

She rammed her hands against his chest and pushed him backward. Tried to. He didn't budge. He put his hands up and grasped her wrists. To keep her from pounding on him next, she supposed. Trapped between the window and large man who held her hostage, she demanded, "What is it you want with me? *What?*"

She had no idea where she was. A private house, that was easy to surmise. In a small, plainly furnished room. Alone. She'd been draped in veils and robes again and the slave dealers had delivered her to the house of her new master, but no one had told her who that master was. She'd been brought to this room by a pair of elderly women, and a tray of food and a flask of water had been provided. Earlier, a woman servant had helped her bathe, and offered her fresh clothes afterward. At first Honoria had wanted to refuse to wear the clothing given by a master to a slave, but she was a practical person at her core. Her black mourning dress was a filthy wreck. She could not stand the thought of donning it once more, though it was the only reminder left to her of her life in England, and of the mother she had lost. She was lost herself, dead to the life she had known. She hated accepting this truth which new clothing represented, but she was too pragmatic and unsentimental not to exchange the rags. The Arabic clothing was exotic, but far from immodest. The vivid colors of the many layers of robes in green and rust and gold suited her coloring. She did her fresh-washed hair in a simple long braid down her back and allowed the woman servant to wind a light, nearly transparent veil around her head and show her how to tuck an end of the draping across her face. Honoria asked questions, but all she received in reply were compliments on how well she spoke the language. Then they left her alone again. She paced like a trapped animal for a while. Eventually she ate her cold meal.

By the time she was done, the woman returned and told her, "Our master will see you now." The servant gestured toward the door. "Please come with me."

Honoria wanted to back up against a wall and fight to be dragged from the room. She wanted to proclaim that she called no man "Master" and obeyed no man on earth—other than the king, her father, and her beloved betrothed. To state haughtily that she was the heiress of a dukedom, who gave orders but rarely took them. She also wanted to beg and scream and cry and crawl under the bed in quaking terror.

She did none of these things, made no foolish proclamations. She could not call on anyone but God for help, which she did silently. She went where the servant directed her, all too aware that if she did not please her new "Master" that any fate he chose could be dealt out to her. She feared that she might be tortured, but being sold would be worse. Lady Alexandra Margaret Frances Honoria Pyne was terrified down to her soul of facing the unspeakable horror of standing on the auction block once more.

She was trembling as she was shown through another doorway, now almost grateful to this stranger who had bought her. The other woman withdrew, closing the door behind her, leaving Honoria alone with their owner. She looked toward the man who had taken her away from that horrible place, and very nearly opened her mouth to say "Thank you."

The tall young man coming toward her was dressed in clean white robes. His beard was trimmed, his dark hair combed back, and there was a bright, cheerful smile on his handsome face.

She stopped dead in her tracks, and shouted angrily, "You!"

"Hello, Honoria," the Spaniard said affably, and held a tattered piece of paper toward her. "I bought you so you could translate this for me."

"What are you doing in England?" she demanded. "Now what do you want from me?"

The Honorable James Marbury stepped back again and bowed to her with elegant polish that did nothing to allay her suspicions. Then he dropped gracefully onto one knee. "Honoria Pyne," he said, sounding sincere and not looking the least bit silly gazing up from his humble position. "Do me the honor of becoming my wife."

After she watched him in silence for quite a long time, James shifted his weight onto his other knee. She stayed very still, barely breathing, though she did blink a few times. It didn't help. He was still there when she opened her eyes.

"Honoria?"

"Yes?"

James came slowly back to his feet. He moved closer. Barefoot, wearing a nightgown and robe, with her beautiful copper hair unbound, she did not look so different than she had in Algiers. Her vulnerability was not so open, but he knew it was there. He hoped it was. Or had she changed utterly, become as sharp and flinty and dead to feelings as rumor claimed? If he took her in his arms now, would it do any good?

A spark of anger lit deep within him, and a bitter voice told him he was giving himself up to a life of sacrifice and penance if he continued with this mad scheme. The voice urged him to walk away, to run from his past rather than embrace a woman who did not want him. Pride kept him where he was, and another type of anger. Was he to leave her to Derrick Russell? If it was to be a contest between them, this time he would win.

Besides, he still wanted her.

"Do you have needs?" he asked. "Do you feel desire? You will be my wife." He took a strand of her long, curling hair beneath his fingers. He looped it around his forefinger almost without thinking, and the action drew her head closer as she followed the tug. He cupped her cheek with his other hand. Her lips were pressed tightly in a prim line. "I should kiss you now," he told her.

"No."

"No, I shouldn't kiss you?" He smiled dangerously as he tilted her face up, bending to brush his lips across hers. The kiss was the lightest of touches. She showed no reaction at all.

"No, I will not be your wife."

"Of course you will," he said confidently. Would she strike him for such high-handed arrogance? Would she order him out of her house? She would rage and shout and he would silence her with kisses, enflame her fury into passion. He would carry her to her big, soft bed and bring her pleasure beyond anything they had once had. She would remember. She would marry him. "It will make our fathers happy," he added.

He held her hands in his, to keep her from hitting him, perhaps. He twined his fingers with hers, then drew her hands up to his lips. He kissed one palm and then the other, and a faint shudder went through her. Not dead, he thought hopefully, just sleeping. "Shall I wake the beauty?" he asked. "Do you know that story?"

"I know many stories. Pirate stories, mostly."

"I know a few of those." He kissed the insides of her wrists. "And tales of Arabian nights."

"Tales of treasure hunting."

He pressed his lips against the inside of her

elbow. "I know one of a beautiful harem girl and her passionate lover."

"I am not familiar with such a tale."

His gaze flashed up to hers. He expected to find her expression soft, her eyes growing dark with desire. Her eyes could be like sapphires, he remembered, or indigo midnight, after making love, like the sea after a storm. Her gaze on his right now was as cold as ice. "You would not look at Diego like that."

"I am."

"How would you look at James Marbury?"

"With the contempt he deserves."

James hooked an arm around her waist and drew her closer.

"I do not know if it is Diego Moresco or James Marbury who is insane," she said, infuriatingly calm. "But I would like you both to leave now."

"We can't," he answered. He kissed her throat and this time a sharp gasp escaped her. "We have only just begun." She felt good filling his arms, like a soft, warm peach. He leaned close to whisper in her ear, and breathed in her scent. "I could ravish you now, if you like."

She put her hands on his shoulders, and for a moment her touch was an embrace, her body molded tantalizingly and arousingly against his. More than memory stirred at being so close to her. He ran a hand down the long length of her spine, laying his palm against the spot where her back curved into the roundness of her buttocks, and felt the soft weight of her unrestrained breasts pressed against his chest. His breath quickened, and his blood heated. Memory was not enough. A small sound escaped him, one of need and anticipation.

Then she stiffened and pushed against him. "Stop this!"

He thought she was admonishing herself as much as she was him. She did not want to be soft and yielding, to remember what it was like to feel like a woman. Why? He fought down the urge to teach her what it was to be a woman, and made himself take a long step backward. "Perhaps you'd rather wait until after the wedding?"

She did not instantly miss being in his arms, Honoria told herself sternly as James stepped away. It was cool in her bedroom; all she was missing was the warmth of body heat that chased away the chill in her blood. Her blood was *not* chilled, she corrected, and the very thought of sharing body heat was distasteful. Everything to do with men, especially this man, was distasteful. How could she ever have been interested in coupling like the basest of strumpets with this, this—?

Animal. Dark and wild and overwhelming. Eyes of honey gold, of amber fire. No, light brown, she corrected herself. Hardly anything to dream about for years. Yet she wanted to see those eyes looking at her the way they had once . . . her palms sweated at the effort to keep from touching him, and there was an ache deep, deep inside her. She would conquer it; she would! The sight of him would not drive her wild! She tucked her hands firmly into the wide sleeves of her robe.

He gestured toward the bed, with his amazing smile lighting his face once more. "I will wait until after the wedding if I must, but—"

"Wedding? Don't be ridiculous. Or do you have some document you would like translated, Mr. Marbury? If that is the case, I can provide you with references to any number of scholars who will require no more than a nominal fee for their trouble. Though if you wish to offer marriage as compensation, there is at least one don at Cambridge who I suspect might be interested in your proposal."

He waggled a finger at her. "Ladies should not know about such things."

"Most women do not have my education. I have traveled extensively, you know." Why was it she could always exchange banter with this man? "We have nothing to say to each other, you and I. I do not know what you want with me, but—"

"The same thing Derrick wants."

"My fortune? My place in society?"

"Your love."

"What nonsense."

"Do you love him still?"

"I have lost the habit of affection. You helped me with that. Perhaps I should thank you."

His eyes narrowed a bit. "I'll make a better husband than your dear Derrick." His tone was edgy, but he did not respond to her baiting. He was, in fact, quite single-minded.

Her hands squeezed into fists inside her sleeves. She said calmly, "I am not marrying him, either."

He beamed again. "Because you want me."

Infuriating creature! "Neither of you wants me." She hated the petulance she heard in her voice. Why was it so difficult to hide her emotions from this man?

"Your father wants you to marry." He crossed his arms over his broad chest. He wore a dark gold brocade vest and crisp white shirt beneath his black evening coat; long stovepipe trousers molded his muscled thighs. It surprised her that he looked as good in Western clothing as he had in Eastern robes, and far more confident somehow, if that were possible. He did not sound the least bit unsure when he added, "It will be me you marry."

"What my father wishes is of no—"

A loud knock on her bedroom door interrupted her words.

Chapter 9

Honoria exchanged a swift, guilty look with her intruder and pointed to the bed without thinking. James was already on his way, and pulled the bedcurtains tightly shut as she reached the door. It was only as she was saying, "Who is it?" that Honoria realized that she should be delighted at this intrusion. She sounded irritated rather than relieved as she demanded, "What do you want?" from whoever was outside her door.

Her father walked in and gave her a brisk hug. "You're tired," he said, when he had her enfolded in his arms. "So I won't keep you."

She pushed away from him, half-afraid, half-ashamed that he would somehow be able to detect that she had been in James's embrace only moments before. "Father!" She backed up quickly, stumbled into a chair, and sat down abruptly. "Father," she repeated, staring up at him. He was beaming proudly at her.

"I haven't seen you so rosy-cheeked and full of life in ages," he proclaimed. "I do believe that young man is good for you."

"What? What do you mean?" She was only able to keep from looking around wildly by force of will. She would not look at the bed. She would not. "What young man? Captain Russell? I daresay not!" Her father's brows rose, but his smile only widened. She was shouting, wasn't she? Blast and curse her wretched temper. She noticed that her fingers were digging fiercely into the tapestry-covered arms of the chair. She made her hands relax, then she rose to stand with a show of dignified calm. Her father's hands were clasped behind his back and he was rocking back and forth on his heels, looking extremely satisfied about something. She was tempted to ask him if he was in his cups, but her father did not overindulge in drink. "Pray, sir," she asked him instead, "to what do I owe the honor of this late night visit?"

"It's not that late." He took out his pocket watch and glanced at it. There was a portrait of her mother on the inside of the case. His glance lingered on the picture for a wistful moment before he said, "It's barely eleven. Some of our guests are still playing cards downstairs, your cousin Kate among them."

Honoria took his words as a reproof. "You're

quite correct. My obligation is to be with our guests, even if I loathe gaming. I will call Huseby and dress again. I should not have left so soon—"

"Nonsense," he waved her apology away. "There's no shame in keeping country hours. Let Kate deal with the card players. We both know asking you to be my hostess was a flimsy excuse to get you into society."

And find me a husband. She couldn't help but glance at the bed. The curtains were sedately drawn. Her father wasn't likely to yank them open and demand what a man was doing in her bed. He might, in fact, be delighted to find a man in her bed. Nonsense. What a wicked, undaughterly thought.

"James Marbury will do, I think. His father and I have already discussed the matter."

Honoria literally jumped in shock. "What?"

Her father simply smiled wider. "I never did like Russell. Too bad it was too late to rescind the invitation for tonight, but it worked out well, I hear. Your cousin told me how you marched him out to the garden and read him the Riot Act." He patted her on the shoulder. "Kate is quite certain you were sincere in your loathing of the fellow."

"Quite," she responded faintly. And James was privy to every word she and her father exchanged. How typical of him to humiliate her while he remained safely in hiding.

"Good for you, my girl."

She was hardly a girl, but she knew he looked upon her as his innocent child, and always would. His love for her shone in his eyes and his beaming smile, causing an almost physical ache at knowing she was not worthy of the regard he felt so strongly for her.

"I—" She felt tears sting behind her eyes. When had her emotions become so close to the surface, so hard to control? Since when did she allow pirates to hide in her bed? "I'm very tired," she finished lamely. She plucked at her father's sleeve, trying to turn him toward the door. She tried to put a teasing smile on her face, and some emotion in her voice. "If you wish me to find a husband, I'd better get some beauty sleep, don't you think?"

The Duke of Pyneham patted her on the shoulder. "No need for that, my girl. No need to look further for a husband, I mean. The Marbury boy will do quite nicely."

This was insane. Honoria's sudden smile was quite genuine as she gazed at her father. She knew that none of the events of the last few hours could really have occurred. She had not had dinner at the same table as the two men who had blighted her existence. She had not threatened one of them in the garden. The second one was not hiding behind her bedcurtains after asking her on bended knee to be his bride. It was all a dream.

"Of course," she said. "I should have thought of it sooner." At any moment her father would leave—or perhaps turn into a parrot and fly out the window. Whatever happened next did not matter so much, now that she knew it was all a dream from which she would presently wake.

"How could you have thought of it? You just met the Marbury lad a few days ago." Her father laughed. "I should have known you'd find a unique way to begin a courtship."

A few days? She almost forgot her vow and spat out the truth. In a dream it would be all right to finally unburden herself of everything she'd kept from her father all these years. But what if this was no dream? She said, "There is no courtship with Mr. Marbury."

Her father patted her on the shoulder, his smile patronizing and insufferable. "My dear innocent," he murmured. "There doesn't need to be."

She recalled that he'd discussed a match with James with the Viscount of Brislay. "Oh, no, you don't."

Her father ignored her. "You have no clue as to what went on between you and Edward's boy at dinner. That's all right. You and the lad keep on as you've begun, and leave the viscount and me to manage the details."

Her father stepped back and took the seat she had vacated. He seemed in no hurry to leave. He gestured for her to take a second nearby tapestry chair. "There are some things you need to know about James Marbury."

She tucked her hands in her sleeves, standing rock still where she was. "Believe me, sir, I know more—"

"You've heard rumors and lies. You believed the tale of his being Edward's bastard, didn't you?"

That was true. She nodded. Did the bedcurtains ripple just now? She turned her back on the bed, and on her father as he went on.

"I'd almost forgotten the tale," he said, as she moved to look out the window. Her hands were still in her sleeves, grasping her elbows tightly. She wanted more than life to be left alone. This was not a dream, and he would not go away until he'd told his tale. James Marbury was not likely to go away soon, either. She was trapped. Again. She damned all men, looked at the moon and tried not to hear.

"I am half English, but I cannot read the language." Diego Moresco put the paper back on the table and came back across the room to where she stood as though her toes were rooted in the deep pile of the jewel-toned carpet. "Some of the letter is in English. I can read my mother's tongue, she taught me well, but I have no other education."

He told her this while he drew her reluctantly forward and made her sit. His touch was gentle but insistent. His expression was kind, concerned, but she sensed fury in him, taut and held hard. Some anger inside him was trying to get loose. He'd held it down for years, but the ropes that bound it were fraying. She didn't know how she knew that, but she knew, especially when he touched her.

"I am impatient," he said, reading her as she read him. His smile flashed, sending a wave of heat through her. "Impatient for many things. It makes me a poor host. My mother taught me to be polite. We will sit and talk for a while." There was a silver pitcher on the table, frosted with moisture. He poured some of the liquid into a crystal goblet and handed to her. The cool glass felt good between her hands. "Fruit juice," he said. "We do not drink wine here. You know the customs of Islam, I think."

"Alcohol is forbidden," she heard herself say. She felt like a parrot, or perhaps a trained monkey, mouthing words, aping human movement. "You practice the faith of Mohammed?"

He crossed his arms over his chest. "When I am in Algiers. My mother had me baptized in her faith. I do not know what faith my English father would want me to follow." He shrugged. "It's not likely I'll ever find out. Drink the juice while it's still cold. It's better that way."

She wondered if she obeyed because he owned her and had given her a command, or because she was thirsty. It was delicious. She felt so very helpless and confused, and hated it. She couldn't take her gaze off the Spaniard. She had never been alone with a man before she met him—now she seemed to be making a habit of it. She couldn't help feeling that being alone with him was better than being completely alone, but it certainly wasn't proper. Did propriety matter now? She belonged to him. The humiliation still burned in her, as if she'd been branded by it.

But she couldn't help but look at Diego Moresco and think, I belong to him, *with something that felt almost like eagerness, and—pride? Pleasure? She did not know what to call her reactions to looking at him, but she simply couldn't stop looking. Her feelings were confused and muddled, as were her normally lucid thoughts. She was so very physically aware of him, aware of the strength in his big, hard-muscled body, of the leashed danger in the economical way he moved. Aware that he was so very* male *that it made her feel small and soft and helpless and female to be near him. He was not a bit like Derrick, who loved her. She should be thinking of Derrick, not staring at a smiling barbarian corsair. Derrick loved her; Derrick did not own her.*

Not yet, some mad voice in her head whispered from out of nowhere. A father owns his daughter, a husband owns his wife. This man, this barbarian, owns you because he paid a few coins for you. What is the difference?

Moresco took the goblet from her and took her cold hands between his big ones, warming them as he began talking again. "My father was an English officer. My mother was at a convent school. She might have been a nun if they had not met."

* * *

"After the wedding Edward and Graciela were separated during the battle of Talavares. He was wounded and shipped home to England. It took him over a year to fully recover." Her father's voice reached her as if from a great distance. She didn't know how long he had been speaking, or what he had said to draw her attention back to the present. "Edward spent years searching for his lady, and years more searching for her grave after the letter he sent to her father came back with one informing him that she was dead. He didn't talk about his quest. Most of his friends forgot that he'd wedded a Spanish noblewoman. I do recall that he would only shake his head sadly whenever any of us urged him to marry again and produce an heir. Though he didn't know about James, he didn't abandon his wife. Finally, on one more visit to the Spanish embassy, he told a newly arrived official that he was searching for burial records. When he gave the woman's name, the official indignantly informed Edward that his sister was disgraced but she wasn't dead. He said that Graciela was living in Malaga and he wrote her letters, even though their father had declared her dead as far as the family was concerned. And then he challenged Edward to a duel for dishonoring the family's noble and ancient name." Her father chuckled.

She did not look at him, but at the heavy bed-curtains behind him. She thought she detected some faint movement within, and was glad her father's back was to the bed. She wondered if the man in her bed was amused at this recounting of his parents' lives. Perhaps he was squirming in embarrassment. She hoped so, as long as he didn't jump out to add an explanation of his whereabouts during the years of his father's so-called quest.

"What," she asked as her father wiped a tear of laughter from his eye, "is so very amusing?"

"You've never seen a Marbury fight a duel."

She had to bite her tongue. "No," she admitted after a moment. She put aside the memory of slashing sabers. "I don't suppose I have." Fighting for his life and hers, yes, but she had never witnessed anything so tame and formal as a duel. Duels involved honor, after all.

"Things would not have gone well with Graciela's brother, I assure you. Fortunately for the man's hide and international relations, Edward found out that Graciela had been found in Talavares by her father and dragged home after the battle. When she explained about her English husband her family were appalled, and unbelieving—there were no witnesses, no records, just a pregnant seventeen-year-old girl's word. Her father tossed her out."

She knew that. Diego had been very bitter about how his mother's family had treated her. She had assumed he was lying; spinning tales to make her trust him, win her sympathy, and make her want to help him. She wondered if her father would toss her out if he knew the truth. She didn't even have the excuse of having married the man she'd given herself to. "So she ended up working at an inn in Malaga and raising her son the best she could."

"You've heard servants' tales, I see."

"Yes," she answered, though Huseby had not reported on James Marbury's past; merely his activities since coming to London. None of the things Huseby had told her had given any clue to Marbury's true identity. Had she had any clue whatsoever, any hint that the man she had thought she'd mistaken for Diego Moresco really *was* Diego Moresco, she would have fled the country rather than gone down to dinner. Perhaps it was not too late to flee.

Recalling what had happened the last time she had left England, her glance was unwillingly pulled toward the bed. Again.

Her father followed her gaze. He stood. "You're tired. I'll be going in a moment."

A jolt of mixed joy and terror went through her. She desperately wanted her father to leave, but didn't want to be left alone with the man behind the curtains, either. Would this waking nightmare never end? Her father came closer and cupped her face with his palms, his touch gentle and warm. He kissed her on the forehead, and Honoria couldn't help but smile for him. There was nothing but hope in his eyes when they looked into hers.

"You and James Marbury will suit." He drew her closer and whispered in her ear, "Trust me, I know the signs." Though he still whispered, there was steel in his voice as he added, "Marry him. Give me grandchildren."

They both knew it was not a request. It was a good thing that he did not command her to be happy. She could not even try to find words to answer him, but he knew her very well. He stepped back with a sad smile. "You are thinking that it's too late to argue. You do look very tired. Go to bed now, Honoria. We'll speak again tomorrow."

Her father was certainly right about how weary she was. She closed her eyes as he turned away. She heard footsteps, and a door opening and closing. She felt weak and faint and as if there was no air in the world. It was far too dark, and she was alone.

The next thing she knew she was being held in strong arms and a warm embrace. She heard the steady thrum of a heartbeat as her cheek rested against crisply starched linen. Her hand rested on a broad shoulder, her fingertips brushed against the soft wave of hair. Someone was carrying her.

"You were trying to faint," she was told.

"I succeeded," she replied, realizing where she was and who held her. She was too weary and too comfortable to fight with him. "Briefly." He must have caught her as she fell. She wasn't alone, after all.

"Hush."

She did not want to be told to hush, but she had nothing to say at the moment, either. She sighed, and rubbed her cheek against his chest. He smelled good, like starch and tangy cologne, and his own spicy scent. Cinnamon, she thought. Or perhaps she wanted to sprinkle him with cinnamon and eat him up. She sighed again, languidly.

A finger slowly traced the curve of her lips. "You're smiling."

"I do. Sometimes." Honoria knew she was less than half awake, but had no strength in her and less sense. It was lovely not to think. Her limbs were heavy, but the rest of her seemed to float, her blood flowing warm and sweet as heated honey. Honey eyes. Honey and cinnamon. Her fingers twined in thick hair. Her lips found his throat. He tasted as good as she remembered. It was his turn to sigh. It was a warm night. Why was he wearing so many clothes? Why was she?

Oh, yes, she remembered now—they were in England. She hated him, but she couldn't make it matter right now. Later, perhaps.

He put her down on the bed and came with her. Bedlinens rustled, and the mattress gave beneath them, embracing and supporting, soft with swansdown. Her eyes were too heavy to open; her hands could not seem to stop clinging to him. He was the one solid thing in the soft, soft world. She felt as if her limbs were made of half-melted candlewax, heated, pliable, and languid. His mouth did not seem to have any trouble finding hers.

It was as if she had never been kissed before, and as though he had never stopped kissing her. It was new and familiar, wonderful and completely wrong. When his mouth left hers and moved down to her throat she murmured, "I despise you," into the soft fall of his hair. *Don't stop.*

"I know," was the response whispered gently against her pulse. "But you missed me."

It was the smugness in his voice that shattered Honoria's delicious, dreamy languor. Her eyes snapped open, meeting his gaze just as he lifted his head to kiss her again. She shoved against his shoulders. There was mocking laughter in those light gold eyes when he sat up. But for being clean-shaven, he looked as disreputable as he ever had in Algiers, with his neckcloth askew and his hair mussed. That she was responsible for his disheveled state was of no moment. Her hair was unbound and curled wildly around her face. Her hand went to her throat and found that the first of the long row of pearl buttons that fastened her nightgown was undone.

"Only one little button, duchess mine," James said with the softest, most wicked of laughs. He reached out, his big hand covering hers, his fingers resting on the line of her jaw. "Only a little flesh showing." He exerted gentle pressure against her throat. She had not realized she was sitting bolt upright until he pushed her back against the thick stack of pillows. He followed her, leaning close. "But you felt it when I touched you there." She shivered as he ran his thumb down the side of her throat. That the shiver was one of need infuriated her.

"I was not made for passion," she heard herself say.

"Once you were."

"That was an aberration."

Amusement danced across his lips and in his eyes. "You use such big words."

She lifted her head haughtily, but could not escape his touch. "I am a large woman. Large words suit me."

He nodded. "Everything about you is large. I like that." He would have kissed her again if her free hand had not shot out and delivered a resounding slap across his cheek. "I was thinking of your large soul," he said as he jumped back to avoid the second swing of her arm. He grasped both her wrists and held them tightly out before her.

"You were thinking of my large dowry, more likely."

"I'm sure it is quite huge. That isn't why I'm going to marry you."

"You are not marrying me."

"Your father thinks so. You have slapped me twice in the last few days," he told her. His hands were quite tight around her trapped wrists, and there was a dangerous warning in his eyes. His cheek was red with the mark of her hand. "I think you owe me perhaps one more. After that I will become very angry with you."

She remembered suddenly, and with great vividness, the long pale scars on his heavily muscled back, and was ashamed of herself for having struck him. Those scars had ached even though years old. She remembered brown skin shiny with fragrant oil, and how he had blessed her and sighed and relaxed beneath her kneading fingers. He would grow boneless and blissful, like some large hunting cat. Then he would turn over, with fire in his eyes and grasp her around her naked waist and—

He had suffered enough physical pain in his life without her adding to it. Besides, wit had always been her weapon of choice. If she *could* keep her wits about her without succumbing to the lure of foolish, best forgotten memories. She said stiffly, "I wouldn't think of laying a hand on you, Mr. Marbury."

He flashed her a wicked smile. "But I want your hands on me, sweetheart."

Perhaps she *would* hit him, just once more, for old times' sake. She drew herself up indignantly to say something taunting, cutting, vicious, but her mind drew a complete blank. All she could think of was hands. His. On her. It had all happened years ago, yet the yearning, the craving, was as fresh and frenzied as it had been in that moonlit room in Algiers. How it could be, she did not know, after all these years of being dead to feeling—but it was so. She *wanted*.

And rejected wanting with all her soul. She had made her choice. She would never again let herself be controlled by desire. Men might control her life, but her emotions and intellect were hers alone to command. She had chosen intellect over emotion and found it offered as much freedom as she was likely to achieve in a man's world. That this man could manipulate her emotions even after all these years infuriated her, but she was more angry with herself than she was with him. It was in man's nature to use women. It was a woman's own fault for allowing it.

But she still *wanted* him.

"You are either about to damn me to hell or draw me down on your bed," he said. Her wrists ached when he let them go, but not because he had held them too tightly. She was frozen with indecision yet burning with longing as he took a step away from the bed. He grasped one of the curtains he'd pulled back, bunching the heavy material in his fist. "If I don't go soon, I won't go at all."

And he'd vowed that he would wait until she was his wife. Honor required it. He would not break his promise, though the sight of her lying so invitingly on the big bed sorely tempted him. Her kisses were like no other woman's, her embrace was sweeter, infinitely arousing, endlessly satisfying. Now he knew why he had kissed and embraced so many others, losing himself in debauchery: he had been trying to recapture what it was like to make love to Honoria. He might never be able to recapture it, not with all the years and the lies and the hidden truths between them. Yet the heat rushed through him as strongly as ever, he was hard with need, and his senses screamed to his mind that vows were for fools—to take the woman now!

He was a weak man, not a paragon of virtue like his father. The woman was before him, ripe and lovely and lush. His Honoria looked as desirable with one button undone and her spectacles askew as any other woman would completely naked and moaning with lust.

He'd given in to the impulse once, but he had not been a man of honor then. Now he must prove that he was.

He reached down and straightened her glasses, though he wanted to caress her cheek and his fingers itched to slowly undo the small pearl buttons and lay her full breasts bare. "I came here to seduce you," he said, and forced himself to move away. "Or at least to remind you of what it is to be a woman." She stared after him as he backed stiffly into the shadows beyond lamplight and firelight and the warmth of her reluctant embrace. He forced a smile, hoping she would not see the strain from a distance. "We'll discuss our betrothal further at the Queen's ball tomorrow night."

"We'll—" She sputtered angrily and started to rise from the bed.

He blew her a kiss and moved toward the window he'd found unlatched earlier. "I'll go out the way I came. Sleep well, my *houri*, and dream of being Mrs. Marbury."

Chapter 10

"She can't be Mrs. Marbury, James," his father told him.

James paused with his cup of coffee halfway to his lips, then slowly set the delicate china cup back on its saucer. The morning was bright and sunny, the coffee smelled delicious, and birdsong from the garden filled the air. The day had seemed to be getting off to a promising start. He stared in frustrated confusion at the slender man across from him. "But you said you wanted me to marry her."

His father had been reading a letter bearing the crest of the Duke of Pyneham when James came into the room, and he smiled as he said, "I do want you to marry her." He tapped the heavy sheet of vellum. "So does her father. But Lady Alexandra Pyne cannot become Mrs. James Marbury."

James had not slept well, or much. He hoped

that his lack of rest was affecting his concentration. "Perhaps I am not hearing you correctly, sir. Why—?"

"Charles II will not allow it," his father said. "An English king," he added, after James stared at him without comprehension. "Your Honoria's ancestor. He was King of England in the late seventeenth century," the viscount went on as James continued to stare blankly, his breakfast forgotten. "It was Charles who created the first duchess, and the law that allows the eldest child rather than the eldest son to inherit the title."

Intense tutoring had left James with a solid working knowledge of the rules of the English and Spanish nobility. "I've never heard of such a thing." He ran a thumb along the freshly shaved line of his jaw, and shrugged. "I had wondered how it was that the duke's daughter followed him in succession. But Englishwomen take their husband's name. She will be—"

"You will take her name," his father broke in, patient but persistent. "That is another part of the special law. The family name remains Pyne, no matter whom they marry or who inherits. There have been only two duchesses, and both husbands took their name. It is a small enough thing, James, to achieve the goal you have set out to accomplish."

James could not explain the sense of loss and betrayal that washed over him at his father's mild gaze and tone. "My name is Marbury." His throat tightened with so much pain that he found it difficult to speak. "I have only just gotten it back." His fist clenched around the fragile china cup, crushing it. Hot coffee splattered his hand, shards of china bit into his flesh, but he barely noticed any pain. "It is not such a small thing for me to give it up."

The viscount's pale skin went even paler, and his large eyes filled with compassion. Not pity; James would have walked out if the other man had shown him any trace of pity. "You are my true born son. My heir. The child I love. Nothing can take that from you."

"Someone already did," James reminded him.

Diego watched Honoria's face while he told her his story. He didn't know why he was telling her his history, or why he couldn't take his gaze off her. He enjoyed looking at her. She was so uniquely attractive. He had thought so from the first moment he saw her. She was certainly the tallest woman he had ever met, but he was no small man. He liked that they were practically eye to eye when they stood together. He had seen many beautiful women, and had not a few of them as lovers. Beauty was easy to come by in the souks *and* bagnios *of the Barbary ports, but lively intelligence and quick wit were less readily available.*

"My mother is very learned, like you," he told her

as she sat on the edge of her chair. "But she had no chance to teach me more than to read Spanish." He waved toward the wrinkled paper on the table. "If she were here, she could perhaps read some of Ibrahim Rais's code. Fortunately, she is safe in Malaga. I pray she is safe," he added with a sigh. After all these years he still missed her desperately. "She is the daughter of an ancient and noble house," he went on bitterly, "but she works in a tavern, or did when last I saw her. Her brother sends her a little money sometimes. I went out in the fishing boats to help when I was eleven."

There was unwavering concentration in her blue eyes. She had the loveliest blue eyes he had ever seen, even if she had to wear spectacles to see. Diego smiled at her, delighted in her company, guarded though it was. They were truly alone together for the first time since they had met. He wanted to kiss her, though he had not bought her to be his concubine. He needed her sharp wits and quick, beautiful eyes for another reason entirely. But he did not think she needed the glasses to see clearly: he had felt her seeing into his soul since the moment they met. He knew he should fear her for that, should be as wary of her as she was of him. Instead he felt as giddy as the wild boy he had once been, the boy he rushed to tell her about as he paced.

"You would have liked me in those days. I would have taken you to the flower market, and we would have bought oranges and eaten them on the long steps above the harbor and watched the fishing boats.

I didn't like fishing, but I love to sail. My mother didn't want me to go to sea, but I was nearly a man. It was time I started to take care of her." He sighed and gestured broadly. *"But there was a storm that blew the fishing fleet off course, too close to the routes sailed by the corsairs."*

He moved to perch on the table before Honoria's chair. Everything he'd felt and feared and been through had been his closely guarded secrets for years. He'd held his privacy tightly, protected it when it was all he had in the world, yet now he handed his life to Honoria Pyne with an eagerness that was almost unthinking. She did not laugh, or repudiate him. She listened gravely, her guard down. She was lost in his story, her bright blue eyes full of innocent interest.

He did not know when he had taken her hands in his, but he found he needed to be touching her when he told the rest. "I was big for my age, and strong. Ibrahim Rais took me for a slave on his galley. I pulled an oar and fought to survive, and tried to escape. Ibrahim Rais does not take kindly to escape attempts. He flogged me, and I tried to run again. Only to be flogged again. He said he didn't intend to kill me if I escaped again—not until he tracked down every member of my family and killed them first. He will have complete loyalty, even in his galley slaves. I've seen him murder innocents, Honoria—the relatives of those who thought they had escaped him. He always finds the ones he calls trai-

tors. He rules through fear, and once you are his, you are his forever.

I stopped fighting him and started thinking. He found out I was smart, and cunning." His laugh was soft, bitter and dangerous. "I learned what battles to fight and when. I learned patience. I was more cunning than I ever let show, but cautious. I've become rich and trusted, but I have never given up trying to escape."

He was on his knees in front of Honoria's chair. He still held one of her hands in his, but his other hand cupped her cheek. Her soft, warm, supple cheek. Her eyes were large and bright as coins. "I will never let Ibrahim Rais hurt you," he promised her. "I will protect you with my life." He did not know why he spoke so; he had not meant to offer her anything but a safe haven inside the walls of his house. Instead he was making extravagant promises, and meaning every word.

She didn't look like she believed it, and Diego was glad of that. At least he told himself it was better for her not to trust him. Despite the prick of hurt, he knew he could not afford to make promises—not when the need for freedom was eating up his soul. He had to think of himself first. He moved back and resumed his perch on the edge of the table.

"I never wanted to be a pirate."

"But you are one." The first words she'd spoken in some time were no more than blunt truth.

"But I don't want to be one. Last year I thought I had found a way out. Last year, I actually per-

formed a good deed. You look skeptical, señorita, *but it is true. I saved the bey's life," he said, drawing himself up proudly. "An assassination attempt while the bey visited the harbor to inspect the fleet. I was rewarded grandly at a ceremony in the bey's palace. The bey himself presented me with a priceless sword made of solid silver." He stretched his hands out before him, to show her the length. "A beautiful cutlass, though of course, silver doesn't hold an edge. I was grateful for the honor, but it was the several pounds of silver and the jewels in the hilt of the sword that I wanted. That, and for the bey to give me safe conduct from the city. I could have returned home a wealthy man.*

But Ibrahim Rais interfered. He insisted the sword and my service rightfully belonged to him. The bey needed Ibrahim Rais's ships and the wealth he brought to the city, so he agreed. I was left with nothing but his gratitude, and all I could do was smile and say that his gratitude was more than enough."

He could still taste the bitterness in his mouth, and dark anger burned in him as though he'd swallowed hot coals. He took a long swallow of the cool fruit drink and forced down the anger that he had kept under control for so long. He had to be patient, to keep his head. But he was so close! And she was so—

What was she? He looked at the red-haired Englishwoman, trying to be ruthlessly objective. She is your tool, he reminded himself. You bought her for her talent with languages. She is nothing more than a means to an end. Use her. That is what she is here for. He studied the alert intelligence on her fine-skinned face, and found himself counting the dust of freckles across her cheeks and nose—not for the first time.

He found himself wanting to trace the soft line of her lips. It would be a sweet mouth to kiss. Her lushly curved body was hidden by layers of loosely fitting robes, but he studied that as well as she sat stiff and straight in the chair across from him. He wanted to do more than to look, he wanted to touch and taste and explore. He found that his hands had curled tightly around the inlaid edge of the table, aching with the urge to draw her from the chair and strip off layer after layer to finally look at all the woman that—

Belonged to him.

Why not do what he wanted with her?

Because that was not why he had schemed to bring her secretly into his house.

Wasn't it? the insidious voice in his head questioned. He ignored the voice that told him he could do whatever he wanted. He had never taken a woman, slave or free, against her wishes. He was not Ibrahim Rais, he reminded himself harshly, to do what he wanted with whomever he wished. But Diego knew he was no better than Ibrahim Rais; that his master had taught him well how to be cruel and indulge every man's natural selfishness. If he had a conscience or any kindness left in him, this innocent *young woman would be safely waiting to be ransomed back to her home and family. What was to become of her, once he'd used her for his own purposes?*

She'll be safe, he told himself as he moved to the other side of the table. It was necessary to put distance between himself and the woman he wanted. He doubted she'd ever been alone in a room with a man before. He wondered if she had the slightest notion of what happened when a man and woman came together when they were alone. To teach her was so tempting.

He fought the temptation, and took up the letter to show her. His hands shook a little. He stared at them, telling himself that, yes, desire ran hot through him, but that it was desire for freedom, desire for the treasure that was rightfully his. Honoria was not the cause of this weakness, or the heat that flared inside him. He was not going to lay a hand on her. She was safe, from his needs, and Ibrahim Rais's vengeance. All she had to do was translate the letter. Ibrahim Rais would never know Diego had stolen his precious letter, or that Honoria Pyne had translated it for him. There was no way any harm could come to her over this.

St. Ambrose Rectory
London, 1838

I am convinced that I know the very girl who is the key to your happiness, my son.

* * *

The Reverend Joshua Menzies read the words aloud slowly, trying once more to make sense of them before he was called to his duties as pastor of St. Ambrose's.

Someone had died in a brawl—no surprise there. Not a night went by in this parish in the slums of London without someone dying in a fight, or from cholera, or in a house fire, or from being attacked by thieving ruffians, or from drinking bad spirits. People died all the time, and were no great loss. That his flock expected him to hold a funeral service in the rain was damned inconvenient. He wanted to wait until he was good and drunk before joining the mourners out in the downpour. If he joined them at all—he might just let the sexton read through the service. The message from his long-lost father made a good excuse to spend the day indoors and alone.

The letter that had arrived at the parsonage just an hour before, delivered by the hand of a grimy, furtive gypsy vagabond, had been written at least a year before. The paper was soiled and torn, the ink faded. The words, from a man he thought dead, were strange. Instructive. Morally uplifting. Full of repentance for the days the old man had spent as a renegade corsair calling himself Ibrahim Rais. The hoary platitudes were even worse than the sniffling breast-beating. This was not the man Joshua remembered, but certainly the handwriting was his father's.

"Abraham Menzies, back from the dead," Joshua mused. "Lucifer probably wouldn't have him." He'd thought the old man dead, or that he'd forgotten his English family completely when he disappeared into hiding in the Ottoman Empire. His wealth and power and cunning hadn't saved him from capture when the pirate city was taken back in 1830. The wonder was that the fierce and feared Ibrahim Rais hadn't met the fate he so richly deserved. Perhaps all his wealth had gone into buying a prison cell rather than a hangman's rope. What really mattered was not that Abraham Menzies was still alive, but that none of his wealth had made its way home to the son he'd left behind.

Joshua Menzies remembered the days when he'd wanted to be a pirate himself, how he'd longed to sail off to Barbary to join his father in raiding and plundering. But his father wanted respectability for his family. Abraham Menzies had deserted the British Navy to find his fortune, but he wanted his family tucked safely away, far from the dangers in the heathen land where he'd found wealth and power. Little Joshua remained with his mother in a sleepy Cotswolds village, living on the money and letters that always arrived by mysterious means, until one day word came that Algiers had fallen. He was well into his studies at Oxford by then—reluctantly, but it had been what his father wanted of him. It was just as well that he'd struggled on and taken a divinity degree, as there was no future in pirating anymore. But not much future in being a vicar with no rich patron or relatives to help him get on in the Church, either. His hope had been to secure a place as secretary to one of the wealthy friends he'd caroused with at Oxford, but no young lord had taken him into their service. And the money from his father had long ago run out, so it was a poor London parish for Joshua Menzies.

Menzies stretched his long legs out under his desk, smoothed the wrinkled paper once more, and continued reading.

> The more I think upon the past, if my mind does not betray me, if my reason has not been stolen, if my hunger for gold and gems has not driven me mad, you will listen to me now. I was wicked then—as vain as the young Spanish captain I loved as a son. He stole my heart, but he did not delve deep enough to reach my words of wisdom. That is still the property of my true son. It is you I will instruct in the way to reach earthly paradise. After all these years in prison, I have had much time to think long and hard on what was and what will be.
>
> I pray that it is not too late for the heart of a good woman to bring all I desire for you to

light. She is a treasure. The key to a treasure for you, certainly. A well-read and much learned scholar with a knowledge of languages equal to your own. In fact, she was able to decipher the long letter I sent to you as a test—the one written by many scribes in many tongues. I thought this most clever in a woman. I'm sure she will remember the contents of this correspondence when you meet. It will give you something to seriously discuss with her. I will tell you what I remember of her so that you may hastily seek her out. Her name is Honoria. A wellborn English lass. I met her aboard a merchant ship called the *Manticore*. She wore mourning black, for the loss of her dear mother, I believe. You must find this girl. I suffer torment and torture because you do not know her. Pain brings out the truth in me. You suffer for lack of knowledge. Honoria will suffer until she gives it to you, but then you will have all the treasure you need.

What the devil was the old man talking about? Had seven years in a French prison leached all the wily sense out of the old brigand's head? Joshua doubted that. The old man was a survivor, clever. Doubtless his wits were as intact as ever. It was Joshua who had little reason to use his faculties these days. No influential connections, and no money to purchase a cushy preferment. He had a leaking roof over his head and made barely enough from the collection plate to keep himself in cheap gin. It was a hell of a way to live, but he'd grown used to it. And used to having no reason to use the wit and intellect he'd been born with and honed so carefully with study. Now, here was this puzzling letter from his father telling that he was to—what? marry?—this Honoria.

"How am I to do that?" He rubbed the three-day-old stubble on his chin, then took a long quaff of spirits from a dented and dull pewter mug. "I'm a dutiful son, you old sod, but what the devil do you really want me to do?"

Menzies read the letter again, and yet again. Someone knocked on the rectory door, but he ignored it. He got up and paced for a while across the creaking, rotting floorboards. Mice scurried along the wainscoting, not in any great hurry to escape from sight. Then it came to him in a flash.

He went back and looked carefully at the ancient, wrinkled, marked-up paper. It was a code, of course! His father would be closely watched. His jailers would suspect him of having many secrets, so if Abraham Menzies went to the trouble to smuggle a letter to his son from the depths of a French prison, the message would be important. And it would be hidden.

Rereading the document, he realized that there were slight differences in the handwriting in some of the words, and faint marks by others. When he read only those words, the message was clear.

Stolen gold and gems. Spanish captain stole way to earthly paradise. Woman bring to light treasure. Key to treasure a knowledge of languages. She decipher the letter I sent to you. Clever woman will remember the contents. Discuss with Honoria. Wellborn English lass. Merchant ship called Manticore. *She wore mourning black for mother. This girl suffer torment and torture. Pain brings out the truth. Honoria suffer until she give it to you. Then you will have the treasure.*

Joshua Menzies rubbed his jaw again. "Well now, isn't that interesting?" He smiled, for the first time in a very long time. "So the old bastard *did* send me word of where he hid his spoils before the French attacked. The letter just never got to me."

Apparently it had been stolen by a Spaniard and the code deciphered by this Honoria chit. What was required of him was to find a girl who had been in mourning while aboard a certain merchant ship. Surely he was still clever enough to find the records of this ship called the *Manticore*. Then, his father thought that all that would be needed to make Joshua Menzies a wealthy man was a little pain and torture of a fragile, delicate woman.

Menzies's smile widened. "I'll enjoy that part."

"I have a letter from your mother," Edward Marbury said after silence had drawn out between them and become uncomfortable.

The statement lifted James's dark, resentful mood. "Is she coming?" He leaned forward with sudden eagerness. "Is she?" A servant had appeared and cleaned up the spilled coffee and gathered up the remains of James's broken cup. He had a fresh cup of coffee beside him now.

"Yes." His father's smile was bright and happy. When the slender, long-faced man smiled, James could see the resemblance between them. His father claimed they were alike in spirit, but James wasn't so sure. "The stubborn woman has finally agreed to sell the inn you bought for her and come live in England. I've never fancied myself as an innkeeper," his father went on. "So I'm pleased to find out that I won't have to spend the rest of my life—" He made a dismissive gesture. "Doing whatever it is innkeepers do."

James laughed. "I can see you standing behind a bar and telling a customer who wants an expensive bottle of wine that the port he fancies is no good. Or insisting that the maids change the bedlinen every day."

His father was not a man who joked easily. He nodded at James's jest, and said, "If your mother wanted me to help her with her inn, she knows I would do it. Though you are correct about my lack of business wit." Unlike most aristocrats James knew, the Viscount of Brislay had no disdain for those in trade or commerce. James did not think his father disdained anyone, except the dishonest and dishonorable.

James finished his coffee and said, "You set a hard example to live up to, sir."

His father gave another dismissive flick of his hand. "Nonsense. I love the woman. You know, sometimes while I spent all those years looking for her I almost convinced myself that I was a fool, a dreamer. I'd go through months of telling myself that I'd put a pretty, but foolish and feckless girl up on an impossible pedestal. That even if I found her, the love I thought we'd had could not have survived the years. I'd tell myself that she was too young to have truly loved me, that she'd found someone else, that she wouldn't even remember me if we met again. I gave myself every excuse I could think of to call a halt to the search. But I could never forget the first time we looked at each other. I could not forget the way that frightened girl helped the others in the burning convent escape when the French soldiers set the town on fire. I could not forget the way she organized a refugee camp and bullied a supply sergeant to feed those terrified people. I could not forget how she nursed the wounded. She was fearless and strong. I remembered how she thought she was too tall and awkward, and how she blushed when I told her she was the most beautiful woman in the world. I remembered how she looked at me when we were married, and the first time we—" He blushed, and cleared his throat.

There were some things about his parents James did not want to know. He glanced up at the pastel cupids and clouds painted on the ceiling. "When will she be here?" he asked as he got up to fill a fresh plate with food from the silver chafing dishes on the sideboard.

"She sailed the day she mailed the letter. I'm surprised it arrived before her. Independent chit," his father complained. "Always has to make her own arrangements and do everything her own way. I could easily have sent my yacht for her, or had a carriage waiting at Dover." For all his complaining, James heard his father's pleased pride at his mother's stalwart nature. "Ah, well," he went on, picking up the duke's letter again. "At least Graciela will be here in time for your wedding."

Wedding. James paused with a bite of roast beef halfway to his mouth, and the scrap of meat dangled in midair while he turned a distraught gaze on his father.

Wedding. He had vowed he would do it, but—

Somehow the thought of having his mother at the wedding ceremony made the whole en-

self in this situation. But if "dear Derrick" had acted like a man—

"Of course not," his father said, and took a sip of coffee. When he put the cup down he asked mildly, "What are you going to do about him?"

James threw his napkin decisively on the table. "I'm going to get a Special Marriage License—that's what I'm going to do."

Chapter 11

"You want me to translate a letter?"

He held the tattered paper toward her. "Here it is."

When she did not move, Diego Moresco tilted his head to one side and smiled his winning smile at her. He exuded bright, brisk confidence, with an undertone of masculine danger. The danger, she suspected, was that she found him the most masculine male she had ever encountered. Faced with the reckless, rascally attractiveness of Diego Moresco, she could scarcely recall what Derrick looked like.

She looked around the room, with its Oriental furnishings lit by the warm glow from brass lamps. The scent of night-blooming jasmine drifted in from a garden through a high latticed window, along with the tinkling of a fountain. Everything was so exotic, foreign, different. She felt lost, not only a stranger in a strange land, but a stranger to herself. She *felt exotic. Anything could happen. Her imagination took flights she'd never anticipated whenever she looked at Diego Moresco. She even felt beautiful when he looked at her. Which was why her gaze inevitably went back to his. His honey-colored eyes held hunger in them. For a moment she thought the hunger might be for her, rather than greed to possess this silver sword he'd told her of.*

What nonsense! Yet—her body grew hot and tight, and there was a needy ache deep inside her whenever he looked at her. And looking at him—it made her feel like her bones were going to melt, made her heart thrum, and addled her senses. She wanted to touch what she looked at, and looking back was something she grew bolder at each time. Looking at him was becoming a craving that she knew could only be of a carnal nature. She had never experienced this sweet feverishness with Derrick, not even when he held her in his arms and kissed her. Diego Moresco had not kissed her, yet she could imagine what it must be like.

Derrick had told her she was beautiful, and she had known it to be a fond, indulgent lie. She was a healthy young woman with good teeth and an expensive wardrobe. She wore spectacles. She was tall as a man, with large feet, and red-haired, besides, when the fashion was for delicate little dark-haired sylphs. Yet for some reason, Diego Moresco, by doing nothing at all but focusing his attention on her, made her feel *beautiful. No—he made her feel . . . desired.*

Perhaps it was the Arabic clothing. All the layers

and veils lent any woman an air of mystery. Perhaps they automatically made a man wonder what was hidden beneath all that concealment. Would even Derrick look at her as though she were a woman and not an heiress if he saw her dressed in veils?

What an unkind thought! And where had it come from? Honoria glared at the pirate as though he had put the thought in her mind, and then realized that he was patiently waiting for her to do as he bid. That was all he wanted of her. She was desired all right, but only for her intellectual abilities! Unreasonably angry, she snapped, "I won't do it."

The sudden crushed hope on Diego's face sent a pang of guilt through her. But for what? And for whom and why? Honoria was so confused for a moment that her vision swam with dizziness, sending the room spinning around her. When the dizziness ended she discovered that she was on her feet, and furious.

"I won't do it," she proclaimed loudly. She brought a fist down hard on the tabletop. "I won't!" She wasn't even quite sure what it was she wasn't going to do. Everything? Nothing?

Diego was on his feet as well. "You must." He pointed at the paper. "It is my will."

She glanced at the much-folded paper. "If it's your will, then you know what's in it. No doubt you have made a large behest to all those you have left widowed and orphaned."

He looked confused for a moment, then laughed

harshly. "Word games. And whom did I leave you to in my will, do you think?"

"A camel merchant, perhaps," she snapped back. "I'm not worth very much."

"You're worth everything to me."

There was something fervent in his tone and eyes that terrified and thrilled her. Her laugh was as shrill as his had been harsh. "I'm worth fourteen drachma."

"You are priceless." He looked surprised and blushed like a boy. Then his expression darkened. His voice held a dangerous edge when he said, "I order you to obey me."

For the faintest flash of a moment, she had found Diego Moresco—endearing. Now she reacted with fury and pride, more to staunch the fearful attraction. She was so very, very confused. "You what!" she shouted back. "How dare you?"

He was suddenly beside her, holding her close. She had no idea how it had happened, or why her arms were wrapped tightly around him as well. "I don't want . . . I don't . . . I want—"

"I do not want to," Honoria told her father, and they were not even discussing James Marbury, for once. She was on her way to a royal ball, dressed in a turquoise gown that Cousin Kate assured her set off her flamboyant hair in a most spectacular fashion. She had not yet taken off her spectacles, and would not until the Pyneham coach reached the entrance to Buckingham Palace. That was not likely to be for a while, as the coaches were lined up three deep and stretched along the street for at least half a mile. Though the Pyneham coach was decorated with the crest of a duke, their coat of arms carried no more privilege than any other on their way to see the Queen. Honoria was perfectly content to wait out the traffic snarl; she'd brought a book with her and the interior of the coach was comfortable and quite well lit. She was never in any hurry to carry out her social duties, especially now that her scandalous past was likely to step up and ask for a waltz, rather than to be merely suspected and decently whispered about behind fans.

Her father moved restlessly on the seat opposite her, probably impatient at having to wait in line to reach the palace entrance, since he did not look annoyed with her. "I don't blame you, my dear," he answered her protest. "I wouldn't want to become a lady-in-waiting to the Queen, either, but think of the advantages."

The Reform Party did not have much access to the young monarch at the moment. An appointment for her to such an exalted position as the Queen's attendant would be quite a feather in the Reformers' cap, she supposed, an indication that the Reformers were not completely out of favor.

"It would be excruciatingly boring," she pointed out. Honoria folded her hands in her lap and attempted to be her most reasonable and logical self while the carriage rolled forward a foot or so. "Her Majesty is—uh—" How to say this politely? "Fond of the more melodramatic plays. And of having maudlin light fiction read to her. I am not sure I could manage to stay awake during such entertainments, sir. Snoring in the royal presence would be most unseemly."

He waved her first sally away. "Boredom would be a small price to pay for helping to bring the plight of Her Majesty's poorer subjects to her attention. You are well known for your good works, my dear. You would be a shining example among a court of frivolous girls."

Honoria did not feel any particular need for her charitable work to be an example, or even noted. There had been speculative jests made about contributions she had made to several institutions that aided fallen women. She pointed out as gently as possible, "My reputation is not quite so unsullied as should be expected of a royal lady-in-waiting."

He nodded. "I have spoken with Baroness Lehzen and have assured the Queen's dearest friend the truth of the matter myself. Her approval of you is essential if you are to serve the Queen."

She tilted her head curiously to one side. "Indeed, sir? What have you told that paragon of Germanic virtue?"

"I told her what happened, of course. That the ship that was returning you home from Majorca after your mother's death was commandeered to help transport troops and supplies to the attack on Algiers. That you were inadvertently present during the fall of the corsairs' stronghold, but that you certainly had no contact with any of the pirate scum who infested the city. That, yes, your betrothed was also on board the same ship and subsequently broke off the engagement, but that was hardly due to any unsavory circumstances. That no honor was besmirched; rather, it was your grief for your mother that drove a wedge between you and Captain Russell."

It was a good story, a believable one. She had spent many pounds in the effort to make it so. No one but she, her loyal maid—and two men who were likely to be present at Buckingham Palace tonight—knew the truth. And only she and James Marbury knew the complete truth, though no doubt they had different versions of it. Truth was a very malleable thing. Gossip even more so, and almost as cruel. There had been much speculation about her adventures in the decadent fleshpots of the East, all with no more evidence than that she had been in Algiers when the city fell to the French. When the malicious whispers had gotten back to her, she had retired from society in the hope of keeping any scandal from touching her father. She could tell by looking at his tightly clenched jaw now that she had not been able to protect him completely.

Lord knew how he would respond if he ever knew the truth. She feared it might bring on a stroke as well as breaking his heart utterly.

"You've led a blameless life," her father proclaimed, bringing a fist down on the thickly upholstered carriage seat for emphasis. "I will see you honored with a place at court."

She kept her voice steady and gentle. "I seek no such honors."

He ignored her. "As soon as you are married to James Marbury, I will push harder for your appointment."

"Married?" She hated women who squeaked like mice, but did it herself more and more of late. "Another reason you wish me married is so I can have the shield of propriety that comes with being a matron rather than a maiden. It suits your politics as well as your paternal and dynastic aims to see me leg-shackled to a male of your choosing."

"Precisely," he responded with a wide smile. He seemed to think she approved of the cleverness of all these machinations. "We have a great many canny, frugal folk in our bloodline, my child. I think I might have some knowledge of getting the best bargain for the least amount of effort."

"It might be a wise bargain, sir. You may even see me married," she conceded grudgingly. Perhaps she should latch onto some fortune hunter to prevent this Marbury match everyone seemed to think was a settled fact. "But I still doubt the Queen will have me as an attendant."

"And why do you doubt it, child?"

"Because she is a woman, sir, with all the vanities our gender is prey to." The carriage moved forward again as Honoria finished, "And no woman as tiny as our little majesty is going to have a lady-in-waiting who towers a foot taller than she. No one," she reminded, "stands taller than the Queen of England." Before he could make any rejoinder, she added, "Oh, good, we've reached the entrance."

Chapter 12

"May I have this waltz?"

"I knew it," Honoria muttered under her breath.

James saw the light that came into Honoria's eyes as Derrick Russell reached her one step ahead of him, and requested to dance with her a second before James spoke. He hoped the light was one of battle rather than welcome, but couldn't tell by the amiable expression on her face. He had watched her for the last several hours as she moved through the ballroom with stately grace, always close by her father's side, always faintly smiling, gracious and correct to all. There was an alert, intelligent dignity in everything she did that he thought as regal as any queen's. But, then, being a future duchess was not so far from a queen, he supposed.

And who was he to aspire to the hand of a duchess?

The son of a viscount, and his noble Spanish lineage went back a thousand years further. He had as much right to be in the same room as the Queen of England as Honoria Pyne, who hadn't seemed to look at him tonight. He wondered if she had seen him make his formal bow before the tiny young queen. Or if she had watched him dancing with other women as the evening slowly passed. Of course, she couldn't see very far without her glasses.

The room was overheated and stuffy, crowded with dignitaries and bejeweled ladies. The orchestra was loud, if not particularly good, loud enough to be heard above the roar of laughter and conversation. James was not here to have a good time, but he was pleased that the palace ball was not the staid affair he'd feared it would be. Refreshment tables were set up against walls which were painted a garish shade of mustard yellow. Huge flower arrangements decorated the tables and were set on marble plinths. White velvet curtains trimmed with gold draped across tall windows that he longed to throw open to let fresh air into the overcrowded room.

Honoria's gown of vivid green-blue and her crown of copper hair stood out like a beautiful beacon in the crush, where most of the women were in fashionable white and pastels or the dark shades suited to matrons. It didn't hurt that she was the tallest woman in the room.

James did not think she was aware that he and Russell were not the only men who took long, slow assessing looks at her. Of course, she couldn't see that anyone looked at her with admiration. That was not such a bad thing for him, perhaps, but what about Honoria? He rubbed his chin thoughtfully, and moved swiftly while Russell waited impatiently in front of Honoria for an answer. The Navy captain preened in his threadbare uniform and looked as though he was doing Honoria a great favor by deigning to consider her worthy of sharing one little dance.

Honoria was glaring at Russell and trying her best to pretend James wasn't there at all. This made it even easier for James to make his move. A boyhood on the streets of Malaga and adolescence in the souks of Algiers had helped him develop swift, deft hands. A fan and small reticule dangled from Honoria's wrist, easy prey for even his rusty purse-snatching skills. He slipped the delicate straps off her in an instant, and had the pretty embroidered bag open as she whirled to him in outrage. He had her spectacles perched on her nose even before she could open her mouth to protest.

"Much better." James tilted his head to one side as he studied his outraged Honoria. "You have the most beautiful eyes, duchess mine," he added. He used a finger beneath her chin to gently close her slightly opened mouth. It took an act of will to close her mouth with his finger rather than cover her lips with his.

Someone behind them tittered. Someone else gasped. An elderly lady smiled benignly and nodded, then swatted the tittering girl discreetly on the arm.

The duke beamed proudly, and crossed his arms. "Well done, son."

"What have you done, sir?" Russell demanded. "Such effrontery!" He held out a hand imperiously. "Honoria, come away from this rude fellow and dance with me. And put those things away." Both Russell's outrage and his orders were completely ignored.

James watched Honoria's cheeks and throat color a becoming, kissable pink. The humiliated blush was quickly gone, but the banked fury remained, arcing like lightning between them. She glared at him from behind the lenses of her spectacles, and he grinned, knowing that she was thinking that at least for once she could see him while she looked daggers at him.

And he knew that she knew that he knew what she was thinking, because a bright and wicked smile broke through her controlled features for just the briefest of moments. For that moment the room lit around them far brighter than the glow of the crystal chandeliers overhead. Far hotter, as well. Lightning, familiar and sweet.

James wordlessly took her by the arm and led

her forward. She came with him without hesitation or protest. Within moments they were amid the crowd on the dance floor, with his arm around her waist just as the waltz began. For once they did not argue, they did not banter—but they did dance.

"I won't dance to your tune, sir. I will not." She stamped her foot as he made himself step back—and looked as surprised as he did at the childish gesture. Her expression was adorable.

Diego came closer, and he was already quite close. "We will dance," he whispered, and did not know whether he spoke a threat or a promise.

The girl's eyes widened, and her lips parted in shocked response that was the most tempting thing he had ever seen.

The intention had been to loom threateningly when he crossed the room to stand close to her. But it was very hard to loom menacingly over a stately, courageous woman who was only a few inches shorter than he was, especially when she came so desperately into his arms. He hadn't meant to kiss her when he came stalking toward her, or to even hold her. He truly hadn't. He'd been determined to keep his emotions out of their dealings. He had to be cold, hard, ruthless. There wasn't much time. He had to take care of himself and escape. The last thing he needed was any sort of entanglement with a woman to cloud his—

He kissed her.

Her mouth was rich and warm and innocent. Innocent, but eager. Her lips were so soft, the inside of her mouth so sweet and heated. He felt her surprise, and her need, and matched it. He found himself as eager as any untried boy, but with the skills of a man who had kissed many women. Yet somehow it felt like this was the first kiss for both of them. A shudder went through him when she made a small noise. Perhaps her dear Derrick had never tasted her, not as a man kissed a woman. He smiled at the notion—and felt her instantly misunderstand what the smile was for.

She pushed against him.

He let her go, though a part of him raged that the kiss was only a beginning, that he should finish what he had started. Another part of him asked when he had started wanting her. It seemed like he had wanted her even long before they had ever met. He ran his hands through his hair in confusion and forced his feet to take a step back.

Honoria backed away as well, blinking back tears. He had not meant to make her cry. He would have wiped away the tears that she fought not to shed, but knew she was too angry to let him touch her again. Angry and humiliated, because she thought that kissing her had meant nothing more to him than a moment's amusing diversion. Perhaps it should have, if he had any sense. If he was as pitiless a man as he needed to be to escape from Ibrahim Rais. "I did not mean to make you cry," he said.

"I'm not crying."

"Of course not. You never cry."

She lifted her head proudly. "I cry. But not for you."

Anger, and something that was uglier than anger, shot through him. "For dear Derrick?" he sneered.

For a moment she looked as if she didn't know who he was talking about, then her pale cheeks reddened. She tossed her head, and the veil that he'd knocked askew while kissing her fluttered gently to the floor. "Derrick. Yes. Of course, I'd cry for Derrick."

Diego looked from Honoria's shining copper hair to the veil now at her feet, and found it hard to breathe. He wanted to touch her hair, to feel the shining curls slide like silk through his fingers while he kissed her lips and her throat, and found his way down the long length of her to those lovely full breasts. She was wearing far too much clothing. For a moment all he could think of was a dancer he'd once seen; a woman who wore many veils when the music first began. She had worn nothing when the music ended. He had never seen anything so arousing as that dance, until now. And he wondered—

"What are you smiling at?"

He rubbed a hand on the back of his neck, glanced away from Honoria, and tried to think of something less arousing. Ibrahim Rais came immediately to mind, and the gruesome scene when Salah had tried to leave the vicious old man's service.

"You are going to help me leave Ibrahim Rais's service," he told Honoria, not looking at her to keep

from being distracted once more. "This man is a murderer and a criminal."

"As are you."

Her voice was calm, yet it stung him painfully. "I have not hurt you," he told her. "I have not taken you by force." He had only cheated her of her freedom so that he could regain his own. His conscience flayed him more for what he was doing to Honoria Pyne than for any crime committed at the corsair admiral's order. Because he *was wholly, selfishly responsible for any pain she suffered. He did not have the excuse that he had no choice but to obey, this time.*

"I am not afraid of death," he heard himself say. "I even tried to die once, when I was younger, though it is a sin. He would not let me. He nursed me back to strength with his own hands." Tenderly, Diego remembered. Like a loving father. Only to beat Diego to within an inch of his life when he'd recovered enough to survive the punishment. The lesson had been quite clear: life was something that only Ibrahim Rais could give or take away. "The city will fall soon, but Ibrahim Rais has powerful friends in the Turkish court. He has a place waiting for him in Istanbul. He has told me that I am to come with him, and I have thanked him while I make my own plans to escape." He looked back at her now, fierce in his determination. "But I am not going back to Malaga a poor man. I will have what is rightfully mine." He gestured toward the tattered scrap of paper on the table. "Decipher the code for me, Honoria."

His explanations and pleading did not move her. "I think not." She crossed her arms, emphasizing the round curve of her bosom. "Oh, I'll help you," she said. "I have my own price for it though, and it is more than a few paltry coins."

It was Diego's turn to cross his arms. Fiercely angry, he demanded, "What is it you want? A jewel-hilted silver sword, perhaps? A bag of Ibrahim Rais's gold?"

She laughed. "Nonsense. I have no need of money."

He laughed in response. "Then you are a fool."

"Some things are more important than treasure."

"Name your price, woman!" Why was he doing this? Why was he letting a slave he'd bought with hard-earned coin get away with such insolence? And what the devil did those glorious breasts look like when they were laid bare? What did they feel like weighed in a man's hands? What did they taste—?

"Derrick."

Diego heard the jealous snarl, but it took him a moment to realize the sound came from his own throat. He didn't know when he'd moved to grab her shoulders, but he shook them a little as he angrily demanded, "What?"

"I want Derrick Russell. That's his real name. The Scourge of Barbary."

"You belong to me."

She pretended not to hear him, or not to understand. She certainly pretended not to notice his anger, or that he was touching her. He knew she was afraid because he could feel her shaking beneath his hands. She was brave. She was foolish. She was—his. He didn't know when she'd become so very important to him, but it was a fact.

He had heard of Captain Russell. His lying tales of pirate-hunting had been reported by the bey's spies, and amused everyone in the city. So that was the truth she hid about—the man she loved. "I will not have you mentioning that man's name." His words were a cold, hard warning. "He is a coward and a fool. You deserve better."

She was pale as milk but for two bright spots on her cheeks. Her eyes blazed, and an eyebrow arched sarcastically at his words. "Who do I deserve, sir? You?"

Diego very nearly tossed her down on the table and took her then and there. "If I choose."

"You would not force yourself on a woman."

He did not know if she believed what she said, or merely hoped it was the truth. He knew that it was, but the temptation was strong. Desire flared higher as he cupped her chin in his hand. "Won't I?" Her gaze slid nervously from his, though he held her face trapped very close to his. "I intend to kiss you again," he told her. "Look at me, Honoria."

She glanced over his shoulder at the table instead. He thought at first that she had read his thought about taking her on it, then realized she was looking at the letter. She remembered what they had been discussing, though he'd forgotten why he needed her—the practical reason he needed her.

"Derrick is a prisoner with the other officers. He is wounded and needs me to tend him. And Huseby is a prisoner as well. They both need my help."

"He's safe."

"No, he's not." She looked frantic and frightened. He doubted she would ever look that way for him, though he was fighting for his life. "If you rescue Derrick and Huseby from their captivity, then I will translate your letter for you."

"You want to strike a bargain?" His voice was soft and menacing. "Do you know what power I have over you? Life and death. I own you."

She tried to pull away from him. When he let her go she touched the spots where his hands had been on her, tenderly, as though he'd left bruises, or his touch burned her. He felt burned, especially when her gaze bored into his. Even behind a pair of glass lenses her eyes carried weight and force—and fire. "I will not obey as a slave."

He knew she believed every word. Perhaps she was strong enough to act on that belief, at least for a while. "I have learned over the years that a strong will is not wise for a slave."

She nodded as if she completely understood, but that knowing the cost of defiance did nothing to change her mind. "Make a bargain with me," she pleaded with him. "Help me for Derrick's sake, and I will help you. That is all I ask."

"Demand, you mean."

She nodded again, with firm stubbornness. "He

needs me. Huseby needs me. I'm responsible for protecting them."

He hated her dear Derrick, her Huseby, and for a moment he hated her. Spoiled, privileged, pampered, and protected all her life, born to wealth and ease. But she was not standing up to him and making demands for herself. She was not raging at the unfairness of what had befallen her. She was bargaining with him for the sake of those she cared for. How could he hate anyone so brave and selfless?

He had never seen anyone so beautiful, a creature of spirit and conviction. He wanted nothing more than to change that blaze in her eyes into a lover's passion, for her to concentrate all her fiery emotions on him.

He wanted her, so she had him. He hated anyone having power over him, even this woman with her blasted righteous convictions. He could not afford to lose control of the situation. He could not let her have her way. Her friends did not need her, but he did. What to do to get her to back down? How to frighten her into doing the one simple thing he required of her?

Fight fire with fire, he thought, and smiled at the simple solution. She was a good girl. A virgin. A prim and proper English miss. "I will make a bargain with you, my sweet. You want Derrick. You want Huseby. That is two things you want of me. I want you to read a letter. That is one thing. For this to be a proper bargain, it must be fair and equal. Shouldn't it?"

She hesitated suspiciously for a few seconds, biting her lower lip nervously. It left her lips moist and red, which made him want to kiss her even more. Finally, she nodded. "Yes, I suppose it would be fair." She looked around the room. "Do you have something else you'd like me to read?"

He shook his head and moved slowly toward her, a large cat stalking a gentle dove. "No more letters," he told her. He drew close enough to touch her cheek, softly, with just the tip of his finger. He drew his fingers across her face, traced the outline of her lips, ran his knuckles slowly down the length of her throat. Their gazes locked. He didn't think she was breathing. He knew she wasn't when he let his hand move lower. He heard and felt her sharp gasp as he brushed his hand over the ripe curves of her breasts. They were safely concealed beneath several layers of cloth, but nothing could hide their sweet softness. He let his hand come to rest on the flare of her hip. "You want me to save—" He couldn't bring himself to say the name. "—Him. Then give yourself to me. I won't force you. But I will have you as the price of a bargain."

They turned and turned again, the graceful movements of the waltz carrying them elegantly around the dance floor. The orchestra was not very good, but James Marbury did not need the musicians' help to dance like a dream. With him leading her he made Honoria feel like a graceful dancer, something neither years of lessons nor practice at a hundred forgotten balls had ever managed to do. For a few priceless moments, Honoria felt like she was flying. Her feet were winged and she wanted nothing more than to dance forever with the man who held her with such calm assurance.

When he was a pirate, he had put her glasses back on her, letting her see at his whim. It was his way of showing her he held power over her. *Or is it done as an act of kindness?* a more reasonable voice whispered. She fought hard against that voice, trying with all her strength to hold onto the tight, stifling sense of anger.

But the music betrayed her, and so did the perfect ease and fit of the way they moved together. Dancing in this man's arms was both sinuous and sensuous.

He was watching her with the most provocative smile on his full, wide mouth. She tried not to be affected by that familiar expression, but an answering smile threatened to break through her resolve. It was even harder not to react to his voice. "You're having fun," he told her.

She tossed her head like a woman flirting with a suitor, responding to him no matter her resolve not to. "Is that a question or a command, my lord?"

He chuckled and the sound was sweeter to her ears than the music. He always could disconcert her with frightful ease. His eyes were bright with laughter, and full of sensual promise. She made herself look away from his face, over his shoulder, and immediately regretted it. She lost the light of his eyes, and realized that people were watching her. People always watched. Why couldn't they all go stare at the Queen just for a few minutes? This was Victoria's ball; let her be the center of attention rather than a mere ducal heir.

Then again, to be fair, perhaps no one was looking at her at all. She was tall and plain, and wearing spectacles. However, the graceful man who held her so surely in his arms was without a doubt the handsomest man in the room, with his broad shoulders, powerful physique, strong jaw and brow, his teasing, wicked mouth and bright, bright eyes. Why would any woman want to look at plain, prissy Honoria Pyne, except for an envious glance before focusing their attention on her partner as they danced past? As for the men, well, her beaming father was understandable. She did not fathom the looks from other men. She nodded her head politely to her father as she and James swooped past him.

Derrick Russell stood tensely next to the duke, glowering fierce hatred. It was plain and ugly on his face. Their glances met for only a moment, and old scars tore open inside her as she saw that all the vitriol was aimed squarely at her. She looked quickly away.

James's hand tightened on her waist. "He is nothing." The words were spoken in a fierce whisper.

"I know," she answered. "I think I've always known." But she was thinking, *Then why did I throw my honor away, if not for him?*

She'd always known the answer to that, as well. He was holding her in his arms.

Chapter 13

He let his hand come to rest on the flare of her hip. "You want me to save him." His voice was low, intense, compelling. "Then give yourself to me. I won't force you. But I will have you as the price of a bargain."

"I—" Honoria turned away from him. She looked around desperately while her heart raced and her insides roiled with fear, and a new, deeply intense indescribable feeling. Not completely indescribable, this ache, this fierce melting heat that grew worse with every encounter with the Spaniard. She had felt the first mad flutter of—desire—the moment he stepped aboard the Manticore. *Even as she tried to help poor, wounded Derrick she had been intensely* aware *of the Spaniard's dangerous presence. She—desired—Diego Moresco. All right. She admitted it, but what did that matter?*

It was base and disgusting, a flaw in herself. She was a woman, the most imperfect of God's creations.

Women were easily swayed by their emotions; Derrick had said so. They needed good, upright, stern men to guide their actions if they were not to be led into error. If they were not to fall prey to the sins of the flesh. It was a point she and dear Derrick had had some disagreement on. It seemed he was right. Her flesh was proving very weak indeed in the face of Moresco's virile demeanor. He had but to touch her and— A tremor of excitement shot through her even at the memory of his hands and mouth on her.

"Forgive me," she whispered, and didn't know if she prayed to God or Derrick Russell for absolution.

"Decide, Honoria. Read the letter for me and I will ask nothing more of you. Pay my price if you want your friends released."

She clutched her arms tightly around her middle and swayed a little as the enormity of what he asked struck hard against her upbringing, her beliefs, her loyalties, and her sense of responsibility.

Derrick Russell was known and hated by the corsairs. If they found out who he really was, the cruel pirates would never ransom him back to England. He would be tortured and murdered if she didn't get him safely away from the prison where he was being held. The pirates would take their vengeance out on a man who was sick and weak from fighting valiantly to protect her.

And Huseby. Maggie Huseby was far more friend than servant, and even a servant deserved the best a mistress could do for her. What if Maggie was molested, or hurt? They needed her.

And she wanted him.

She turned back to Diego Moresco before cowardice and propriety overwhelmed her. "Very well," she told him, head held proudly high. "I accept your price."

The dance was over, but she and James Marbury still had their hands on each other. Even with her glasses on, the ballroom was a blur to Honoria. The only object that had any clarity was the man who faced her, so close the heat of his flesh was indistinguishable from her own. The orchestra struck up another tune. People changed partners. Honoria and James stayed where they were, unmoving as figures swirled around them.

James finally seemed to notice. "Shall we dance?"

The sound of his voice brought Honoria out of the past. They were in London. Eight years had gone by not in a blink, but as slow, inexorable torture. She felt the weight of every lonely moment all of a sudden, and it crushed her spirit. Moving very carefully, she stepped away from the man with whom she had sinned.

"I cannot afford the price," she said, her voice tart and astringent. She liked it when her sharp edges showed. It kept people away from her.

It didn't seem to affect James Marbury any. He kept her hand in his as they left the dance floor. She didn't think he intended to let her go.

"Why are you doing this?" she finally questioned, just before they reached the knot of people that consisted of both their fathers, cousin Kate—and, inevitably, Derrick Russell.

"It's complicated," he answered as they stepped closer to the waiting group.

"Ah, but I prefer a simple life," she said in a normal voice, and with a smile that might have been coquettish had she not put so many teeth into it. At least he hadn't tried to tell her he loved her. If there was a part of her that ached for such a nonsensical declaration, she pushed it down and ignored it.

Derrick, however, would not be ignored any longer. He deliberately forced himself between her and James Marbury. "You will dance with me now," he informed her, as firmly as if he were ordering a sailor to swab down the deck of his ship. Though he spoke to her, his furious glare was cast at the other man. She saw the flash of dangerous anger in James's eyes, and the way that his stance subtly tensed for a fight.

Did the two fancy themselves rivals? She was almost amused at the thought—the sort of amusement that threatened to lead to hysterical laughter. But that would cause a scene, as would allowing herself to be squabbled over by two equally despicable curs in fine clothing. So she gave in to the unpleasant inevitability and let Derrick take her arm. "Very well, Captain Russell. Let us dance."

She heard James murmur, "Are you sure you can afford it?" as she turned to move back to the dance floor, but she refused to acknowledge his bitter words.

James watched Honoria in the arms of her former fiancé with fury. The two of them moved together with a certain familiarity that set James's teeth on edge. They had been a couple once. Russell wanted them to be a couple again—for all the wrong reasons. Honoria knew that, but still she put up with Russell's touching her, making demands of her. Why? What did the woman think she was doing? Playing her suitors off against each other? Or was she merely trying to torture him, and using Russell as the means?

He was thinking like a jealous fool and he knew it. The woman drove him mad. But, then, she always had. He smiled, though memory and desire took his breath away.

Very well? What did the woman mean, very well? Diego was of two minds as the enormity of her response slowly sank into his brain. Well, not two minds; rather, his mind and his body reacted almost as separate entities to Honoria's agreeing to become his lover. Part of him, the part that was supposed to be such a cunning schemer, was flummoxed and in shock, aware that he'd bluffed and she'd called it. And now—he had to go through with it. And what was wrong with that? He knew she was not a great beauty in any conventional sense. He'd had great beauties, and been pleasured but never impressed. Honoria was impressive. *She was intriguing. Proud. Purposeful. Emphatic. Impossible. She looked like an amazon out of legend, tall and strong-limbed, and as wild as any ancient warrior-woman beneath her prim British exterior, he was certain. Something in her called to something in him. He'd wanted to free that wildness from the moment they met. He'd been able to think of no one else, had barely been able to accomplish his escape scheme for wanting to be with her every moment. He didn't want to need her, but the pull had been there from the first time he laid eyes on her in the heat of battle.*

This is not honorable, the very soft voice of his conscience told him as he stalked purposefully forward. *She is a maiden. She is under your protection. You will dishonor not just her, but yourself.*

"Honoria," he said, as he put his hands on her shoulders.

"Oh, do be quiet," she snapped. Then she grabbed him by the hair, and determinedly pulled him into a kiss.

It took him some struggle to pull away from her lips. They were both breathing heavily as they gazed for a long, burning moment into each other's eyes. How desperately his body demanded that he claim her. How vulnerable she looked, how utterly desirable.

He was no gentleman. Honor was a luxury.

So was Honoria, he decided, as he took her spec-

tacles off and laid them on the table. Then he took her in his arms and taught her how to kiss. Her mouth was rich and hot, and the ample bosom that pressed against his chest was soft enticement to hands that began to roam of their own will. He brushed a thumb against a swelling nipple and a shiver went through her. She moaned against his mouth, and her tongue ventured to dance shyly with his. This was a real kiss, a promise of ecstasy.

When their lips parted, she looked stunned and dazed, but there was a dreamy glow about her. Her arms clung around his neck, and her breath came in sharp, excited gasps. He did not detect regret or repulsion or any hint of dutiful submission. The one thing he did not want to see was that she was thinking of another. He didn't want her to bring "dear Derrick" into bed with them.

He put his hands on her thighs and drew them intimately closer, hip to hip; made sure she felt his growing hardness. He watched with avid greed as her eyes widened in surprise and the color deepened with growing desire. She made a small whimpering sound that spoke volumes about longing without any concept of what this desperate, growing hunger inside her meant. It filled him with pleasure and pride at being her first. There was a great deal he was going to teach her.

Most important, he was going to make her forget about Derrick.

He shifted his hold on her and took her hands in his. "Come to my bed," he whispered. "It isn't far."

* * *

He was looking at her—Honoria could feel it even though her back was toward that side of the ballroom. The intensity of his stare gave off a wavering haze like the heat given off by a blacksmith's forge. It was as though the man was branding her with a look.

Perhaps she was coming down with a fever. A brain fever, perhaps; one that caused hallucinations. Yes, that must be it. After all she'd been put through in the last several days, was it no wonder that all sorts of impossible, fanciful notions were intruding into her normally quite unimaginative thought processes.

Unimaginative? She almost laughed, and couldn't help but catch her breath as memory played a nasty trick on her, and a flood of primal images and sensations broke through the carefully constructed walls of years of denial and shame. Unimaginative? This time she did laugh. Derrick said something, but she didn't bother to answer. Derrick was as unimportant as a flea, and about as repugnant.

She did take note of Derrick's frown as he guided her steps on another turn of the dance. He was far from handsome when he looked like that, all spoiled and petulant. She reveled in wearing her spectacles, in noticing the faces in the crowd as they flashed past her. Pale faces with carefully controlled expressions looked back at her. She saw a row of dukes and dowagers, and debutantes in diamonds and pale lace, dignitaries in bright sashes, and generals and admirals in all their glittering medals. They danced past the Queen sitting among her ladies and a host of solemn German relatives. No one looked like they were having a very good time. Of course, no one dared show too much emotion in this gathering of the great and powerful. It could be remarked upon, talked about, used against them; this was a Queen's court, after all.

They all had their secrets to hide: some simple, some grand, some hideous. And they all wanted to suspect that she had done something shocking and scandalous, simply because she had dared to have an adventure, to step outside the small, narrow world of the *ton*. So she walked carefully among them when she must be in society at all, showing a bland, unimaginative face.

She laughed again, unable to stop the mirth from bubbling out. It was a small release for the tension that roiled through her. She felt like a volcano about to come boiling violently to life, especially as another turn brought her face to face with James Marbury for a moment. She was right; he was staring—and how well she knew that look in his honey gold eyes. They looked like that when they made love, almost glowing with the intensity of his desire. She'd been branded with that look years ago, and the mark was as fresh as ever.

Wildness, recklessness, everything mad, forbidden and damning in her flung against the prison bars of reason and begged to run to him. Oh, the things she'd done, basking in the glow of that look! And would do again, quite possibly in public, if James Marbury kept looking at her like that.

Plain, proper, staid, dull, dreary, bluestocking, overgrown and uninterested, unimaginative Honoria? Her gaze swept around the crowd once more. If only they knew. No woman alive could come away from four days in bed with James Marbury and be considered anything but very, very imaginative.

"What's that?"

"It's a book."

She rolled over on her stomach and propped herself up on the bed on her elbows. "I can see that."

He flashed her a smile, and ran his hand down the length of her bare back. It sent a shiver through her, but it didn't take her attention off the leather-bound book he held in his other hand.

She sat up all the way this time, and his hand moved to cup a breast and he bent his head to flick his tongue across her nipple. "I like books."

"I know. You like this?" His mouth settled and suckled, but he had to bend a bit awkwardly to do it and hold the book as well.

Desire rippled through her, and she made a sweetly satisfied sound, but took the large volume from him. She wasn't wearing her glasses; in fact, she neither remembered nor cared where they were. It made it a bit inconvenient to look at the book as she opened the pages. Fortunately, there wasn't much in the way of text. "It's a picture book."

He made an agreeing noise as he pushed her gently onto her back and his lips settled between the furrow of her legs. Honoria kept the book pressed closely to her face. What Diego was doing only made the beautifully detailed illustrations seem more graphic.

"Oh, my . . ." she said, after she flipped a few pages, and then turned one particularly instructive *picture this way and that for a while. "Oh, my, my."*

Diego left off the quite delectable things he'd been doing to pluck the book away from her and have a look at what she'd found so interesting. He had a devilish smile on his face when he put the book down and bent close to kiss her. She tasted herself on his tongue, and was delighted by sweet, salty, musky taste of sex.

After they'd kissed for a long, sultry time he asked, voice teasing, eyes bright with desire, "You liked what you saw in the picture?" She raised her head from the pile of bright pillows at the head of the bed to nod enthusiastically. "Let's try it."

"Oh, yes, please!"

He was snatching pillows out from under her and rearranging them elsewhere even as she spoke.

"What the devil are you smiling at, Honoria? Honoria? Are you listening to me?"

Derrick's waspish tone brought her out of her reverie, but she couldn't manage to wipe the wide smile completely away as she focused on him. She supposed she should be blushing in shame, but she couldn't manage that, either.

"What am I smiling at?" she inquired mockingly. "Why, you, I suppose. If not for you . . ."

He did not take her meaning, of course, and preened with vanity instead. "Ah. That's my Honoria." His grip tightened a little on her waist. She could hardly wait for the music to stop. "When shall we announce our engagement?"

She sighed. The man really believed he could make her change her mind. Amazing. "We've already had this discussion. Don't be repetitive."

"You're not very good at being coy, Honoria."

No, she didn't suppose she was, nor could she think of why she should try to be. She looked around boldly, reveling in being a red-blooded woman, or possibly a wolf set loose among a herd of sheep. It was James Marbury she sought, the wolf mate who'd set her emotions tumbling wildly free all those years ago. Her Spaniard, who'd returned from the dead to claim her as his lover once more.

Then reality hit. What nonsense—though for a brief moment she let herself believe it. The Spaniard was no more interested in her than

Derrick was. Fortune hunters, that's all either of them were. The only difference was, Marbury was dangerous. Marbury knew her weaknesses. He *was* her weakness. No matter how strong she tried to be, no matter the walls she'd built high and thick around her emotions, she remained vulnerable to him. Malleable, changeable, unable to stop her mind from flying off on fanciful roads that always led back to the bedroom and the long, sensual nights she'd left behind. How she hated the weakness he incited inside her that threatened to destroy everything she was and stood for. She liked her placid existence; she really did! She would not shame her father in the eyes of society. She would *not* lose the emotional control that kept her sane.

As soon as the music ended, she peeled away from Derrick's clinging touch and marched purposefully up to the Honorable James Marbury. He stood tall and proud beside his father, and his eyes held a spark of anger deep in their core. Anger toward her, she knew, though she had no idea what *he* had to be annoyed about.

She ignored his dangerous look and told him quietly, "This has to stop. Do you hear me?"

"I hear you," James answered, even more quietly, but his voice was as edged as a dagger.

Jealousy roared almost uncontrollably through him. Watching her dance and smile and laugh with the other man, while he stood on the sidelines consumed with desire, galled him. He wanted to take her and shake her and demand what it was about Derrick Russell that attracted a woman as fine as her. He kept his gloved hands clasped tightly behind his back as they glared hotly at each other a moment longer. If he touched her, he wouldn't shake her; he would make love to her to prove that she was his, then and there. What would dear Derrick say to that?

"You say you see, but do you understand? These games must stop."

He nodded. "They will stop. Very soon. I promise you that, duchess *mine*."

The possessive emphasis he put on the last word sent a melting shiver through her. Damn the man! How could he make her react so with one small word? She didn't dare to look at him any longer. "As long as we understand each other."

"We understand each other very well."

Honoria backed away from the man's intensity. Turning, she found that her father had come up beside her. She thanked God for his steadying presence, and put her hand on his arm.

"Are you well, my dear?" he asked worriedly. "It's been a long night. Would you like me to take you home?"

All she could do was nod, and try not to drag the poor man from the ballroom when he led her off.

Chapter 14

Four days. Honoria sighed; she couldn't keep the words from running through her head. Possibly it had been longer, but she could piece together enough erotically detailed memories to count four days and night for certain. Time had disappeared for her in the Spaniard's bed. What had she been thinking? She *hadn't* been thinking, of course; that was the obvious answer and shameful truth. Some madness came over her and she became lost in a sensual fantasy world. It had seemed quite real at the time. In fact, nothing that had happened in her life since had been as real as those four short, glorious, ecstasy-filled days when nothing existed but him, her, and every pleasurable sensation that had ever been.

How she hated being reminded of those days.

Her dreams last night had been predictably vivid. His hands had been on her in her dreams, and his exquisite mouth. She'd smelled the musk of his skin, and the strength in his hard-muscled body. Worst and best of all, she had felt him inside her, possessing her, his thrusts driving in a hard, fast rhythm that drove her . . .

Needless to say, she had awoken agitated and with the restless ache of longing she'd fought to kill for years. Only this time it was worse. They had touched and spoken and her body had been pressed to his as they danced. The brush of his strong thighs against her had not been imagination. His lips were very real, and the impulse to kiss him had been almost too strong to bear last night. She had fought her wild passions down in public, but they had run rampant in her dreams. She'd woken up panting, aroused and unsatisfied, and had to fight off the urge to find the man and have her way with him.

She had these dreams often enough in the country, but there she could deal with them with simple activity and hard work that wore her rebellious body down to exhaustion that put her beyond dreaming. She was in London now, where she could not take a ten-mile walk across the countryside, or work beside stable hands or housemaids, or go for a long swim in the deep, cold pool hidden in the Lacey House woods.

She was in London now. And so was Diego, her Spanish corsair, James Marbury. They were both in London, and all she could do was think of him, and remember. As if she ever did anything else when she was in the country, she admitted reluctantly, even though she hid her thoughts from herself by reading books and performing good works. She sighed at acknowledging this obsession, and hated hearing herself make such a weak sound.

"I am a weedy creature," she murmured. "An utter weed." She could not bear to meet her own gaze in the dressing table mirror as her maid finished arranging her hair. It was not a withered weed she would see there, but a lustful wanton, no matter how much she pretended to be a dried up stick of a spinster. Being a red-blooded woman had distinct disadvantages, especially considering the course she'd chosen to steer in life.

"Men," she muttered. "Who ever invented the masculine gender, Maggie?"

"You've asked me that before."

"So I have. I believe we came to the conclusion that they are useful for lifting heavy objects and caring for horses."

Maggie stepped back from the table, and the conversation. "You are keeping your callers waiting, Honoria."

It was nearly two in the afternoon but the day was only officially beginning here in the city, and it was going to be a busy one. She was scheduled to be downstairs soon to meet her "morning" callers.

"The devil with callers," Honoria decided. "And to the devil with Mr. Marbury." She rose decisively from her seat. "Send my regrets to whoever wants to see me today," she ordered Huseby. "I'm going to spend the day with my real friends."

"You'll be in the library, you mean?"

"Precisely, Maggie. With lots of tea and a stack of books."

Honoria walked into the library with firm, brisk strides, determined to read something uplifting and morally improving. Which did not explain her marching straight to the shelf where a copy of *Tom Jones* rested. She took out the leather-bound tome and flipped it open. The first thing she noticed, as she always did, was the personal note from Mr. Fielding to her great-grandmother. The book about the amorous adventures of a wild orphan lad was scandalous, and a family favorite since it was first published in the middle of the last century.

Honoria shook her head. "Is it any wonder I've turned out the way I have?" She was wanton by nature, lust ran in her blood at a constant simmer, but that didn't mean she had to give in to base impulses. She fought off the depraved urge that had sent her to pick out this of all books, and placed *Tom Jones* back on the shelf.

As she walked toward another shelf she noticed that the room was chilly, and dampness from the early afternoon rain permeated the air even though a fire burned in the grate. She glanced toward the windows behind the library table and noticed that one was open. As she passed the table to close the window, she saw the book lying open there.

The edge of one side was singed, as though the book had been snatched from a fire. The ill-treated book was clearly out of place resting on the alabaster tabletop. Honoria forgot about the window and picked up the small, open book.

She got a good look at the illustrated pages, gasped, and promptly dropped the book. "Oh, good Lord!"

She turned to flee, but it was too late. James Marbury blocked her way—and the fiend was smiling. It was enough to make her heart race and her bones melt.

"I brought you a present," he told her. "I remember how much you like books. Especially that book."

"Oh, good Lord," she repeated.

James found her expression priceless. "It's a memento from Algiers," he told her. She tried to step around him, but he moved to prevent her, coming closer to her in the process. The color of her gown was golden yellow. The color was as vivid as her personality, but the dress itself was buttoned all the way to just beneath her chin. What a pity to cover such a lovely long throat and the magnificent swell of her bosom. Her hair was a braided crown on the top of her head.

"I want you to go right now!" She pointed dramatically at the window.

"I know you do," he answered with more bitterness than he intended. "But you won't be rid of me this time. You belong to me, remember?"

She tried to dodge around him again; he took a step closer to her. They were eye to eye and very nearly nose to nose. "I will make you remember. Say thank you for the present, Honoria."

"Thank you?" Her chin tilted up at an even prouder, more stubborn angle. Her eyes flashed fire that sizzled along his nerve endings.

"Remember?" He brushed the tips of his fingers across her cheek and ear. Her head tilted sideways at his touch, her cheek briefly resting in the wide palm of his hand, her eyes half-closing.

She straightened abruptly, turned and walked away from him. "Remember what?"

He shrugged. "Page fourteen, perhaps?" He grinned. "That was quite a favorite of yours. Let's clear off the tabletop and try it," he suggested. "Or would you prefer being closer to the fire? It's too chilly in here to be naked on alabaster."

"Naked!" Honoria whirled around. "Stop looking at me like that."

"How am I looking at you?"

His large amber eyes glittered in a way that sent heady waves of desire through her. No man should have the power to make a woman weak and ready to swoon simply by looking at her!

I have a wicked nature, she reminded herself. "You are the devil, James Marbury."

"Yes, I know."

"I will not be tempted." She planted her hands behind her back and faced him with bright spots of color staining her cheeks.

Outrage? Or interest? It would be far more than interest by the time he was done with her, he vowed. He knew his Honoria.

"You look lovely naked. How can you move in so much clothing, anyway?"

"I move very well, Mr. Marbury. And I think you should move, as well." He picked up the book and came toward her. She pointed at the open window. "I meant that you should leave the way you came. I don't want you to be seen."

"I enjoy seeing you. I always have."

"I do not wish to be seen."

"Yes, you do. And touched, and made love to." She backed up toward the fireplace. He followed slowly after. "I should have taken you home with me last night," he told her. "We could have studied the book together. Then we wouldn't have spent the night imagining and remembering. We would have made new memories."

"My old memories are quite enough to occupy me, Mr. Marbury."

He smiled triumphantly. "At least you don't deny remembering the way we made love. Do you know what I remember the most?"

He watched Honoria's curiosity get the better of her. She leaned forward just a little, her breasts rising and falling with her quick breathing, eyes shining as she reluctantly asked, "What?"

He whispered the answer. "The rapt look on your face when you climaxed."

She moistened her lips, the quick gesture infinitely and unconsciously sensual. "Oh."

James knew he was right to have obeyed the impulse to leave the book here and wait for her, when his original plan had been to sneak into her room and leave the erotic picture book on her pillow. Leaving her a reminder of the pleasure they'd shared wasn't nearly as rewarding as reminding her in person.

"It is customary to say thank you for a present," James reminded her. He came closer and put a finger beneath her chin. Then he traced a finger around her lips. He did not think that she noticed her lips open at his soft touch. "Or would you rather show me your appreciation instead?"

The man's low, sultry voice sent a shiver through Honoria. She tensed as she looked at him, her body thrummed with it, but there was no fear or trepidation within her. What she felt was rich and heady desire, growing with every passing moment. The man had a gift—with a word, a look, a sure, seductive touch . . .

And that was what he was doing, seducing her. For some reason, she had lost track of her wits for a few moments. Honoria blinked, and closed her mouth. She blazed with anger as she snatched the erotic picture book from his hand. She shook it at him. "You left this for my father to see, didn't you?"

"Of course not. Are those real gold buttons?"

"Then why bring *this* book into this house? This room?"

He touched the top button of her gown. "It's very pretty. A gold rose."

"Yes, it's a gold rose. What about the—"

"Excuse me." He grasped the gold rose button and twisted. The button popped off; he barely heard it ricochet off a bookcase as Honoria gasped in outrage. With deft fingers he popped off a second, third, and fourth button before Honoria was able to spin away.

He grabbed her wrist and pulled her back to press close to him. He wanted to feel her naked thighs molded to his, but was frustrated by her layers and layers of skirts. "Silly European clothes," he murmured, his lips close to her ear.

Then he kissed just the right spot on her throat beneath her ear. She moaned just as he expected. The book thumped on the rug as it dropped from her hand. Honoria pushed him roughly away.

Then she grabbed him by the hair, pulled his head up, and kissed him. The taste and scent of her filled his senses. Her perfume was roses, and she tasted hot and fierce and utterly fearless. She inspired passion like no one else he had ever known. Their tongues danced together as he caressed her shoulders and the nape of her elegant neck. He plucked the pins from her hair, then answered the urgent need to touch her through her damned chemise and corset. He wanted her breasts free. And the skirt which barred access to the rest of her rich body—that definitely had to go!

Honoria couldn't stop herself and didn't want to. She pulled him as close as she could, wildly cupping his buttocks and kneading the taut muscles of his back and shoulders. Things were getting out of hand. How unwise and how lovely. He had said something about using the tabletop. Well, why not? She threw her head back and laughed, and James took the opportunity to kiss the base of her throat. She clutched at his shoulders and moaned again with her eyes closed. The heat of the fireplace was behind her, and the heat from James's touch grew deep inside.

Fire. Burning. Passion. *Don't you see what you're doing? What he's doing? Stop it, you fool! You can't lose yourself in desire!*

Why not, she argued with the stern, logical voice inside her head. That logical voice continued, though she wanted it to stop: because the man was attempting to manipulate her weakness, to use her for his own purposes. Because emotion of any kind was not to be trusted, passion most of all. He claimed to want to marry her when he had no reason other than to tell her it was "complicated." No doubt it was nefarious, as well. Perhaps he was involved in some scheme with his father to cheat her father of his fortune, or use him politically. Whatever was going on, she must think of her father's welfare first. She could not think in the throes of lust.

Oh, really? I seem to be doing a pretty good job at the moment. I want to shut up and let myself enjoy this.

The door to the library opened. "My lady?" Huseby said.

Then the maid gasped.

James was at Huseby's side in an instant, his hand over her mouth before she had a chance to shriek. "It's all right," he told her. "We're engaged."

"We are not." There was annoyed tartness in Honoria's voice, beneath the breathlessness.

James didn't argue, but concentrated on reassuring the servant. "There's nothing to be alarmed about." He slowly took his hand from her mouth. "Nothing at all."

"I'm fine, Maggie," Honoria said, coming to stand near her maid. "And Mr. Marbury is leaving now." She held her bodice together with one hand, and jerked a thumb at the open window with the other. "Now," she repeated.

Her hair was down around her face, her lips were red and swollen from kissing, her cheeks and throat were flushed with color. He didn't want to stop, or to leave, not when things were just getting interesting.

Huseby gave him a stern look, then concentrated on her mistress. "My lady, you must come quickly. Baroness Lehzen is in the drawing room."

"Baroness Lehzen?" Honoria asked. She looked around aghast. "Here?" She crossed both hands over her bosom. "Now?"

"The queen's Baroness Lehzen?" James asked. "What's the queen's best friend doing here?"

"She's come to see my lady, of course," Huseby answered, in a tone that reminded James that *his* Honoria outranked any jumped-up governess, no matter whose best friend Lehzen was. "You shouldn't keep her waiting," Huseby addressed Honoria. "His Grace sends a message that you are to convince the baroness that you are worthy of being a lady-in-waiting to Queen Victoria. You had better go change clothes first, though," she added.

James looked at Honoria, adorably disheveled and disconcerted, and couldn't keep from laughing.

She pointed angrily at the window again. "I believe you know the way out, Mr. Marbury."

Despite her frosty tone, he howled with laughter. She gave him one furious glance, then went to the library door. A visit from Baroness Lehzen was important to her future; he would not jeopardize that again. Damn it—just when things had been getting interesting!

"Don't worry darling," he called just before the door slammed. "I'll see you soon."

Chapter 15

The next morning, Honoria looked at the stained and scorched cover of the book, then hurriedly opened a drawer in her dressing table and hid it away as Huseby came to work on her hair. Honoria had given her huge array of servants the day off, leaving Huseby to do all the work of making Lady Alexandra presentable. Honoria had also cancelled all her invitations to balls and parties, though she planned to keep her charity work appointments today. She needed to be alone as it was possible for her to be.

She couldn't stop thinking about the book, or James's suggestion about page fourteen yesterday. She couldn't even remember what was on page fourteen. To the best of her vivid recollection, there had not been a single position of the many they had tried that had not been her favorite at the time. The blasted book was like

Pandora's box. She was certain that looking inside would release all the demons that resided bottled up inside her. They'd certainly come close to breaking free when she'd been with James yesterday. Thank goodness Baroness Lehzen had put in a timely appearance.

She ignored the part of her that damned the Queen's confidante to perdition for interrupting a perfectly good tryst, and said a small prayer of thanks that she'd been able to snatch the book off of the library floor before a maidservant found it while cleaning. The last thing she wanted was for the lurid, and very well done, drawings to come to her father's attention.

Besides, it had not been a tryst. James Marbury had been attempting to seduce her for his own nefarious purposes. *And doing a fine job of it,* she admitted with a certain wry chagrin. *And who kissed who, my dear?* Only he would think to seduce her with a book! If there was one ploy that might succeed with a bluestocking like her—

She should have thrown the book away, or tossed it into the fire. Instead, she'd hidden it beneath her pillow when she returned to her room yesterday afternoon to change clothes. She'd then worked so hard to hide her emotional upset from Baroness Lehzen, and then her father, who talked court politics with her for hours afterward, that she completely forgot about the book.

She'd remembered that it was beneath her pillow when she woke up from another restless night this morning, too aware that she was in the same damask-curtained bed where James had hidden and spied on her a few nights before. She would not have been surprised to wake up to find him lying beside her. The sneak.

Perhaps she'd half-expected and half-hoped that he'd pay her another surreptitious visit.

"At least the instruction manual would have been handy," she murmured now. She made herself look straight at the face in the mirror. Yes, there was definitely a weak, dreamy and foolish look about her features right now. "Wanton slut."

"What's that, my lady?"

Honoria touched a finger to the carefully formed sausage curls that framed her face. He had always liked to play with her hair. "I am a very confused woman, Huseby." She was not, she thought firmly, in the least bit disappointed to have woken up alone. She was a spinster and proud of it!

But not for long.

Honoria was surprised at the thought, then remembered that she'd formed a plan to get out of the dire situation her father's determination had put her in. Of course, that was what she meant. If she must have a mate, she would choose one who did not arouse a single ounce of her foolishly passionate nature.

Maggie Huseby did not sound like a servant, but a friend, when she said, "You've been confused for years, Honoria. It's the Spaniard's fault."

Honoria tilted her head back to look at Huseby. "That it is, Maggie."

"The nerve of him, courting you after all these years. Not that it's all that long," Huseby added swiftly as Honoria spun around on the bench to face her. She dropped the brush in her hand, and hairpins scattered as the maid backed across the room. "You're still a young woman, after all."

Honoria couldn't help but laugh. "Good lord, woman. Do I look that angry?"

"It's only been eight years," Huseby answered. "You are young. You just act old most of the time. Makes me forget that you're but six-and-twenty. That gives you plenty of time to wed and make babes. To please your father, and yourself," Huseby added, taking a brave step forward. She eyed Honoria cautiously. "You going to let that temper of yours loose for what I've said?"

Honoria crossed her arms beneath her bosom. She was dressed in green and black plaid taffeta, trimmed in black piping and a bit of lace at the sleeves and on her collar, with a cameo brooch of her great grandmother pinned at her throat. She was dressed in the armor of fashionable propriety, but felt like talking about harems and—sex.

She meant to ask Huseby—who knew almost everything about nearly everyone—whom the maid thought was weak-willed and biddable enough to make Honoria the sort of husband she wanted. Instead she clasped her hands nervously together in her lap and leaned forward, as though afraid they'd be overheard. She was a cautious, private woman who'd held her silence for eight years. Huseby had loyally done the same. She was not sure how to start now.

"I—in Algiers. Do you remember the house you were brought to from the fortress?"

"Certainly, my lady. It was a lovely, peaceful place. For a heathen's house," she added, with stout British superiority. "Very nice garden it had." She tilted her head to one side, recalling. "Very peaceful until the old pirate and his men showed up, that is. You recall the old pirate, my lady? Ibrahim Rais?"

"The man held a dagger to my throat. I'm not likely to forget him anytime soon." She twisted her hands together as Huseby's eyes widened. "That's right, you weren't there for most of the altercation between the old man and—the Spaniard." She gave a slight shrug. "Suffice it to say that we both survived the event. Just."

"Well, that's a mercy, isn't it?" Huseby echoed Honoria's dry tone.

Honoria chuckled, and rose to pace back and forth across the dressing room. Huseby stood with her back firmly against the small room's door, assuring that they could not be interrupted. There was not much space in the windowless room. It contained the mirrored table, a full-length mirror, a hip bath behind a painted screen, a dress form, a chair, and several chests. The walls were lined with shelves and clothes racks. It was an altogether feminine place, perfectly suited for intimate conversation. The thick Turkey carpet on the floor muffled Honoria's footsteps, but she suspected Huseby could hear the loud pounding of her heart.

Finally, she stopped in front of her friend, and said, "We were lovers, the Spaniard and I. Even while you and Derrick—my own betrothed—were in the house. I don't know when he sent for you, how he got you out of the fortress, or how long you were in the house before the night of the attack. I asked for his help in getting you out of the prison; then . . . I . . . simply . . . forgot everything but . . ." The heat of her shamed blush burned her face. She turned her head away as she finished, "Him." After a long moment of silence, she added, "Everything Captain Russell accused me of back on the *Manticore* was quite true. I was the Spaniard's whore. And"—the final words came out in the faintest of whispers—"I'm desperately afraid that it could happen all over again."

Huseby folded her arms beneath her bosom. "Am I supposed to react with horrified shock, Honoria? After yesterday?"

Honoria frowned, then shrugged. Dear, circumspect Maggie Huseby. "I suppose you've known all along. You've done a very good job of pretending you believed I was still a maiden."

"All I know is that Captain Russell had no right to treat you the way he did. Whatever you did, you did for him. I thought you were very brave."

What nonsense! What she'd been was reckless and wanton. She'd let her emotions run away with her sense. "I think I was very foolish. I've tried to make up for my sins since, but they seem to be catching up with me fast and hard at the moment."

"Both of those men at once. You deserve better than either of them, though I must say the Spaniard cleans up better than most men I've seen." Huseby nodded. "It would serve them both right if you went off with some nice man and left the two of them rot."

Honoria smiled. "That's my plan, exactly. That's what I wanted to talk to you about."

There was a tentative knock on the door behind her before Huseby could answer. "My lady," her secretary called. "You said that you would meet with Mrs. Oglethorpe at two."

Honoria glanced at the clock on the dressing

table. It was indeed nearly two, and she was well-known for her punctuality. She possessed too few virtues to slack off on any of them, even once. "We'll continue this conversation later," she told Huseby, who stepped aside as Honoria moved toward the door. "After I've given away a substantial amount of money to the poor and downtrodden."

The Reverend Joshua Menzies almost chortled with glee as he walked boldly into the home of his quarry. The quest to find Honoria Pyne had proved so easy he might have put his luck down to divine guidance, if he believed in such a spineless thing as a loving creator. He'd relied on his own native wit and trained intelligence once he'd sobered up enough. It had been no complicated matter to find the meticulously kept records of one particular voyage of a merchant ship called the *Manticore*. He'd only had to seek out the offices of three different shipping companies before finding the one that owned the ship. Then, using the story that he was trying to find information on a sick parishioner's missing son, he'd talked a sympathetic clerk into giving him access to all the *Manticore*'s records.

Soon he found out something his wily father had not known: that the young woman who went by the name Honoria Pyne was the heiress of the Duke of Pyneham. How he'd laughed, knowing that his father would have considered the duke's daughter a far more valuable prize than the treasure he'd so carefully hidden. Even more amusing and ironic was the fact that Joshua Menzies was already well acquainted with the worthy Lady Alexandra, though only through her reputation for good works. She was quite the famous philanthropist, known for receiving petitions from needy clerics and charity representatives wherever she happened to be in residence. Her *noblesse oblige* was quite touching, most worthy, and thoroughly convenient for the Reverend Menzies, since the lady was naturally in London for the coronation, along with every other member of the peerage. A few more inquiries had brought him to the door of Mrs. Oglethorpe, and a story about hoping to found a home for wayward young women had Mrs. Oglethorpe inviting him along with her to plead his case to the generous Lady Alexandra.

Menzies touched the newly cleaned and starched white collar at his throat, thinking how a divinity degree had come in handy at last, as he waited on a chair set up in a hallway outside a wide, dark door. He was but one of a half dozen waiting men and women left to cool their heels. He was the only one not perched on the edge of their comfortably upholstered seats. He was quite relaxed and happy to be the last in line, though he wished the rabble would get their begging over with so he could have the duke's daughter to himself. Time passed slowly. The only diversion came whenever a footman appeared from within the inner sanctum of the library to see someone out and then announce another name.

Mrs. Oglethorpe had been shown immediately into the generous lady's domain, and had left some time ago, with a beaming smile on her fat face and a kindly nod to him. That had been three or four supplicants ago. There was only one person left in line before him now. Menzies sighed, and tilted his head back. He closed his eyes and tried to nap while waiting his turn. The attempt must have been successful, since he did not know how much time passed before the footman shook his shoulder, and told him, "My lady will see you now, Reverend Menzies."

Menzies sprang to his feet. He felt more alert and alive than he had in years. He had no fixed plan for confronting Honoria Pyne, but he knew he could outthink any fool chit of a female. He was his father's son, born to be a pirate, to take bold, ruthless action and to think on his feet. The woman in the library held not only the key to a lost treasure, she was a treasure in her own right. He would have his father's fortune from her, and another from her private coffers as well—interest for the years he'd been forced to wait for what was rightfully his. He would enter the lady's presence an impoverished minister, but he would leave a king!

A large clock beside the door chimed melodiously as Menzies came into the library, announcing that the hour was five o'clock. There were several people in the large, book-lined room, but Menzies paid no one any mind but the young woman seated regally behind a desk in the middle of the room. Even sitting down she was tall, a stately, striking woman with copper red hair and large blue eyes. He noticed the intelligence in those eyes as he drew near, but he was quick to discern something else as well. Lady Alexandra gave every outward impression of having a serene, dignified nature, but Joshua Menzies was a man used to hiding his own true nature, and he recognized a similar talent in the young woman seated before him. He could tell that serenity sat like a thin veil on her, barely covering a core of temper and passion. He instantly decided to find out what she was like in bed. Unwilling would be best, he thought. Yes, how delightful it would be to have her under him, clawing and screaming while he did exactly as he pleased.

His smile was one of genuine pleasure as he bowed before her, and rose to say, "My dear, I have waited a long time for this day."

"Indeed? And how is that?" Honoria replied tartly, as she stiffened at the most inappropriate greeting from the last man on today's appointment list.

The notes given her by her secretary said that

he was the rector of a poor London parish, St. Ambrose's, come to seek aid for wayward girls. Having firsthand knowledge of being a wayward female, she was happy to hear his case. She was not happy at his overly familiar attitude, so her tone was stern. His smile only grew wider. There was something chilling about it. He was a tall man, lean and long-faced. There was something about him that reminded her of a feral tomcat. And something disturbingly familiar about him as well.

"Have we met?" she asked before he could answer her first annoyed question.

"We should have met years ago," was his enigmatic answer. "Forgive me, my lady." He put a hand over his heart, and attempted to look contrite. "Let us begin again." He bowed once more, and rose to say, "I am your humble servant."

"I thought you were a servant of God."

He folded his hands over his flat stomach and lowered his eyes. "Indeed. But it is to the house of Pyneham that I come seeking favor."

He did not have much talent for humility, she concluded, nor was he making much effort now. How odd, as ministers of his lowly rank were usually quite skilled at being obsequious. She might have been pleased with his attitude, as she had little patience with sycophants, but there was something very disturbing about this man.

She wanted to tell him to go away. Responsibility required her to ask, "What is it you seek?"

A glint came into his eyes that was more than a little disturbing. Where had she seen a look like that before? On someone older, yes, but . . .

"It is a delicate matter, concerning the reputation of a lady." He looked at her secretary, at Huseby, who sat working on a piece of sewing near the fire, at the footman by the door. "We must speak alone, my lady." The minister's expression turned earnest, his voice genuinely pleading. "Please."

"That would be most improper," Honoria reminded him.

"I am a man of the cloth," he reminded in turn. He was surprisingly persuasive as he continued, "Your spotless reputation is in no danger from a minister of the Lord, now is it, my child?"

It was late. She wanted desperately to get her duties over with so she could concentrate on solving her personal problems. Or, even better, to hide in her room and forget her personal problems. She'd listened to other peoples' troubles all day and did her best to be of some help, but now she was tired. "I have very little time," she told the Reverend Menzies.

"I will not take up much of it," he promised her. "But we must speak in private. For the lady's sake," he leaned forward and whispered.

Honoria still did not like the look in his eyes, but she sighed, and nodded. Both her secretary and Huseby looked unhappy when she gestured for them to leave, but they didn't comment. The footman glared suspiciously at the minister, but slipped out the door to wait in the hallway in case Honoria should call.

Once they were alone, Honoria stood and moved to one of the chairs by the fireplace. It seemed to her that if they were going to discuss some poor young woman's fate, a more intimate setting might be more conducive to discussing delicate matters. Menzies did not hesitate to follow close behind her.

In fact, he was quite uncomfortably close when she turned to say, "I was given to believe you came seeking funding for a home for young women." She gestured to the chair Huseby had vacated. "Please be seated."

"No," he said, somehow managing to put a hiss into the sound. "I think not."

His attitude almost frightened her, and it occurred to her that perhaps being alone with him was a very bad idea. She reacted to her uncertainty with a show of arrogance. She turned an imperially cold look on the Reverend Menzies. "What did you say to me?"

He reached a hand toward her. She backed up a step, her instinct to slap his hand away, but the door flew open behind him before she could move. Menzies wheeled around, and she took a quick step toward the door and the large man who filled the doorway.

Relief flooded her when James Marbury came striding briskly into the room. A dark coat highlighted the impressive width of his shoulders. Buff trousers outlined the long, powerful muscles of his thighs. He looked strong, competent, and utterly male. He was carrying an armful of roses. She almost ran to him and threw herself into his arm as if he was rescuing her from some dire, wicked fate. But James Marbury *was* the wicked fate.

The roses were white and yellow, her favorites, which pleased her immensely. She had never much liked red roses, and pink was not only insipid, but clashed terribly with her hair and complexion. Fragrance filled the room, much the way James Marbury's presence did. The library was not a small room, but James was a large man. Not just in size, but in personality, in exuberance and charm, and most particularly in spirit.

Honoria shook off the warm feelings with a stern warning to herself. She was just being fanciful, to think anything but the worst about the former corsair who so bedeviled her, wasn't she? But then he smiled at her, and she practically basked in it. She was unaccountably happy to see him, whether he'd come to her rescue or not.

Which was why she crossed her arms and

said waspishly, "What the devil are you doing here?"

"Change your dress, Honoria," he replied, ignoring her tartness. "We're getting married. Do you own anything white?"

"No."

"That's all right. I liked what you wore at the ball. The green-blue one. You probably never wear the same dress twice, duchess mine, but if you have a gown like that one, it will do nicely." He held out the roses. "I even brought your bouquet."

Honoria was frozen in place. "No." After she spoke, she forgot to breathe.

James hadn't expected her to take it well, even after yesterday, and she wasn't disappointing him. He knew there was no use in trying to court her properly. The best thing for them both was to simply go through with it, before either of them could back out. Looking at her, pale and perturbed but so very strong, he knew he didn't want to back out. He just wasn't sure what to do once the deed was accomplished. He had never thought farther than finding Honoria Pyne and making her his wife.

He'd think of something, he supposed. Right now, the object was simply to get them both through the wedding part of the great scheme to redeem himself in his own, his father's, and God's eyes. He was going to do the right thing by this woman whether she wanted him to or not! This time she wasn't getting away. And that meant moving fast, before she could find some way to worm out of it. Or before "dear Derrick" could show up to attempt to stake his own claim.

Jealousy ground into James as he came toward Honoria. She was still as a statue and pale as marble. It was not until he stood in front of her that he noticed the man dressed in somber black standing at her side. It wasn't as if the other man was small and unobtrusive, or trying to hide. James had simply been far too focused on Honoria to notice if there was an army in the room. He only vaguely remembered the footman who had tried to stop his entrance. Now he glanced at the thin man with the disturbing face, and grinned as he took in the significance of the man's long threadbare black coat and stiff white collar.

He clapped a hand on the man's shoulder, and thrust the roses at Honoria. "A priest," he announced. "Perfect!"

"I'm not a priest," the man announced. He stiffened beneath James's touch. "Get your hands off me, sir. Have you no respect for a man of the cloth?"

"Infinite respect," James replied. There was something familiar about the minister, but James couldn't place where he'd seen him before. It didn't matter right now, anyway. "And I have a need for a man of your profession."

"I'm sure you do," the vicar responded dryly, eyeing him with deep distaste. "Begone, sir," he said. "Can't you see that you have disturbed a private meeting?"

"I had to," James replied, tilting his head to one side. "There was no other choice. The guests are assembled, but the bride was missing."

"Bride?" the minister asked. He glanced at Honoria, then back to James. "You are quite mad, aren't you? Or is this some sort of joke?"

"No joke. I have a ring, too. And her father's permission. And a special license. All I lacked was a priest. The Bishop of Bath and Wells was supposed to be here by now, but he sent word he'd be delayed. That's all right." James clapped the minister on the shoulder again and the man winced at the force of it. "You'll do," James told him. "It's a lucky thing you were here."

The vicar looked stunned. "Lucky . . ."

James turned to Honoria, whose bright blue eyes were round behind the lenses of her glasses. She did not look well. "Honoria?"

She turned her head toward him at the sound of his voice, but he did not think she saw him. She was holding the roses, her face lovely and pale above the soft white and yellow blossoms. No, not pale, he realized of a sudden. She was turning blue. She began to sway and fall forward, roses scattering on the floor all around her. He had to move swiftly to catch his intended bride in his arms before she fell unconscious onto the floor.

Chapter 16

If it were not for the scent of roses and the feel of wool, linen, and hard muscle beneath her cheek, Honoria would have thought the whole incident a particularly detailed farcical nightmare when she awoke. But she could smell the roses, and she could feel him breathing, and knew that she was in his arms and that he was—

"James."

"Yes, my love?"

She listened for mockery, but his voice sounded particularly kind and solicitous. He was in the process of carrying her somewhere, but she couldn't find the will to open her eyes to find out where. "Put me down," she ordered, without lifting her head from where her cheek rested over the strong rhythm of his heart. "Or you'll do yourself an injury."

"You are a tall girl," he answered easily, "but light as a feather."

He sounded like he believed it. Well, he was a big man. She never felt large and awkward standing next to him. Or lying down beside him, either, come to think of it. This wanton thought finally caused Honoria to open her eyes and look up at her nemesis.

"We cannot do this," she told him flatly. "I cannot."

He set her down before her bedroom door. She wondered if anyone along the route had noticed that James Marbury was familiar with the way to her suite.

He reached past her to open the door, smiled, and kissed her cheek before stepping back. The chaste brush of his lips sent her senses reeling in a way no passionate kiss could have managed at the moment. Huseby stood just within the sitting room doorway. She reached out and tugged the flushing and flummoxed Honoria inside and firmly closed the door in James Marbury's face.

"He kissed me," Honoria announced in the stunned tone of a woman who had never been kissed before. Part of her knew how ridiculous this reaction was. Part of her recalled that in his time, Diego Moresco had certainly done far more than kiss her. But somehow, this time . . .

Huseby shook her. "What is the matter with you, Honoria?"

Honoria firmly fought off the pleasant, perplexed numbness. "It seems Mr. Marbury intends to marry me." She was outraged, she truly was, but something prevented her from working up the energy to express it. She suspected it had something to do with the way he'd held her. The kiss. The roses. She made a frustrated gesture. Oh, bother! Sometimes she suspected she was no better than any other soft, squishily sentimental, romantic female. She had not been sentimental even at eighteen. And especially not over *him*.

"It's worse than that," Huseby told her. "Your father commands you to marry this very afternoon." She hustled the nonresisting Honoria across the sitting room. "I've got orders to get you dressed and down to the music room as quickly as possible. I'm afraid there's no escape this time, Honoria."

She was naked under the stars. She had never known such freedom and abandon. The night was beautiful, alive. The tinkling of the small fountain was the richest music in the world; the scent of flowers and rich earth were enrapturing. The evening breeze on her bare skin left a sparkling tang of sensation as it cooled the sweat of passion. And Diego's tongue was circling the hard tip of her breast as she leaned over him. They'd taken turns straddling each other, rolling over and over, laughing and panting as first one and then the other was on top, joined together, him inside her. She knelt over him now, her hips rising and falling, taking him with the slowest, longest thrusts of her hips that she could manage. Her inner muscles rippled and closed around the solid, hot length of him. They fit together so well, like a sword into a sheath. No, like a man and woman who were made for each other! She threw back her head and laughed at the stars exploding above. This was heaven, the paradise garden of the Persian and Moorish poets. Her laughter was full of joy, and of amusement at the innocent girl who had sat in a chilly English library reading those poems with wonder, but with no understanding of what the words tried to convey.

How could she have known? How?

That girl was gone, and the woman in the garden was blind with desire and delight. Her laughter turned into a long gasp of pleasure as another climax took her. Her back arched and Diego grasped her hips, thrusting up as he pulled her down hard on his erection, his climax following hers by only a moment.

They ended up stretched out side by side on the tiles by the fountain. There was a small crack in the fountain basin, so the ground beneath her was slightly damp from the constant small drip. Honoria didn't mind. She was in Diego's arms and she didn't mind anything while she was there. Her world had spiraled tightly into the circle of Diego's arms. Day into night and into day again.

"You are," he said, brushing a hand through her tangled damp hair, "fantastic."

His face was close enough to hers that she saw him clearly, though his handsome features were shadowed and shaded by the darkness, and silvered by moonlight. She did not mistake the intensity in the depths of his honey gold eyes. She did not expect him to speak words of love, but she basked in the warmth of his gaze, and drank in whatever words of praise or affection he had to offer.

She did not dare to offer him words in reply. She could not bear to speak tonight. She feared the truth about how he made her feel would spill out if even one word were to escape—how she'd come to feel about him. He looked as if he wanted her to speak. As though he waited for something—praise, reassurance, commitment? She had given him everything, but she could not give him words. Words were too important to her; words made things real. If she spoke what was in her heart, she was certain her heart would be broken when this time out of time came to an end.

Because it would come to an end—she was not so besotted not to realize that forever wasn't possible between her and her corsair. But not yet, she prayed. Please, not yet.

She traced a finger slowly around his full lips, then drew his mouth to hers for a long, slow kiss. As their tongues speared and circled, the heat began to build inside her again. Deep in her belly the sweet liquid ache centered, then spread. Her thighs opened like a blossom at the merest touch of his hand. The bud within the intimate folds of flesh was already swollen and throbbing. It took but the slightest pressure from the pad of his thumb against it to send an orgasm jolting through her. Her muscles stiffened and she clung to him as he coaxed a second flash of intense pleasure from her, and another. She was weeping when he entered her again, awash in a world of passion, where there were no words and none were needed.

After that they slept for a while under the stars, exhausted, limbs entangled, with her long hair covering them like a blanket. When she awoke the moon was still high, and she remembered that there were words that she could *give him.*

It took some effort to get him to wake. She thought he looked like a ravished angel when he finally opened his eyes and sat up with a yawn. That she was responsible for his dissolute condition pleased her no end. She put out a hand and he helped her to her feet. She giggled when she realized that she could barely stand. She was weak, and not a little sore, from all that lovemaking, but she didn't mind a bit. She was still laughing as she snatched up a white silk caftan. First she put on the spectacles she'd dropped on the pile of cloth, then pulled the caftan on over her head. The nearly sheer silk was an erotic caress against her skin. As her head emerged from the neck of the caftan, she saw that Diego had pulled on his robe. The way he belted it on left most of his chest bare. She marveled at how exciting she found the glimpse of skin framed in the long vee formed by the edges of the robe. She could not get enough of the man.

"Come," she said, reaching a hand out to him. "There's something you wanted me to do, remember?" He looked confused as she led him toward the house. "A letter to be read," she reminded him.

A light spilled out from the high lattice window of his work room, catching them in a square of illumination. She could just make out her lover's features by squinting hard. Diego looked as though he didn't understand her for a moment, then he nodded. It pained her that he looked as if he was waking from a dream. She sighed, but was comforted by his arm coming around her shoulders.

They were still arm in arm when they walked into the work room. She froze in the doorway when she saw the people waiting within. Diego's arm tightened around her.

He breathed a curse that was also a name. "Ibrahim Rais."

A white figure rose up from the chair behind the table. "My son," a deep voice intoned sadly. "I fear that you have been trying to escape me."

There really was no escape, Honoria knew. Oh, she could have jumped out a window and run off somewhere, but in the end she would have had to explain why to her father. She was as trapped now by her father's expectations as she had always been. Trapped by circumstances, history, duty, and habit, too, she supposed. Honoria always did what was proper. She was used to attending and participating in ceremonies of one form or another. Whether it be lending her countenance to the christening of village children on the family estate, or wearing a coronet at the Queen's coronation—or marching down the aisle at her own wedding—she always did what was expected and correct. What else could she, the heir of the Pyneham line, do but put on the shimmering silver-gray gown Maggie chose for her, let the family diamonds be clasped at her throat, and walk with proud dignity into the music room?

She brought Huseby with her. If she must face this ordeal, she was determined to do one unaccustomed thing—though it had taken a short, sharp argument to get her maid to agree to stand with her as maid of honor.

"You're my best friend," she had finally argued. "After all we've been through together, you can do this as well. Please."

Huseby didn't agree until the butler knocked firmly on the door and said His Grace demanded Honoria's presence right now. "I suppose I can't let you face the Spaniard alone," she said.

Her father was waiting by the music room door when the butler opened it and bowed them inside. He handed her the bouquet of white and yellow roses she'd dropped in the library. Habit kept Honoria's spine straight, her head high, and her steps stately and dignified as she advanced on her father's arm between a row of chairs, with Huseby walking slowly ahead of them. She was aware of a great many more flowers in baskets and vases, resting on every surface in the room. The room was full of people, but she saw none of them even though she was defiantly wearing her spectacles. She had no idea where they'd come from, and didn't care. The only person she was aware of was the large man who stood next to the black-clad vicar in a spot precisely between the two tall French windows. The windows were not of stained glass, yet Honoria felt the chapel-like atmosphere of the place, and for the first time her knees began to wobble with nerves. Her stomach clenched and her breathing grew shallow.

This was really going to happen.

This was really going to happen!

Dear God, this was really going to—

To the devil with duty and habit! she thought wildly, and would have hiked up her skirts and run like the wind, if James Marbury had not appeared suddenly before her. He was taking her from her father and gazing steadily into her eyes. She wasn't sure if he gave her strength or turned her into a complete coward, but she did go with him to stand before Reverend Menzies. James's hand over hers was large, strong and warm. Huseby took the roses from her.

Honoria almost laughed when she saw the sour look on the minister's face. James noticed the minister's annoyed look as well, and he and Honoria shared an amused glance. "And I thought you would be the one in a tearing fury," James whispered to her in Arabic.

Reverend Menzies turned a sharp glower on James, and looked as if he was about to retort. Then he cleared his throat, waved them to stand directly in front of him, and intoned, "Dearly beloved . . ."

Honoria looked at James, ignoring the ceremony meant to join them together as man and wife. The concept was patently ridiculous, despite being legally and religiously binding. All she wanted to do was get him alone and wring his true purpose for this farce out of him. But all she could do with her father watching was meekly reply, "I will" to the vows to love, honor and obey. She was forsworn even as she spoke, but this was not the time or place to point out her insincerity. Besides, she kept slipping into the fantasy, the falsehood, the foolishness of looking into honey gold eyes and believing she was a beloved and cherished young bride.

That helped get her through the ceremony, until the moment came when Reverend Menzies said, "You may now kiss the bride."

James had sworn to himself not to do anything to frighten or upset Honoria, but when it came to kissing her, he couldn't stop the instinct to take her in his arms and cover her mouth hungrily with his. Whether her lips opened beneath his with surprise or desire held no importance to him. Her hands moved to his shoulders. For a moment she tried to fend him off, then her fingers clutched his coat, dug into his shoulders, and pulled him to her. The heat of contact flashed through him, the softness of her lips enticed and invited. The satin of her dress was smooth beneath his hand as he caressed the long length of her back, feeling her arch against his palm. She was a creature of fire clothed in silver, like a marvelously wrapped present waiting to be opened. She was his and his alone. He had only to strip away the trappings and—

"Ahem."

He was vaguely aware of restless murmuring behind them, then far more aware of the sudden withdrawal of the woman in his arms. She had heard and reacted to those faceless others, when James wanted her attention to be completely centered on himself! Her standing in society was more important to her than he could ever be.

"Excuse me, but I said you should kiss the bride, not ravish her." The sanctimonious minister's voice was stern, but so soft that only James and Honoria could hear him.

Honoria dropped her hands from James's shoulders as though she'd been burned. Her head came up proudly.

James had no choice but to let her go, and take a step back. He was afraid she would start fighting him if he did not. He felt like such a fool, all of a sudden. His physical attraction to Honoria was a very real thing, but his reasons for marrying her made no sense to him anymore.

She didn't need him.

James forced his fears out of his mind. He wasn't sure if he was more angry at her rejection, the minister's words, or all the people he'd joyfully invited to witness his wedding and now wished were gone, as he turned toward them and forced himself to smile. He knew his delight would not seem forced; he'd been taught to be an accomplished actor by Ibrahim Rais. And Honoria was an excellent actress after a life spent in public. Out of the corner of his eye he saw her force a smile, and give a regal nod toward her father.

His family and hers stood, and applauded. He couldn't help but notice the jaded smirks on some faces. The sight was enough to make him hope, just a little, that perhaps Honoria needed him a little after all. Though how he could protect her from the sophisticated cruelty of courtiers, he didn't know.

He took Honoria's arm and led her forward.

Her maid followed after, still holding the armful of yellow and white roses, their heavy, sweet scent perfuming the air. Reverend Menzies brought up the rear. A trio of people came from opposite sides of the room to meet them in the middle.

The kiss had left Honoria reeling, and very nearly senseless. She was mortified at having forgotten herself so completely, so quickly, and in front of everyone. James Marbury was a danger to her, and she wanted nothing more than to escape his wicked presence.

Then she remembered: she was his wife.

How the devil had she allowed this to happen? She glanced back over her shoulder at the minister, half tempted to demand he do something. But what? What could she do? Thinking was hard with the sweet residue of James's kiss still buzzing through her veins, but she did her best.

A wedding wasn't legal just because of a few words, was it? Maybe in the eyes of God, but surely the State required more, especially from a peer of the realm. Weren't there papers that needed to be signed by the bride and groom and witnesses? There must be some sort of marriage contract, with solicitors from both families involved, that had to be hammered out. This was not the joining of a pair of peasants, but the matrimonial arrangements of two old, titled, landed, established, wealthy families.

Did the Queen know about this? Was her permission needed for a ducal heir, someone who was in the line of succession for the throne of England, to wed? Honoria certainly hoped so.

Surely there had to be some legal recourse for her to escape a second bondage to the man who had once bought her as a slave, and now enslaved her as his wife.

Menzies looked back at her with a venomous glare. She found something disconcertingly familiar and frightening in that look, and quickly turned her attention to her father, Viscount Brislay, and the tall, statuesque woman on his arm. Yet still, she seemed to sense the minister's gaze stabbing her in the back. She blamed James for her sudden flight of fancy. Why not? He was responsible for everything else; he might as well take the blame for any insane responses that invaded her normally logical thought processes.

"You're looking daggers at my mother," he whispered, his lips suddenly very close to her ear. The proximity, and the warning in his soft voice, sent a shiver that had nothing to do with fear through her.

Honoria turned her dagger glare on him. Before she could say anything, Viscount Brislay stepped between her and—her husband. She gritted her teeth at the thought, even as James's father bestowed a light kiss on her cheek. "Welcome to my family, my dear." His voice was calm, his gaze assessing, yet there was something warm and welcoming about the man despite his outward reserve. It was easy to believe that he did welcome her, and that he truly cherished her as a member of his family.

But she would not let herself think that her father-in-law wanted the marriage for any altruistic purpose. She knew to the farthing just how much her dowry, and her future title, were worth. This man had to be scheming with his alleged son for some greedy purpose. Still—

"Lady Graciela Almeda y Gonzaga Marbury, Viscountess Brislay," Viscount Brislay introduced his wife.

"Mamacita," James added proudly.

The affection and pride in James's voice tugged at Honoria's jaded heart. She turned to Lady Graciela and realized to her dismay that the woman was nearly as tall as she was, and as amply proportioned. "Good Lord!" she murmured, before she could stop herself. The older woman had graying dark hair, a high-arched nose, and a warmly tinted complexion. Her mouth was rich and full, the same sensual shape as her son's, her eyes were so dark they were nearly black. They did not look at Honoria with any warmth. Her gaze pierced like a dagger made of ice.

"You will make my son happy," she said in aristocratic Spanish. It was not a question, a wish or a request.

So, this was what it was like to have a mother-in-law. Honoria was tempted to gulp, curtsy, and back slowly away from this stern female who looked her over with such a gimlet eye. Lady Graciela Marbury was yet another reason for obtaining an annulment as swiftly as possible.

Her father drew her away from James and into a fierce embrace. "My dear, dear child," he whispered, his voice choked with emotion. "Be happy. All I've ever wanted was for you to be happy."

She did not doubt that he meant it. But she had stopped expecting happiness so long ago that she no longer knew what the word meant. All she wanted was peace and respectability. She had married the last man who could provide her with either, and it was what her father wanted! Still, she managed a smile for him, and wiped away a tear at the corner of his eye. She gestured around the music room.

"How did you arrange all this?" she asked, to distract them both. "When?"

"Oh, not I," he answered. "Your cousin Kate began hatching this plot the day after the dinner party. I've only worked on the details of the marriage contract. There's still a slight difficulty about Marbury becoming a Pyne, but I think we'll agree on a hyphenated version and on heirs' names soon enough. Cousin Kate assures me that arranging the wedding supper and the guest list on such short notice was far more complex than marriage settlements."

He was so ridiculously pleased with all they'd been up to. "I see." Honoria threw a furious glance at her husband, who was speaking to his mother. Honoria felt the crowd closing in around her, and knew that they were all laughing at her behind their bland well-wishers' expressions. "My fate has been known to everyone but me for some days now. How—charming."

Her tone must have held some of the temper she was trying to conceal. Her father moved quickly to place her arm on James's. James turned his attention from his mother to the duke.

"Your lady wife," her father said formally. "I commend her to your tender care, sir. Make sure she is happy."

Honoria took pleasure in hearing her father sound as serious as Lady Graciela in his admonition to James. James, however, took the duke's words with a charming smile, and patted Honoria's hand on his arm. "I will do everything in my power to do so, sir," James responded, beaming at the duke, sounding for all the world like he meant it.

What do you want with me? Honoria thought with desperate anger. *Why are you doing this? More important, how do I escape?* She refused to let herself feel trapped, despite the crowd and the weight of having taken vows before God and man alike.

"There's supper laid out, I believe," her father-in-law said. "Let us seal this celebration with a few joyous toasts."

Her father clapped a hand on the minister's shoulder. "Join us, Reverend, and accept our thanks for a job well done."

Reverend Menzies rubbed a thumb along his jaw. "Thank you, Your Grace," he said with a slow nod and a toothy smile. "I believe I will."

Chapter 17

Now, this, Joshua Menzies thought, as he found himself among the great of the land, *is a truly interesting situation.*

There were almost more servants than guests in the dining room. Dressed in silver and blue livery, footmen carried silver trays laden with fine crystal wineglasses, constantly replenishing the supply for the numerous toasts wishing the couple well. Menzies was happy to accept every glass that came his way. It took a great deal for him to get drunk, but he intended to try to reach that longed-for condition this evening. He'd been far too sober lately, while searching for the girl from the *Manticore*. Well, he'd found her. He threw back his head and laughed, despite his sour anger.

His life had taken quite a turn since he'd received his imprisoned father's letter. He'd dutifully gone on a quest looking for a well-educated merchant's daughter, and found one of the greatest ladies of the land instead. Then, poof, before he could make any progress toward his goal, he'd found himself officiating at the great lady's wedding. To a man with a Spanish accent and a knowledge of Arabic. How very very curious.

He sipped another glass of the finest wine he'd ever been privileged to taste, and breathed in the scent of obscene wealth along with the bouquet of the dark liquid in the crystal glass. Both were aromas he liked very well indeed. Covetousness burned in him like a fever.

He knew that he would have all that Lady Alexandra and the Honorable James Marbury possessed. Somehow, in some way, he would take from them the fortune his father had spent years risking life and limb for—with interest. And if this Marbury should prove to be somehow connected with the Spaniard in his father's letter—well, he'd take revenge, as well.

Menzies did his best to remain inconspicuous amid the well-dressed guests, lest he be shown to the servants' dining hall rather than be allowed to stay in the room with his betters. He sneered as he stood across the opulent dining room and looked at the bride and groom, she in silver, he in tight buff trousers and a dark, finely tailored jacket. Oh, they made an admirably matched couple, the spark of sexual attraction strong between them. She scarcely looked Marbury's way, but there was no doubt that there was a deep, dark attraction pulling her toward the husband her father had arranged for her.

He sensed that she had a deep undertone of barely restrained passion, rather than the boring nervousness of a blushing and virginal bride. She was too striking and vivid to be considered a beauty by insipid fashionable standards, but when he looked at her, Menzies saw a woman made to stoke and satisfy a man's lust. Not pretty, but beddable, and that was better. His groin tightened at the sight of her full breasts and the way the proud set of her head showed off the length of her throat. His hands ached to weigh those fine soft tits in his hands.

Marbury stood too close to his wife for propriety's sake; the look he turned on her was too openly lustful. Here was a man who knew what he had, and was eager to take the woman to his bed. Not for the first time; the vicar had no doubt of that. Marbury had sampled the merchandise before accepting it, for certain. Did the heiress's father know that, and was there any way he could use it against the woman who held the secret to his own father's fortune?

A long buffet table was set up nearby, laden with more food just for this small gathering than he was used to seeing in a year. Menzies intended to leave here as full as he was drunk.

As he determinedly approached the table

once more, there was a stirring in the dining room doorway. He couldn't help but turn and look, along with everyone else in the room, to see a tall blond man in a Naval uniform push past a pair of footmen and stride arrogantly toward the bride and groom. *What's this?* Menzies wondered, drawing closer as the crowd parted to let the officer through. There was an avid interest on many faces that told him that they expected quite a good show.

The actors in this little drama didn't disappoint them.

Marbury stepped between his wife and the newcomer.

The officer wove drunkenly to a halt and peered angrily past Marbury's wide shoulders. "Honoria!" he shouted. "Is it true? What they're saying at the clubs—that the Spanish bastard won the bet to be the one to marry you? That the fortune is his? It should have been mine!"

"Bet?" the heiress asked from behind Marbury. "Is that what this is about, Derrick? A bet to see who could marry me?"

"Of course!" Derrick shouted, full of snide, ugly sarcasm. "What else?"

"I see." Her voice was soft, cold as ice at the top of the world.

"That is not what this is about, Honoria," Marbury said, but he did not turn his furious, dangerous gaze from the intruder. "You, sir," he said, dropping his hand on the man's shoulder, "were not invited to this wedding."

Derrick sneered and pushed Marbury's hand away. "Don't touch me, bastard." He took a step back and looked Marbury over disdainfully. "You took what was mine."

"A long time ago," was Marbury's quiet, confident answer. "Not that she was ever meant for a coward like you to begin with."

The intruder bristled indignantly. "Coward? I'll show you who is a coward!"

Menzies wasn't surprised when Derrick slapped Marbury's face. Nor was he surprised by the thin smile that briefly lifted Marbury's lips. Marbury clearly hated this man, and had just goaded the fool into doing exactly what he wanted.

Marbury touched his marked cheek as shocked silence rippled out from the center of the room. There was not a person present but himself who was not frozen in place, fascinated by the drama. "My choice of weapons," he said. "My choice of place. My second will call on yours. Now—" he gestured dismissively. "Get out of my wife's presence."

Having made a fool of himself, disillusioned the bride, and ruined the wedding party for everyone, the intruder turned on his heel and stumbled drunkenly out.

Menzies rubbed his chin and watched him go. There was something there, he thought, some old feud. Something to do with Algiers?

He didn't know, but he would find out. The party was over, anyway.

He followed Derrick out.

She had not spoken to him, not one word, in all the hours the carriage had been moving steadily through the night, taking them to a brief honeymoon at the Pyneham country estate. The weather was fine, but there was only so much countryside that could be made out by moonlight, no matter how hard James tried to concentrate on the passing view out the carriage window.

Honoria sat across from him, as still as a statue. She wore a black traveling dress and bonnet. Even the gloves covering the hands held clasped tightly in her lap were of black kidskin, so all that was visible in the dark enclosure of the coach was the pale oval of her face. He alternated staring out the window with watching her, but her gaze had yet to lift to his face. The silence wore on him, for it was shaded with equal parts fear and fury.

She had never feared him when she had reason to, back in Algiers. Now she was his wife and— He sighed, and wondered if this was how they were to spend the rest of their lives. No, he decided with a sudden rush of temper and determination; it was not. It was time for him to take control of the situation, to make his marriage what he wanted it to be.

"We made the vows," he said. "We will live up to them."

Honoria continued to ignore him, but he expected that. He already knew how stubborn and headstrong she was. Once she got a notion in her head she followed it through, right or wrong. She had a great many notions about him, and it was up to him to prove to her whether they were right or wrong. She was a challenge, and he suddenly looked forward to continuing what they'd already started. He needed it. And he wanted her as strongly as during those long, sensual Arabian nights. But he had to get her attention first, the same way he had begun when they were alone in the library.

He shifted her wide skirts aside and sat down beside her. Honoria had to scoot over quickly from the center of the well-padded bench to avoid his landing in her lap. There was plenty of room in the luxurious coach for two people to sit side by side, but James moved close to Honoria. She backed off, until she was wedged into the corner of the compartment. She remained stiff as a board when he put his arm around her shoulders.

When he undid the ribbon tying on her bonnet she finally spoke. "Don't."

He ignored her and took the hat off, tossing it across to the other seat. "You need to relax," he said. "Get comfortable."

"I am."

"All that heavy black must be hot. You look more like a widow than a bride."

"Black is practical for travel." Her voice was as stiff as her spine when she replied, "I am quite comfortable as I am . . . my lord."

"My lord?"

"You will find that you have acquired a title along with a wife . . . my lord. You are no longer the Honorable James Marbury—not that you ever were. Honorable."

"Ah," he said, leaning against her. "I see."

"I doubt that."

"Well, it is dark in here."

"You are being facetious." Her tone was as crisp as starched linen.

"I know." He put his head on her shoulder. "Why are you so angry with me, Honoria?"

"It would take weeks to enumerate."

He could tell that she did not want to speak to him. He heard the anger at herself for talking to him every time she answered him. He took her not being able to stop herself as a good sign. Then it occurred to him that perhaps she had not had anyone she *could* speak to as herself in a long time.

He knew how that felt. Until his father had forced the whole story of his life in Algiers out of him, he had lived in unnatural silence. He had had outlets—women, drink, brawling. He was infamous in the streets and taverns of Malaga. A respectable woman had no such recourses.

He decided to deal with the most recent cause for her to be angry rather than to dwell on the past. "I knew nothing about any wager, I swear to you. No, that is not quite true. There were wagers in the betting books of several sporting clubs concerning whether or not the Duke of Pyneham's daughter would wed. The odds were running against, by the way. It would seem that dear Derrick took the bets, but I did not. I swear. I cared nothing about the matrimonial prospects of this duke's spinster heiress. I was looking for you."

Honoria tried not to be affected by the sincerity in his voice. It did not help to feel his soft hair against her cheek, or that there was something comforting about the warm weight of his body against hers. It tempted her to relax in kind, to fit herself against him. She remembered all too well how naturally their bodies molded together. He was quite impossible, and so very *physical*. She didn't want to answer him. All she wanted was to get to Lacey House, run to her room, and lock herself inside until he went away forever. She said, "Then why else did you marry me, if not to win a wager? How many fortunes do you need, my lord?"

"I escaped Algiers with enough to buy a tavern for my mother."

That did not answer her question. She had to

bite her tongue to keep from pointing this out. After she remained silent for a while, he made his own assumption.

"It disgusts you, doesn't it? Knowing that I went into trade? That you married a man who has worked in a taproom, and has helped hang up the clean laundry, and picked herbs from the kitchen garden? Hardly proper occupations for a gentleman. You would prefer to marry a true, lazy, useless nobleman, rather than an honest man."

His descriptions of such homely tasks actually sounded quite soothing to her. She said, "When I met you, you were a pirate."

"A pirate is romantic," he informed her. "An innkeeper is not."

"Depends on the innkeeper." She cursed herself for the way he might take such a comment—and, in truth, she wasn't quite sure what she meant by it.

He went on. "Then I found myself the heir of a viscount. There's an unexpected fortune there. In many ways," he added softly.

"So you didn't marry me for the money," she answered tartly, refusing to let herself be affected by the deep emotion he seemed to feel toward his newly found father. "You no doubt decided to take on the challenge of winning the wager."

He propped his chin on her shoulder, and whispered in her ear. "Oh, you are a challenge all right, fox-haired duchess mine." His voice was smooth as silk, as seductive as she had ever heard it.

She could not stop the shudder of reaction that went through her, but refused to acknowledge what he made her feel. "Yours for now," she said. "But not for long."

He sat up straighter. She missed his weight when it was lifted off her. "You're worried about the duel, aren't you? Afraid I'll be hurt, or longing for me to be killed? Shall I choose swords or pistols?"

She laughed. She couldn't help it. Her iron control slipped far too easily around this man. She looked at him for the first time, and was aware of the dangerous glimmer in his eyes even in the dim light inside the carriage. How well she remembered that look in his eyes. "Afraid? For you? Ha!"

"Escape?" Diego gave her a warning look and motioned for her to stay by the door as he moved to the center of the room.

She ignored him, and followed closely on his heels—though what she could do to help in this situation, she did not know. All she knew was what Diego had told her of Ibrahim Rais. She only knew that she wanted to save Diego from whatever punishment the corsair admiral intended for him. Protect him somehow, or share his fate. When she slipped her hand into Diego's he squeezed it tightly, reassuringly, though the quick look he flashed her was exasperated that she had not stayed put.

Ibrahim Rais had two guards with him in the room. As she and Diego moved forward a third one entered, pushing Maggie Huseby ahead of him. Huseby saw her and ran forward with a startled cry. As she embraced her servant and friend, a deep sense of chagrin overcame Honoria. She became aware that days—days—had passed since she had thought of her fellow captives. She had been living for the rapturous pleasure she found in Diego's bed, and nothing else had mattered. Kisses, caresses, the shattering delights of lovemaking had driven out the higher callings of duty and responsibility. The realization that she had betrayed her position, her friend, and the man she was betrothed to ripped through her. If someone had thrown a bucket of icy water over her, the sensation of waking from a long, luxurious dream could not have been stronger.

"What have I done?" she rasped, guilt almost overcoming awareness of the danger posed by the vicious old corsair. "Where is Derrick?" she finally thought to ask.

"I was so worried, my—Honoria," Huseby quickly stopped herself from using Honoria's title. "Derrick is asleep, or pretended to be when the guard came for me," Huseby added, almost under her breath. "I have been tending his wound. It is nearly healed, as far as I can tell."

"Good, good," Honoria answered. She meant the words, but was too distracted by what Ibrahim Rais

intended to do to Diego to work up much concern for Derrick.

Huseby went on hastily, her hand on Honoria's arm, "When we were brought to this house I was told I would see you, but—"

"Silence," a guard ordered, and pulled Huseby and Honoria apart.

"You may take the servant away," Ibrahim Rais ordered. "I only wanted to show my dearest Captain Moresco that I had proof of his treachery."

As Huseby was taken out again, Honoria was pushed forward to stand with Diego before Ibrahim Rais.

"I am no traitor," Diego declared to Ibrahim Rais's accusation.

"Aren't you?" the corsair admiral asked mildly. "Do you think you can hide your plans from me forever? I've had you watched all your life, boy." His gaze shifted to Honoria. He looked her over from head to foot with bold interest. "I confess I did not know you had purchased this one, or why you bought her when you could have had her as a gift." His fingers caressed the hilt of a knife stuck in the wide sash at his waist. His smile was slow, evil, and anticipatory. "No doubt I will learn everything you both know by the time I am finished with you."

Diego moved protectively closer to her. His gaze did not leave Ibrahim Rais's face. "But I have done nothing."

"You sent a large bribe to the Bey to obtain the release of prisoners due to be ransomed," the corsair

informed him. "Why would you do that if you did not plan on taking them with you when you go?" Ibrahim Rais was still looking at her. His eyes reminded her of a reptile, a particularly poisonous snake. "No one leaves me. Especially not you." He moved close to Diego and grasped the edges of his robe, pulling them face to face, holding the cloth tightly in his old, strong hands. "I made you everything you are."

"A pirate," Diego responded with cold disgust. "A schemer. A man who has learned to live in shadows. A man who has no chance to live with honor and honesty." His voice was full of bitterness as he added, "You turned me into scum like you. I would rather you had left me as a galley slave."

"I'll make you much worse before I'm done with you." The corsair cast an ugly look her way. "Did you do it for her? Why? I would have given her to you."

"I wanted something in my life not tainted by you. At least I bought her with my own coin."

Honoria had forgotten for a few days that she was a slave, a piece of property. She supposed she should be appalled and offended by Diego's words, but she was deeply affected by them.

It did not seem that Ibrahim Rais had yet tumbled to the fact that his second in command was not only trying to defect, but to take the pirate's treasure with him. She knew why Diego really wanted her, yet she thought—hoped—that she meant more to him now than merely a means of escape. The look he turned on her after he spoke told her he felt something for her, but it was too brief and fleeting.

She looked around desperately at the trio of guards filling the room. She saw the hopelessness of the situation, the madness in Ibrahim Rais's eyes, and realized how very afraid she was. She had no idea what they were going to do.

Everyone jumped and turned when sound exploded up from the harbor, louder than thunder. The house shook in response to the many voices of booming cannon. Heads turned. Bodies jerked defensively as the cannon roared out again. Then the barrage started in earnest.

One of the guards shouted above the booming, "The city's under attack!"

So was he, a moment later. Diego moved in the space of a breath, faster than Honoria's racing heartbeat. In one swift move he broke from Ibrahim Rais's hold and was on the guard. An instant after that he had the guard's scimitar and the other man was on the floor, bleeding. When Diego turned again, he held the sword in one hand, a pistol in the other. "Down!" he shouted.

Honoria had the good sense to get out of his way. The sound of the pistol was louder in the enclosed room than the cannon fire from the harbor. Another of Ibrahim Rais's men fell. The third guard rushed forward, sword raised. There was a brief flurry of blows, metal ringing on metal. Then there was blood and the third guard was down. Then Diego turned on Ibrahim Rais.

Honoria shrieked in pain as Ibrahim Rais grabbed her by the hair and pulled her from where she knelt against the wall. The old man was strong and held her easily, though she kicked back, hitting him in the shins. When he rested the tip of a knife at her throat she had the sense to go perfectly still.

"Good girl," he murmured, holding her before him as a shield.

The sword dropped from Diego's hand. He still held the empty pistol in the other. Honoria watched him move very cautiously forward as the tip of the knife blade slowly pierced a spot just above her collarbone. She didn't feel any pain, but was aware of the trickle of blood that seeped from the small wound onto the white caftan. Her spectacles were tilted askew on her face, but she had no trouble making out Diego's grim, hard expression as he slowly advanced. All the while the cannon in the harbor continued to shake the small house while attacking the city. But the chaos within, with a madman holding a knife at her throat, was worse.

"Let her go," Diego said.

"I think not. I will slit her throat in front of you, of course." The man sounded far too cheerful about his intentions for Honoria's peace of mind.

"If you touch her you know I will kill you."

"She's bleeding already."

Diego smiled. It was chilling, yet she found it somehow reassuring. "Then you're a dead man, aren't you?"

"She'll die first."

"Don't you know what's going on?" Diego asked, gesturing with the pistol. "There's a French fleet in the harbor. The English Navy is probably with them. We've known they would strike for months. We've all made our escape plans; our world is ending. Let her go. Let me go. Save yourself, old man."

She felt the strong arms holding her begin to tremble. There was a waver in Ibrahim Rais's voice when he said, "My treasures."

"Get to your house," Diego urged, voice low and rushing with warning. "Gather what you can. Escape. Hurry."

"My—"

Diego threw the pistol. The heavy gun whooshed past Honoria's head to hit Ibrahim Rais squarely in the forehead with a bone-cracking thud. He grunted and fell, the knife clattering to the floor a second before he did. Suddenly released and off-balance, Honoria fell forward. Diego caught her and drew her into a hard embrace.

"Is he dead?" she panted, breathless after a swift kiss.

"I think so," Diego answered. He gave only a swift glance to the old man in passing as he hurried her toward the door. "Let's get out of here."

Honoria touched the small scar just above her collarbone as she recalled her last sight of the four men James had defeated to secure their escape from Algiers, just before he abandoned her to her fate. She had seen the man in a real fight;

she would not fear for him fighting a duel.

"Well," he persisted. "What shall I choose?"

"Swords or pistols?" she questioned back. "Choose what you will, my lord."

It was not as if any choice she ever made had any meaning for him, anyway.

Chapter 18

"We're here."

Honoria came awake at the touch of James's hand on hers, and at the sound of his voice. For a moment she had no idea where she was, other than that her head was resting on his shoulder and that his arm was around her. She was quite comfortable, or as comfortable as one could be sitting upright in a traveling coach.

She blinked her eyes open as a flood of memories from the day before rushed back to her. She was married. To James Marbury. And they had traveled through the night at her insistence, rather than stop at an inn to reach—

"We're here," James repeated as a footman threw open the carriage door. "Lacey House." He slipped out the door and turned, holding a hand toward her to help her descend.

Honoria stared at the Palladian mansion that

loomed behind Marbury's imposing breadth of shoulder. Its domed façade, the design a cross between an Italian villa and an ancient Greek temple, was of white polished marble that gleamed brightly in the early morning sunlight. Lacey House. The family seat. Her beloved home. She knew every room from garret to cellars, knew every pathway through the extensive woods and gardens; knew every servant, every horse in the stables, every dog in the kennels. Lacey House had been her haven and refuge for the last eight years, and now her nemesis was here in the one place she'd felt safe from the world and all its betrayals. Worse, her nemesis had brought her here and was waiting for her to follow him out of the carriage. For a panicked moment Honoria nearly shouted for the coachman to drive on.

James reached into the carriage and put his arms around her waist. The next thing she knew, she was cradled in his arms and he was marching resolutely up the shallow steps that led to the grand entrance of the ducal mansion. A long row of liveried servants stood on either side of the door waiting to greet them, and she realized that her father must have sent word of her returning with her husband. They served the Duke of Pyneham first, and perhaps they would serve her husband before answering to her. It galled her, but there was nothing she could do. Some of the maids held bouquets of flowers in their hands, and there were welcoming smiles on all the faces. Everyone but the blank-faced butler gaped as James carried her forward. To them this was a joyous occasion, even if the groom made their entrance less than dignified.

She did not demand that he put her down as they reached the doorway. She said, "I sincerely hope you are straining your back."

He laughed. "No you don't. You need me healthy."

"I can't think for what."

"I'll remind you shortly." She made a disgusted sound and he went on, "You're tall, not heavy. I like you tall."

"I am an overgrown cow, and everyone knows it. Don't flatter me. I won't have it."

He paused on the top step of Lacey House, and looked at her with great seriousness as the butler bowed and held the door open for them. He ignored the people to either side of them, seeming to have eyes only for her. The intensity of his look took her breath away. "Someone gave you the idea that you aren't beautiful," he said softly. "I'm going to teach you how beautiful you are."

"How do you plan to do that, break every mirror in the house?"

He smiled as he put her down, letting her body slide down the length of his. Then he kissed her, right there in front of the butler and everybody. Honoria was vaguely aware of applause breaking out around them, but she was far more aware of the texture of his lips and of the questing tongue that teased her mouth open beneath his. She knew intellectually that she did not want to be kissed, but her arms went around his neck and her body molded itself to his and relaxed in the shelter of his embrace. For a long, luscious moment she *soared.*

When James lifted his mouth from hers, her glasses were tilted askew. He didn't even seem to notice straightening them on her nose, but the offhand gallantry of the gesture left her nearly as weak and shaken as the kiss had done. What was the matter with her? Probably lack of sleep, she concluded, and steeled her resolve to confront him once more.

He disarmed her with one of his roguish smiles. "Tell me what the protocol is, duchess mine—do I now carry you over the threshold? Or do you carry me?"

"I am not a duchess."

He tilted his head to one side and studied her gravely. "But I am now a Pyne. I am not happy about that—"

"Neither am I," she interrupted.

He completely ignored her words as the look on his face turned bold. "You might not have my name," he told her with assured arrogance, running his hands slowly up the long length of her waist. "But you will have my children. You will have no reason to doubt that you are my wife."

A shiver went through her, half thrilled anticipation, half hysterical terror. In an instant, every ounce of control she possessed shattered. She turned and ran across the threshold of Lacey House.

"Go away!"

James sighed. He could hear the tears in her ragged voice through the thick wood of the bedroom door. Well, at least she had answered his knock this time. He scratched his ear and shrugged at the worried-looking butler, a large man named Huseby.

"Virginal bridal nerves," he offered to the concerned man.

A flash of skepticism played across the butler's face before he said blandly, "Of course, my lord."

"I think we need to think of something else."

There were a great many family retainers named Huseby. James had met several in the last hour, as they'd tried to persuade the hysterical woman to come out of hiding. This Huseby was more commonly known as Charles. Charles held a ring of keys he'd secured from the housekeeper, Mrs. Huseby. They'd already discovered that having a key to the door of Honoria's suite did no good, as she'd barricaded herself inside. James could imagine the stack of furniture shoved across the doorway. She was going to hate herself for this loss of control once she came back to herself.

This could not be allowed to go on, for both their sakes. A frontal assault had proved impossible; it was time for different tactics. "I think we should go now," he said, drawing the butler down the hall.

Honoria breathed a sigh of relief when several minutes passed in silence after James and Charles's footsteps faded away. She hadn't hidden in her room since she was thirteen, but she felt as vulnerable and out of control now as she did then. She almost smiled, recalling what a terror she'd been to her parents during her gawky, stormy adolescence.

Honoria moved away from the door. She was tired from the journey, her face was salt-stained and aching from too much crying. All she wanted was to take off her traveling clothes and climb into a hot bath. But calling for bath water would mean having to open the door. She couldn't hide in here forever, but she was not prepared to face James Marbury until she had regained her usual composure. At the current rate, she estimated that would take up to a year for her to fight her way back to her normal serene control.

"Drat the man," she muttered as she unfastened her buttons and hooks with inexpert fingers. Once she'd stripped down to her underthings, she found a china wash basin in her dressing room and dumped the water from a vase of fresh flowers into it to bathe her face, hands, and neck. The water held the aroma of newly cut greenery and pleased her strained senses more than any exotic perfume. "Ah, the simple life," she murmured ironically, and then unpinned and shook out her curling red hair. She picked up a brush and began stroking it through her hair as she walked back into her bedroom.

Only to throw the brush in a whirling arc in automatic reflex at James, who stood with his arms crossed in the middle of the room.

He snatched it out of the air before it hit him. "Honoria! Be good."

There she stood, with her hair undone, without a corset or even a robe. She wore nothing but a thin white cotton chemise. He stood there with his arms crossed, looking her up and down with a slow, assessing stare. "It is nice to see you dressed for the occasion," he said, grinning roguishly.

She resisted the urge to modestly cover her cleavage with her hands. She knew that far more of her bosom would be showing if she were wearing a ballgown. But she was not wearing a ballgown, or even the armor of a corset. She was in her bedroom, and from the way he looked at her, she might as well be naked. Under present circumstances, what she was wearing and where she was wearing it was shocking and scandalous. And dangerous.

"No need to blush," he said, taking a step closer. He gestured around the bedroom, then looked back at her, eyes bright with amusement and something that sent a hot rush of desire through her veins. "You look lovely, by the way."

She ignored the compliment and reverted to basic annoyance. She put her hands on her hips and demanded, "How did you get in here?"

He pointed to the open balcony window. "Mr. Huseby—the gardener, not the butler—was kind enough to loan me a ladder. You look like you're feeling better now. Good." He began to undo his cravat. "Your skin has such a fine, healthy glow."

"My skin is none of your affair."

He tilted an eyebrow. "Isn't it?" His coat followed his cravat.

Honoria was appalled. "What do you think you are doing?"

"Taking my clothes off." His vest went next.

As he began unbuttoning his shirt, she ventured to ask, "Why?"

"We have a great deal to discuss. Which 'why' are you referring to at the moment?"

She hated that he sounded so confident, so amused, while she feared she was turning into a raving madwoman. She looked around her for means of defense, or escape. She had shoved the heavy table across the door herself. If she ran for the barred doorway, he could catch her long before she had time to move it out of the way. Her gaze went to the balcony, where soft white curtains fluttered in the breeze from the open doorway. Perhaps she could—

"I shoved the ladder to the ground after I used it," James told her, guessing her thoughts. "You're trapped here with me, Honoria. Face it. It is *kismet* that brought us together, then and now."

"Nonsense," she responded. "Fate has nothing to do with it."

He moved forward. She took a step back, and stumbled on the edge of a plush rug that had been turned up when she moved the table, but James had her in his arms before she hit the floor.

"If not fate, then what?" he asked.

He was very close to her. Very large and strong, very masculine, with his white shirt undone to reveal the dark vee of hair on his muscular chest, and the rippling hardness of his stomach. She had to catch her breath before she answered. "Bad luck, that's what I call it."

His golden eyes narrowed. His face was very close to hers, so close that her spectacles were quite unnecessary. He reached up and took them off, placing them gently on the top of a nearby chest of drawers. This forced her to concentrate exclusively on him rather than any other distraction the room might offer. Not that she could do anything else, anyway. She could not help but look at his beautiful, sensual mouth as a slight smile quirked up the edges of his lips.

"You're afraid of feeling any emotion, aren't you? That's what this is all about. Why?"

"Emotions take me out of myself, make me forget who I am," she answered. "I will never let that happen again."

"Who told you that?"

"It was you who taught me." She wasn't sure when he began touching her. She should have been, as he was drawing slow, caressing circles with one finger on her throat, dipping inexorably lower with each widening sweep. It set her tingling with arousal. No, it accentuated and heightened the arousal even the merest thought of him always brought her.

"Emotions don't take you out of yourself," he told her, sounding so very certain and seductive. "They reveal who you really are."

"Thoughtless. Reckless. Irresponsible, then." She could barely speak for the rising heat that threatened to engulf her. Anticipation and longing curled inside her; a needy ache only he could satisfy. She didn't want it satisfied. She tried to pull away from him, only to discover that she couldn't move at all.

"Passionate," was his answer. "It isn't a sin to make love." He smiled, lighting up the world, and her. "Especially with your husband."

She couldn't even think, anymore. She hated that all she wanted to do was make love to this magnificent, glorious, overwhelming male—who was in her bedroom, who was her husband.

"Husband," she managed to gasp. "No." She shook her head. "We can—should—we *will* have the marriage annulled."

He picked her up again—he was making quite a habit of it. Throwing his head back, he laughed as he took her to the bed. "Annulled?" He chuckled, and she felt the sound deep in his chest. "I don't think so."

Honoria wanted to tell him to stop when he set her down on the soft feather mattress and stretched out beside her. She put a hand up, but found herself stroking his cheek rather than pushing him away. The skin beneath her fingertips was rough, and the abrasiveness sent little ripples of sensation through the pads of her fingers.

"You need a shave," she said. What a needless, silly thing to say. "I miss your beard," she added. "It made you look like the devil."

"I am the devil. Your devil."

"I know." The words flowed out of her, slow and heavy. And why did her limbs feel so deliciously heavy as well, full of a slow, growing heat? Everything tingled. And her breasts—she didn't want to think about the languid heaviness, or the tightly puckered tenderness of the swelling peaks.

His mouth descended, not to hers, but to cover one of those nipples that stood out so prominently beneath the delicate fabric of her chemise.

She gasped, her spine arching off the bed at the intensity that flowed from the spot where his lips covered her, suckling and teasing with his tongue. She should be fighting this. Why wasn't she fighting this?

"More?" he asked, raising his head just a little. He didn't give her time to answer before he took her other breast in his mouth. This time, though, he slipped the material down, freeing her breasts completely from their confinement.

She did not want any part of her to be free. If she lay very still and closed her eyes, she wouldn't feel anything. He could have his way and then go away; she didn't have to be emotionally involved with this.

She tried, but she soon found herself grinding her teeth with the frustration of trying to ignore the delicious flickers of sensation that rushed like wildfire through her. She'd bunched fistfuls of bedcovers in her hands, and her heels were drumming against the mattress. Uninvolved? How could she possibly remain uninvolved when he made her feel—

"Get off me!" she demanded, bringing a fist

up to bang it against his upper arm. "Please, Diego!"

"James," he said. "Please what?"

He moved a little. She bolted into a sitting position. "Please don't sound so insufferably smug. It's only sex," she added. She leaned forward, squinting to get a better look at him as he rose from the bed. "What are you doing?"

"Taking off my shoes and trousers."

"Oh." Her spine stiffened in shock. She waved a hand wildly at him. "No. Wait! Don't do that!"

"I'm afraid I have to," he replied, with a solemnity that covered a great deal of amusement.

What did the man find to laugh about in a situation like this? Her, probably. She crossed her arms beneath her breasts, barely noticing that she was half naked in her annoyance. "I see no reason why you have to take off your shoes and trousers."

"The maid who changes the linen—I'm sure her name is Huseby—would. We may get the sheets tangled today, my wife, but the garden muck I got on my shoes from using the ladder isn't likely to come out as easily as—"

"I have no intention of discussing soiled sheets," she interrupted hastily.

"Move over," James responded, and shoved her toward the center of the mattress, hip to hip as he got back into bed. "They're a fact of life,

Mrs. Marbury; nothing to be ashamed of. But there's no need to have mud in your bed."

"You seem to be in my bed at the moment."

He put an arm around her. "And here I intend to stay." He used his free hand to fluff up the pile of pillows behind them.

"You're naked," she observed.

"Nice to know that you can tell without your spectacles on."

"You're built like a bull; of *course* I know you're—Oh, my!"

Not only built like a bull but as randy as one, she thought as his erection brushed across her belly. Her instinct was to stroke the hard, velvet-sheathed length of him and lovingly cup the heavy sacs of his testicles, but she managed to keep her hands from the remembered delight of touching the most intimate, private part of him. He was beautiful naked, brown-skinned and hard muscled. That hadn't changed. He filled the bed, and her senses. The scent of his skin was so achingly familiar. She wanted to bury her face against his chest and in the hollow of his throat and simply breathe him in for hours. The scent and feel and sight of him were overwhelming, and quite wonderful.

The traitorous admission that she welcomed being out of control flitted through her mind. She was in his hands. She could not stop him, so why try? Somehow that didn't seem as awful as it should. In fact, she was filled with a bright sense of curiosity, a wonder at what would happen next.

He knelt over her. "Lie still," he said. "While I get reacquinted."

Honoria really did mean to protest when he unbuttoned her chemise, but she only moaned, a long, low needy sound that was eloquent in its own way. She felt the material part, baring her to his view and touch from the waist up. She could not lift her hands to cover herself, or push him away. They were no longer even holding on to the bedclothes, but relaxed, palms open at her sides. She was made of candlewax, melting in the heat of the sun. Then his hands began to move over her, heating her inside and out. He bent forward to run his tongue slowly down the cleft between her breasts.

How could she help but move in response as his skilled fingers smoothed over her flesh? She closed her eyes, more aware of the tiny sensory details around her that way. She was lying on satin, quilted and embroidered, and she could feel every rich, sleek, soft strand of thread as though it was imprinted on her skin. She could almost *feel* the color, green as the first spring grass. The rest of her garments were removed, with the gentlest of tugs and the sighing slide of fabric down her hips and legs. Morning sunlight spilled across the bed from nearby windows and the light pressed against her totally bare skin, adding its mild heat to the building fire from James's touch. Air flowed gently over skin naked but for the swift fluttering kisses around her navel, then at the top of her thighs.

He had forgotten how much of her there was to love. From the top of her fiery red head to the shapely length of her amazing legs, and all the glorious curves and mounds in between, she was all earth-goddess: wide-hipped, large-breasted, ripe, lush, totally female—beautiful. Every erotic detail he held in his memory proved to be true, not the flight of his over-heated imagination.

He rose to his knees to simply study her for a moment. His erection arced over his belly, urging him to sheath himself deep inside her. He controlled the impulse, intending to savor—and seduce. She was so very responsive, but she had to remember that she was made for the taking and giving of pleasure. She was the sort of woman a man loved to make love to.

"Beautiful," he said worshipfully. His hands hovered over her, absorbing the heat from her skin. He studied the line of freckles that dusted like a curve of stars across her collarbone and the tops of her breasts. He could only look for an instant before cupping the soft weight of her breasts. Her nipples were large and pink and tempting. He leaned forward to kiss them again, one at a time.

"Beautiful," she repeated as though speaking in a dream, her head turned on the pillow, exposing the vulnerable line of her throat. He saw her lips lift in a slow, utterly seductive smile. He had forgotten the power of that lover's smile. It tugged equally on his heart and on his manhood. Then, with a purring sigh, she stretched her arms slowly out across the bed. She seemed as languid as a cat but he felt her trembling with desire. He did not think she could hide her passion from herself, or from him, very much longer. He knew he could not hold his in check too much longer, either.

He smiled knowingly as he parted the vee of her legs and kissed soft white skin. She moaned very softly, and shifted her legs wider, slowly, like a blossom opening. He had told her to stay still, and knew that she was trying to will herself to feel nothing. But she moved, subtly, sensuously, reacting to his every touch and kiss. "Time to wake, Sleeping Beauty," he whispered. "It is your wedding night."

Honoria opened her eyes very slowly. The fire in them was unmistakable. "It is the middle of the day," she pointed out. Her words were punctuated by sharp little gasps of arousal as his thumb circled and teased the swollen folds of flesh between her legs.

"Does it matter?" he asked her, voice husky with desire.

She shook her head, very slowly. Then she reached for him.

He'd forgotten the speed of her reflexes,

though he welcomed her supple strength. She had him on his back after a brief, breathless, laughing tussle. "What?" he demanded on a gasp of pleasure as she slithered her long body down his.

Rather than answer, her mouth settled around his erection, taking his whole length. She controlled his pleasure with a sure rhythm that sent waves of concentrated heat through him. He wanted to beg her not to stop when she lifted her head, but he knew from her wicked smile that begging would do no good.

He lifted himself on his elbows instead, and met her bold look for bold look. "As good as you remembered?" he asked. He sat up and held his arms out.

She hesitated for an instant, but the mask of iron calm she'd hidden behind could not be called back, not in this bed, not now. He waited, making and letting her choose, shaking with need, and controlling the urge to throw her onto her back and enter her hard and fast and long.

Honoria felt tears wet her cheeks as she moved into James's embrace, but she didn't know whether it was the past or the present she cried for; whether her heart was broken, or if they were tears of elation and happiness. She only knew that if she did not have him inside her soon, completing her, she would surely die from one more instant of utter loneliness.

He did not make her wait, but settled her on his lap. He thrust upward as she lowered herself onto him and he came inside her, face to face, mouth to mouth, arms and legs and all of them entwined. He filled her, hot and hard. She surrounded him, sheathing him in soft, tight folds. They remained like this for a while, unmoving, statue still while fever built in maddening intensity.

Then slowly, very, very slowly, Honoria began to rock her hips, her inner muscles rippling around his length at the same time. He moaned and his hungry mouth came down on hers, ravishing, thrusting to match the rhythm of her hips.

Finally, when he could take it no longer, James shifted their positions again, tumbling her backwards. He thrust into her the way his body demanded, hard and fast, her cries of pleasure urging him on. Her legs wrapped tightly around his hips; her fingers dug desperately into his back. The sight of him, his features transformed with wild desire, filled her vision and her world.

Honoria was completely out of herself and soaring free, tied only to the connection of pleasure she shared with James. The knot of arousal grew and grew, it curled and twined inside her, the spiral widening until an unstoppable firestorm burst through her just as his seed spilled inside her. She shrieked, he bellowed, and they both gave a shaky, breathless burst of laughter as his weight came down hard on top of her.

Honoria lay sweaty and satiated, with a man the size of a small house draped over every naked inch of her, and stared in amazement up at the ceiling. Her hands stroked the heavy muscles of his back and shoulders with absent affection while she reveled in this new feeling, this mixture of surprise and fearful promise. Her amazement, a feeling that went deep into her bones, was not just at having made love. It was because he had reminded her how good it felt to laugh.

Whether she could forgive him for that had yet to be seen.

Chapter 19

After some time passed, James rolled over and propped himself up on his elbow. He yawned and scratched his chest. Honoria lay on her back, head propped up by a pile of pillows covered in yellow and green satin casings, her red hair spread out like wildfire across a spring meadow. She looked lovely and wanton, with her lips tender and swollen from kisses, her pale skin still flushed from lovemaking. He remembered the last time he had seen her looking this way, and held in the sadness for all the years in between now and the last time they had made love. Memory had not idealized her, as he had been afraid it might have. She made love like the Honoria he'd longed for for seven years, even if she wasn't the woman he thought she was.

"And why is it," he heard himself asking, though he didn't know if she was awake to hear, "that you didn't tell me who you really were?"

Honoria came awake with a start. She hadn't realized she'd dozed. Finding James stretched out beside her convinced her instantly that she had not dreamed what had happened between them. She shifted and rolled to face him when his hand across her waist prevented her from sitting up. "Why didn't you tell me who *you* really were?" she demanded in turn.

"I did."

"Well, yes, all right," she conceded, after a stubborn few seconds. His earnest expression was far too appealing, and the hint of anger in his eyes lent a frisson of danger. After a moment she went on, "But I didn't think it was relevant at the time."

"Neither did I," he conceded in turn. "I knew I was a viscount's son, but the best I hoped for in life was to go home to Malaga a wealthy man." He touched the upturned tip of her nose. "But you . . . I don't understand why you hid the truth."

She fought not to find the gesture endearing, but this small intimacy shook her emotions as strongly as having sex had done. She wanted to pretend it was simply that she was not used to being touched in any affectionate way by anyone but her father, but it seemed ridiculous to try to make excuses while lying naked in bed beside the man she'd married the day before.

And why was it that she did not feel awkward, did not feel even the least bit of shame to be lying naked in bed with a man? Perhaps it was because she'd had so much prior experience of being in the same situation with this particular one. She should at least feel vulnerable as he asked her questions, but all she felt was languidly comfortable and vaguely hungry.

"Would knowing who I was have changed how you treated me?" she asked curiously.

"No," he answered promptly. "I needed you. Duchess or merchant's daughter, I needed you." He took her hand and kissed it—the back, the palm, and each individual finger. "I still need you."

"Liar." She would have snatched her hand away, but his grip was unbreakable.

"Never." He indulged in one of his roguish, charming smiles. "Not much, at least, or often. Besides," he defended his behavior, "I did nothing to harm you."

This time she did manage to sit up, though he still held her hand in his. "You arranged to have me sold at a slave auction! To have me locked up all alone in a dreadful prison cell!"

"For your protection, yes. I did everything I could to protect you." He sounded genuinely surprised at her being upset.

"It was dreadful! I'd never been alone before in my life!" The words spilled out of her without any control. "I was eighteen, innocent. I was grieving for my mother and lost in a foreign land. The man I thought I loved was wounded and feverish, and there was nothing I could do to help my best friend. Then I was left alone in that awful place!"

"Better than in a dark, filthy cell with a hundred stinking, ragged prisoners."

His words painted a harsh picture for her. For the first time she realized that what she, spoiled aristocrat that she was, had considered inhumane and hideous, had indeed been the best treatment he could provide for her in a bad situation.

A situation he got you into, she reminded herself sternly. *He was trying to escape his own hell.* She sighed, understanding all too well about personal hells. *How can I blame him for that?* She wasn't sure, but she wanted to. Holding onto the anger would help her regain the control that shattered from being near him.

"Why?" he asked again.

She remembered his original question, despite the change of subject, and this time she gave him the answer. "Because I was a fool. Derrick pleaded with me not to let our captors know who he was—the scourge of the corsairs."

James's eyes narrowed. "The what?"

She laughed bitterly. "Indeed. I discovered later that his vaunted reputation was of his own making. Just one more lie he told me." Once that truth was out she couldn't stop the words. "I haven't a clue to how the man managed to deceive me so. I was eighteen and in my second Season, for heaven's sake, when we met. I'd been courted by every manner of fortune hunter from the moment I first had my come out, and not been fooled by any of them. But I thought Derrick was different—thought he shared my interests and concerns. Thought he cared for me, and not my inheritance. Maybe it was simply because he was taller than me. I am a terrible judge of men," she concluded.

James sat up and put his arm around her shoulders. "So," he said, companionably. "Is that why you haven't married until now? Because you trusted no man?"

"Precisely," she snapped. "Between you and Derrick, I have quite learned my lesson about romance."

"Oh, no," he said, voice low and sultry. "You haven't begun to learn anything about romance, Mrs. Marbury."

Honoria's spine stiffened, and she lifted her chin proudly. "I am not Mrs. Marbury."

"Perhaps not in name," was his smugly satisfied answer. He squeezed her shoulder as he helped her to her feet. "I'll tell you what," he offered. "If it will make you more comfortable, you can call me Huseby. I'll just be another one of them around the house. You'll hardly notice with so many of us Husebys about."

Despite herself, Honoria laughed. It felt so good to laugh. The carpet beneath her bare feet was somehow deeper and softer than she remembered it, the sun streaming through the high windows more golden. Impossible, of course, but her senses, so long kept in check, were sitting up and taking more notice of the world than she liked. "That is quite all right. A generous offer, but not necessary." She tossed hair back off her shoulders. "There really are quite a few of them, aren't there?"

"Quite," he mimicked her usual clipped tone. And made her giggle again. The fiend.

"I am going to get dressed now," she said, and he let her slip out of his hold. They were both aware that he was physically in control of the situation. She decided that she could cope with that; it was the emotional and mental control that she must strive for and win, of herself if not of him.

You will not feel, she told herself with every step she took away from him. *You do not feel his gaze on you. And it doesn't matter if it is.* But that didn't change the fact that she knew her walk was somehow different, that there was a provocative sway to her hips, that every step sent little tingling aftershocks of passion through her.

She found her spectacles, then found clothing in the dressing room that was simple enough for even the heir of dukedom to struggle into without a lady's maid. She knew that Maggie would arrive shortly in the second carriage that carried James's valet and both their wardrobes. Maggie would soon put her to rights: tighten her corsets and button her up from chin to toes with all the armor of propriety and habit. Until then, she could make do with a loose-fitting morning dress and her hair in a long braid—for she had no intention of calling in another maid who would see the subtle marks of love-making on her as she helped Honoria dress.

She didn't want to leave the dressing room, especially not after she got a good look at the woman in the mirror as she braided her hair. Honoria knew that heavy-lidded, voluptuous woman. She'd left her behind in Algiers. She turned her back on the mirror and attempted to be prim and proper when she marched out to face James again. Fortunately, he had also taken the opportunity to don his clothing. He had moved the table away from the door, as well.

She frowned at his presumption at touching what was hers; then the frown melted into something that wasn't quite a smile as she recalled that he'd been touching more than just her belongings this morning. Morning? She glanced at the mantel clock. Yes, it was still morning, but just barely, being only a few minutes before noon.

"A Huseby came to the door. I sent for something to eat," he told her. "And tea."

"I prefer coffee." She recalled with a blush that it was James who taught her how to make proper coffee during the idyll in his house. She had painstakingly taught Lacey House's cook the procedure.

"So do I. I asked for that, too."

"You won't be disappointed."

He smiled. "You remember." He looked flattered, pleased, as though a cup of coffee was some sort of precious gift from her to him.

She allowed herself a shrug. "A liking for Turkish coffee is one of several bad habits I learned from you."

"You remember how to make love, too," he said with an irrepressible smirk. "You have a natural talent for lovemaking. But you need more practice, Honoria. There are a great many things in the book we haven't tried yet."

She stood in the middle of the luxurious bedroom and crossed her arms beneath her bosom. "You are insufferable."

He nodded. "I know."

His gaze shifted below her face, and his expression became very intent. A surge of heat rose in Honoria. She found herself fascinated by watching him watch her, until she finally said, "You are staring at my breasts, Mr. Marbury." Several layers of clothing covered her bosom, yet she could *feel* him as strongly as though he was touching her, and the tips of her breasts responded, straining hard and sensitive against the material of her dress.

"Men look at women," he told her. "Women look back. It's wonderful." He was standing by the unlit fireplace, his hands behind his back. He took a step toward her.

She retreated toward the door. "Oh, no. We are not repeating that."

"We will," he assured her. "But not until we've had breakfast."

As if in response to his words, a knock sounded on the door. A moment later Charles Huseby entered, followed by two housemaids and a footman. They all carried food-laden silver trays. "A selection of delicacies, as you requested, my lord," Charles told James.

Honoria stood in the center of the room, determined to ignore everything and everyone. Then the rich aroma of coffee tickled her nose, and she couldn't resist the temptation to move closer to the table James had shoved back into its accustomed spot. The servants set out dishes of strawberries with cream, meat pies, custards, poached salmon, gold-crusted bread still warm from the oven, popovers, dishes of butter, and dark berry jams. There was tea and coffee. Scones and a heavy dark cake dotted with dried fruit. It all looked and smelled seductively delicious. Seduction was what this was all about, of course, and it worked very well indeed. She could not recall when she had eaten last, or even when she had wanted to eat. There had been food at her wedding reception the evening before, and a cake, but she had tasted none of it.

The dishes were set up, linens spread, chairs held out for them. She and James took seats on opposite sides of what was not a very large table and let their plates be filled and drinks be poured before the servants were dismissed. It was James who sent them away, just as he had ordered the meal. She was not happy about this presumption of place, but legally it was his right, so she couldn't complain about it in front of the servants.

When she and James were alone, she said, "Do you mind?"

"Eat," he responded. His honey-colored eyes twinkled as he added, "You need the energy."

"Don't you twinkle at me, James Marbury." She tapped a finger on the tabletop. "And I will not put up with any innuendo, either. Do you understand?" She knew she sounded ridiculous, and he had only to tilt an eyebrow at her before she broke out laughing at the foolishness of what she'd just said. "You infuriate me," she told him. She took a bite of custard, then a taste of scone, while he chewed on a slice of thick, warmly toasted bread slathered with butter and jam.

She found the silence frighteningly compatible while they ate their way through a good sampling of all the dishes the butler had brought them.

Finally, after he'd cleaned off his plate and pushed the chair back from the table, he said, "You like it when I infuriate you. Admit it."

Honoria drew herself up stiffly. "Nonsense. There is nothing pleasant about what you do to me." He glanced significantly toward the bed, and to her chagrin, she couldn't keep from smiling and going warm all over once more. "Point conceded, Mr. Marbury—Pyne—Huseby—Moresco, or whatever you wish to call yourself at the moment."

"Husband will do."

His voice was soft but edged as he stood slowly and came toward her, demanding an acknowledgment she was not prepared to give. She was at a loss as to how to combat her visceral reactions to James when he gave her no time to find calm and gather her defenses. He was purposefully keeping her off balance, and doing a very good job of it. The question was, why? He had what he wanted, which apparently was to make himself her husband. Why couldn't he simply leave her alone now that he'd accomplished his goal?

They stood silently face to face for a few moments. He waited for her to speak, to give in and call him husband. She knew exactly what words he wanted from her. She could not bring herself to give them. His muscles were taut and tense, his eyes practically glowing with anger by the time he put his hands on her shoulders. She knew he wanted to shake her, but all he did was draw her closer.

"Is it because of my past? Is that it? Because my mother worked in a tavern? Because I've been a fisherman, and a galley slave, and owned a tavern? Aren't I good enough for a duke's daughter because I've gotten my hands dirty?" he asked with hurt bitterness. "Oh, and because I've been a pirate," he added sarcastically.

Honoria listened with shock that he would think her so shallow. But then, what did he truly know of her and hers? She shook him off with a sharp, "Oh, for God's sake!" Grabbing his hand, she ordered, "Come with me," and paraded him out the door. She refused to answer his questions as she marched him swiftly along, but at least he let himself be led for once. In fact, at one point he said he liked having her hold his hand, but she ignored this provocation.

She took him to the Long Gallery, which took up a large part of the second story of Lacey House, and which was designed to impress. The floors were marble; the ceilings were decorated in frescoes of heroic figures and ancient naked gods painted by the finest artist of the early eighteenth century. The tall windows looked out on impressive formal gardens, and the walls were lined with numerous portraits.

"Welcome to the Rogues Gallery," she said, bringing James to the portrait of a thoroughly naked woman stretched out on a velvet divan. The woman was quite lovely, blonde and buxom, with a sensual mouth and huge, bold eyes of bright blue. "Her eyes and breasts tend to run in the family," Honoria went on.

James looked the rather erotic painting up and down appreciatively. Then he ran the same look over Honoria. "They certainly do. Who is she?"

"My great-great-great-great-great-grandmother." She counted on her fingers. "I believe that is correct." She pointed at the painting. "That, oh, son of an honest, hardworking tavern wench, is Maggie Pyne. The founder of the family. The first duchess. She was a whore. Worse, she was an actress. A very good one, apparently. She was also the mistress of a king, by whom she had a son, who had a son, who had a daughter, and on down to me. She was smart enough to get King Charles the Second to make her a duchess, and to pass a law that allowed the eldest child to inherit the title and property no matter what their gender. Whore she might have been," Honoria added proudly, with a fond glance at the founder of the line, "but she was sharp as a blade and took care of what was hers."

"You are descended from a commoner?" James asked.

She wasn't sure if the horror in his voice and expression was genuine, or if he was joking. "Who isn't descended from a commoner at some point?" she asked back. "What's a nobleman, but the descendant of someone with a big sword and an overinflated sense of their own importance?"

He crossed his arms and tilted down his chin. "Do you think so?"

"I do," she affirmed. "And that's not the worst of it. Let me show you what sort of family you've married into." She led him down the long row of portraits. "That's an aunt from last century who was locked up in Bedlam. She escaped the madhouse and ran off to America with the estate steward—whose name was not Huseby, by the way. And that's an uncle named Joseph, who fought bravely in the American Revolution. On the American side, I'm ashamed to say."

"Shocking."

"*And* he married a Scottish Dissenter." She pointed to another woman's picture. "Aunt Samantha married a Mohawk warrior."

"A what?"

She waved the question away. "You still haven't heard the worst." They stopped before a portrait of her great grandparents. "That's the second duchess, the second Maggie Pyne, as well. It's said she also enjoyed acting." She pointed at the slender man standing proudly beside the blonde and beautiful duchess. "James McKay," she told her own particular James. "Highwayman. I believe he went by the professional name of Jamie Scott. He and the duchess met while he was robbing her coach."

"How romantic."

She couldn't stop her own smile at the merriment in his eyes. She put her hands behind her back, and rocked back on her heels. "Yes, quite. But my point, my lord, is that the Pyne family has no cause to be high sticklers about the professions of others. Especially the people we marry." She chuckled wickedly. "In fact, your lady mother might insist we break off the alliance when she finds out about *my* ancestry."

He nodded solemnly. "Perhaps it would be best not to tell her. At least until the first grandchild is on the way. She could forgive anything for the sake of my baby."

It finally occurred to Honoria that she was having a perfectly normal conversation with her worst enemy about *their* marriage. Even worse, when he mentioned their having children, her first reaction was not a cringe of horror, but a warm and totally unfamiliar feeling of sentimental longing.

"I need to sit down now," she said, as her legs would suddenly not hold her. Fortunately, there was a velvet-cushioned bench just behind her. She dropped onto it like a stone.

James sat down quickly by her side and took

both her hands in his. The fiend would not let the subject go. "Perhaps you're with child already." He sounded unutterably pleased about the prospect. "We should get started soon. I want lots of children." He massaged his thumbs across her knuckles, setting her stomach to fluttering pleasantly.

"Soon? Lots? Of children?" She blinked after each squeaked question.

"So do both our fathers," he added. He gestured at the rows of ancestral paintings. "We have to do our duty for our families."

This reminder of familial obligation helped settle her for a moment. Then, as she looked at him, a fist formed around her heart and squeezed hard.

"Honoria? What's wrong?"

Even though he'd moved closer to her on the bench, his concerned voice sounded very far away. She could not see for the pain. For a moment the world went white around her. One word, one concept, dropped like a burning coal into her mind.

"That's why you married me, isn't it?" she asked after the spasm of betrayed anguish lessened. She understood this pain; she had lived with it for years. But right now, it felt like it would break her wide open. "It has to do with duty, and not with me. It's never anything to do with me." She was not important to anyone, and never had been.

The pain transformed to anger as she focused her hatred on James Marbury. "You care nothing for me," she stated flatly. "You never have."

Instead of protesting his undying affection, he sprang to his feet and glared accusingly down at her. "And you've never cared for me! You've never felt anything but contempt for me, have you?"

She surged to her feet. "That's a lie! I love you!"

"I love *you*!" he shouted back. The words reverberated down the length of the Long Gallery as he continued to shout, "I've loved you from the first moment I saw you. Not that you cared."

"What do you mean?" The family portraits gazed down silently on her shriek of outrage. "You're the one who bundled me onto that boat and then walked away!"

"You never said you didn't want to go with dear Derrick, did you?"

"You never said you wanted me to stay!"

"You never said you wanted me to *ask* you to stay!"

They stood toe to toe, hands on hips, mirror images of fury, surrounded by the staring painted eyes of her illustrious and notorious ancestors, their unguarded words echoing around them.

Chapter 20

Nothing was going right. Nothing was going as expected. He had a plan, but it was not the original plan that was supposed to give him his freedom and untold wealth. Honoria had changed everything.

The streets of Algiers were ablaze from the invader's cannon fire. All his carefully made escape plans were going up in flames and smoke like the white buildings of the Casbah, but his plans weren't important to him anymore. The treasure wasn't even important. He'd worry about his own hide and grabbing what loot he could after he was sure Honoria was safely away from the danger of the attack. It wasn't the attack that was the worst danger; it was the looters he feared. He could hear the screams of helpless victims as his party cautiously moved through the town. This was a city full of pirates who knew their time was up. They understood pillage and rape, and were turning on the helpless for one last rampage while the city burned. Getting Honoria to the ship was safer than remaining in his house, especially after cannon fire had breached the wall. But they had to get through the looters and frightened mobs to do it.

The narrow, twisting streets of the ancient mountain fortress were full of panicked, frightened people. The high white walls would be no protection from invaders this time. He pushed through the crowd, saber in one hand, pistol in the other. Honoria followed close behind, with Huseby holding onto Derrick and bringing up the rear. Diego noticed that the supposedly feeble Englishman moved quickly enough to save his own hide after Honoria explained the plan to him.

Diego knew that taking Honoria toward the harbor might seem an act of folly when the danger came from the French Navy that had sailed into the bay, but she had agreed readily to his plan. Too readily, he thought bitterly. "Oh, yes," she had said after a cannonball knocked down the garden wall and they were battling a fire that started in the kitchen. "The roof is going to come down on our heads at any moment. Derrick and Maggie must be gotten to safety." Her face was covered in soot, but it was the most beautiful face in the world, calm in the face of danger. She nodded emphatically. "It's my place to take care of them."

She said not a word about what had passed between them in this falling-down house. She made no protest that she didn't want to leave. They might as well never have been lovers. It was obvious that all she cared about was getting away. Very well, he would make sure she got away from him.

"I want you out of here," he lied, wanting nothing more than for her to stay with him forever. He couldn't stop adding callously, to hide his hurt, "Consider it payment for the pleasure you've given me."

Her eyes narrowed briefly at his words. It was the slightest of flinches. She let out a long, sighing breath, but that was all the reaction he got. He had hoped she would slap him as he deserved, berate him, and tell him she cared. But all the passion he'd discovered in her was now covered by stiff English reserve.

By the time the housefire was out, Huseby and dear Derrick were ready to go. Diego gave instructions to his servants, then he led the English contingent away from the wreckage.

There was a naval battle raging between corsair galleons and modern European ships. He did not think the fight would go on for very long. The corsairs were too smart not to see it was a useless fight. Those who could not cut and run would soon surrender and try to make deals with the victors. The merchant ship Manticore *was one of many prizes sitting in the middle of that battle, unmanned, very likely going carefully untouched by both of the warring sides. Those ships were valuable prizes to both sides: spoils for the victors, bargaining pieces for the losers. Being onboard the* Manticore *was the safest place for Honoria and her friends.*

* * *

"I got you to safety."

Honoria nodded. "I said I was grateful." How well she remembered helping to row the small boat away from the dock. The water around them had reflected the fires. It had been so bright she'd expected steam to rise up off it. "You kissed me goodbye," she said, desperately. "Then you were gone."

"What else could I do? What was there to say when you wanted *him*?"

"You told me you wanted me to 'get out of here.' "

"I didn't mean it. How could you think I meant it?" He wasn't sure when he'd taken her in his arms. He held onto her for a long time, and felt her shaking with sobs.

After a while she lifted her tearstained face and said, "I hate melodrama."

"But you're very good at it," he teased gently. "Besides, if I'd told you I loved you then, I would never have let you go."

She turned her tear-soaked face up to his and he kissed her, tenderly at first, but neither of them needed tenderness right now. The intensity of contact deepened and sparked through them quickly. Honoria knew they had much to discuss, but did not care. She drew him closer, pressed herself against the long, hard-muscled length of him. She wanted contact with him, every kind of contact, the more the better.

It was James who looked around after a while

and said breathlessly, "We'd better get back to your bedroom."

Honoria adjusted her askew spectacles and responded practically as she took his hand, "There are over thirty bedrooms in Lacey House. We simply have to find the nearest one."

Honoria slipped out of bed and into a robe without waking James. Dawn was just breaking and she walked out onto her balcony to look down on the neatly tended gardens below. A maze of blooming rose bushes was laid out beneath her bedroom. Bright color and heady aroma filled her senses even though she could not make out details without her spectacles. She wasn't quite sure where she'd left her glasses this time, and didn't much care. Huseby would find them, and Honoria had several spare pairs. Maggie had arrived from London yesterday and put herself in charge of picking up all of Honoria's and James's dropped and misplaced items.

Honoria was not sure how many times they had made love, or in how many places in the last twenty-four hours. She shook her head as she curled her hands around the balcony banister and tried to work up a sense of chagrin. She had sore muscles and was seriously underslept. She was starving, and wanted a long, hot bath. But all these were physical reactions to what she'd been doing with her husband. She was also deeply, deeply satisfied, physically and mentally. She searched for a sense of shame within herself, but could find none.

She smiled out at the dawn and spread her arms wide to the world. The rose-scented breeze blew coolly across her skin, teasing tender nipples to hardness beneath the thin turquoise silk of her robe. When James came to stand behind her, naked as the day he was born, she leaned back against his sturdy body. He put his arms around her and she tilted her head back against his shoulder.

"Come inside," he said. "It's cold."

She smiled at this reminder that he was a creature of the sunny Mediterranean. "It's a beautiful morning."

"Which in England means it isn't raining."

"You are always *so* grumpy before you've had your morning coffee." He only held her tighter. She paused for a moment, then added, "I, on the other hand, am always grumpy."

"It's one of your chief attractions for me," he responded, and drew her backward off the balcony. He shut the glass door behind them, to keep the mild air out and the warmth in, she supposed.

"Shall I ring for breakfast?" she asked.

He kissed her and ran his hands over her body, sliding the silk erotically over her skin. "I'm hungry," he said, after she was quite mad with desire. He picked her up and tossed her back on the bed, then he jumped on top of her.

Sometime later, warm and content with the afterglow of passion, she tried again. "Breakfast?"

"Mmmm."

She nudged his shoulder. "I'll take that for a yes, why don't I?"

She started to get up to ring for a servant, but his hand shot out to grasp her wrist. "We need to talk," he said when she turned curiously to look at him.

Oh, no, she thought. *We most certainly do not.* Her blood ran cold at the very thought of conversation. She did not want to communicate in any way other than through touch and taste and the other senses. For the first time in years she was free of anger, resentment, and repression. She did not want to analyze, she wanted to live! She was out of control, and perfectly happy to stay that way. "I'm happy," she said. "Leave me alone."

"You don't want to hear what has to be said."

She nodded emphatically. "Precisely."

He sat up, and they sat on the green satin bedspread, cross-legged, facing each other. His look of concern disturbed her. He reached over and ran his fingers through her tangled hair, spreading it out like a copper blanket over her shoulders.

"You've been asking me why since we met

again. Don't you want the answer?"

She shook her head. "I don't need answers."

He bent forward, peering at her from an inch away. "Excuse me, madam, but I seem to be in bed with a stranger."

She bent back and pulled on her discarded robe. "You're here. That's enough."

"It would not be enough for my Honoria." He put his hands on her shoulders. She, who had become so very pliable, stiffened beneath his touch. He did not ask what was wrong. He said, "Ah, that's better."

She was not amused. "I hate being like this! I hate always having to think. To watch what I feel and do and say! If we start talking now, we'll argue, and I'll hate you for only marrying me out of duty—because that's what you want to explain to me—and then I'll go all cold and hard and turn into *her* again!" She sounded foolish and childish and did not care. She was so very sick and tired of being mature. She was so very—tired.

He pulled her into a warm, tender embrace and they settled down on the bed, lying face to face. He brushed hair out of her face, and tears from her cheeks. "I like you all tart and testy," he told her. "I love your wit and intellect. I don't want to lose those parts of you."

"What does love have to do with duty?" she asked, curious for an explanation despite having denied wanting one. She had a mind that wasn't good at not thinking, even if she wanted to escape that part of herself.

"Everything," he answered. "Though I didn't realize they were one and the same until sometime yesterday morning. He continued to stroke her cheek with the pad of his thumb. She found it very soothing. "It is a long and complicated story."

"You've said that before."

"You know my parents' history," he said after a few moments. "How they lost each other during the Battle of Talavares? They set a very good example to me about honor and duty and the strength of love."

"I can see that, but what has that to do with—"

"My own life took a very bizarre turn. Even more bizarre than their story."

"Thank you," she said tartly. "I enjoy being referred to as 'bizarre.' "

He smiled. "That's my Honoria. I did try to forget you, you know."

"As I tried to forget you," she conceded. "I failed miserably."

"As did I. I escaped from Algiers disguised as an English sailor. I had a small chest of gold and jewels that I managed to take out of my house with us . . . along with a certain book." He grinned wickedly.

She flashed him a smile in return. "I do not have the decency to blush, James, so you might as well go on with your tale."

"What I brought with me was nothing compared to what I would have claimed if I'd gotten to Ibrahim Rais's treasure."

"Sorry about that."

He managed to shrug while lying down. "What I truly wanted was the silver scimitar. It was rightfully mine; the rest was corsair plunder. But what mattered most was your safety. After that, I concentrated on returning to my mother and providing for her."

"You never thought to search for your father?" She put her hand on James's chest, directly over his heart. She hadn't noticed before, but she realized that her leg was thrown over his. She needed to be touching him, even when she wasn't aware of doing so.

He put his hand on the curve of her hip. "I assumed he was dead. It never occurred to me to claim my English heritage. Then, one day, on a day when I was roaring drunk," he added, a faint blush coloring his cheeks, "this Englishman showed up at our tavern and claimed to be Edward Marbury, my father. I wouldn't have believed him if my mother hadn't rushed into his arms. They were happy; I went on being drunk. And whoring. And brawling," he added unapologetically. "I was empty inside," he went on, his eyes full of pain and regret. She touched his cheek, and he kissed the back of her hand. "I missed you."

"Did you? Why?" She was genuinely curious. "I mean, after all those years . . . all those women . . ."

"Women who weren't you."

"Hmmph."

"It's true. Why is it that *you* didn't marry? Was it because you missed me?"

"No. It was because both you and Derrick betrayed me." After a moment, she added, "It was also because I knew I could never make love to anyone but you. I suppose you are infinitely smug to hear such a confession?"

"Infinitely. But I didn't think I'd betrayed you: I thought he'd married you. That you were happy in England, with lots of babies."

"He threw me over the first moment he could when we were out of Algiers. I had been compromised in the eyes of society, as far as he was concerned. He thought that even though I was the daughter of a duke, my soiled reputation would jeopardize his career. Bloody fool didn't seem to recall that I could buy him the Admiralty! His breaking the engagement did start rumors about me, and tainted me in the eyes of the *ton*. The rumors were quite true, of course, but for my father's sake, I went on pretending to be a paragon of propriety."

"And for my father's sake I began a quest to find the young woman I seduced and abandoned—his words, not mine."

"Really?" she asked sarcastically. "I thought you thought I was happily married."

"Malaga is a port town," he told her, "and Captain Russell's ship put in at the harbor a few months ago. I found out through an acquaintance—a very nice lady of the evening—that she knew for a fact that Captain Russell was not married. In fact, my friend—"

"I thought you said she was an acquaintance."

He ignored her jealous tone. "He wanted my friend to come to England to be his mistress. But he told her that he needed to find a rich wife first, so that he could afford to support a mistress properly."

She laughed softly, without rancor. "That's my Derrick."

"He won't be anyone's Derrick much longer," James promised grimly. "I was angry enough to kill him when I heard that he hadn't married you, but his ship had left Malaga by the time I heard the story. I didn't know what to think, or do. I thought that perhaps you'd been happily married to the lout and died in childbirth. It happens. But my lady friend was certain he'd never been married at all. I knew then that he'd abandoned you, and that letting you go with him was the biggest mistake I'd ever made."

"So you then romantically ran off to England to look for me?" she asked eagerly.

He shook his head. "I nearly ran off in a blind rage to find you, but my father had a better plan, and I listened to him." He touched the tip of her nose, then kissed it. Her eyes crossed as she watched his lips come toward her. "But not until after he made me into a proper English gentleman. My father is very convincing in the matters of duty and obligation. He insisted I owed it to the woman I had seduced and abandoned to find her and make amends, and practically dragged me by the ear to London to start the search once I was polished enough to fit into society."

Honoria had gone tense; there was a bruised tenderness about her. The confident, teasing young woman of the last two days had been replaced by the wary creature he'd help make her into. But wary, hurt or not, he owed her the truth. He went on, though the very air around them seemed to darken and become more chill with each word. "In my own way I was as hurt as you were. I had survived life under Ibrahim Rais, but was still lost and soul-weary when I returned to Malaga. I had nothing to live for, and a great deal of guilt on my conscience. I did many evil things as a corsair, even though I did them reluctantly. I did not even return with the one thing I had earned. My father suggested that if I tracked down Honoria Pyne and married her, then I would have at least made reparations for some of my sins. I had his example of spending his life finding my mother. I admired him, and wanted his approval. It was my duty."

"You found Lady Alexandra instead." Her voice was so soft and colorless he barely heard it.

He nodded. "I felt like a fool, but a vow is a vow. I was determined to marry you."

"A fool. Of course."

"Honoria—I—"

She shook her head and rolled off the bed. By the time he caught up to her she'd donned her spectacles and was scrutinizing herself in the dressing table mirror. "Just as I thought," she said before he could ask her what was wrong. "Still as plain as a plank. Any man would feel like a fool married to me."

"That isn't what I meant."

She seemed not to hear him as she continued to peer into the mirror. He saw the unshed tears shining in the reflection of her eyes. "For a few hours I half had myself convinced I was someone worthy of sparking deathless passion over." She sighed. "But I understand duty to one's father very well. I hid my shame to protect my father. I agreed to marry because my father wished it." Her eyes met his in the mirror, full of resigned sadness. "At least I know you didn't marry me out of greed." She sighed again. "I have lived my life as my father wished. You are obeying yours. There is no shame in that. We will deal very—dutifully—together. I apologize for being a cow, and thank you for dutifully trying to make me think you had a more than conjugal interest in me. Perhaps I am with child already. In any case, you can drop this farcical show of passion."

James grabbed her shoulders and turned her forcefully to face him. He didn't know if he was more furious with her, himself, or their damned paragon parents! "What are you talking about? You're the most beautiful woman I've ever seen. Do you have any idea how I missed making love to you?"

She lifted a hand weakly. "Please, don't—"

"An amazon is what you are! A valkyrie. You are a descendant of Hippolyta, Boudicaa and Zenobia. You are kindred to Alexander's beloved Roxane, meant to be mated with a warrior—with me. Any real man would happily kill to have a woman like you in his harem."

"Oh, really?" she asked disbelievingly. "Then why is it that only one person bothered to bid on me at a slave auction? And that man wanted me as a translator?"

"You didn't end up a translator, though did you?" He drew himself up proudly and took a step away from her. Then he looked her over quite thoroughly from head to foot. "With that hair and those breasts, you would have fetched a fortune. I couldn't afford a fortune. So I started the rumor that the Turkish ambassador was thinking of buying you for the Sultan's harem."

"Boudicaa?" she heard herself croak, barely intelligibly. "Breasts? Rumor? Sultan? What are you talking—? Are you mad, or am I?"

Honoria put her hands up to her temples. She didn't know what to think, or to feel, and shied violently away from doing either for now. "I am so very tired," she murmured.

"I know," he soothed. "We're working too hard at this."

Her head ached from being bombarded with so many facts and conflicting responses. All her protective walls were tumbling down in disarray, the barriers against emotion breached and broken, though she tried to rebuild them. She was naked and vulnerable in every way. Every little word and gesture, every memory, every nuance of meaning in word and gestures and looks scratched across her tender nerves. Her head ached from too much information.

James gently lowered her hands from her temples. He began to massage them in her stead, in slow, steady, heavenly circles. Her eyes closed of their own volition. She couldn't help but begin to relax beneath this gentle ministration.

"Maybe we shouldn't talk for a while," he

suggested. "Maybe we should get that breakfast you suggested earlier."

"Yes," she murmured, though it was more of a purr of a sound. Then she pulled away from his touch. She looked around. "We need to get out of here. It is time you and I got dressed, behaved like civilized people, and sat across a dining room table from one another while having a meal."

He shrugged nonchalantly. "If you want. As long as I get to take you back to bed eventually."

"That remains to be seen," she informed him with an echo of her old tartness, but not very much conviction. "But first we are going to eat breakfast. And then I am dutifully going to give you a tour of your new home, Lord James."

Her maid and his servant Malik entered the instant Honoria rang the bellpull, and the next thing James knew, Malik led him away to his own rooms to be bathed, changed, and dressed. He did not care that this was customary for great families who lived in great houses with plenty of spare rooms; James did not want to have separate quarters from his wife. He knew he had the right to order a suite of rooms redecorated for them to share, and hoped Honoria would enjoy choosing new furniture and drapes and whatever. Women were supposed to like that sort of thing. The one thing he was going to insist upon commissioning from the furniture maker was a new bed. A big one.

Honoria would balk, would say it wasn't done for husbands and wives of their station to live so intimately. They would fight. He grinned. It would be fun.

He was smiling with anticipation as he was shown into a dining room an hour after leaving Honoria. He was in the proper black trousers and jacket of an English gentleman, a cravat neatly tied over his crisply starched white shirt. He felt constrained and conservative in such clothing, but he supposed that it was its purpose: to remind the wearer of his exalted place in this exclusive society. Here was another rule to change. Let the servants be shocked; he and his wife would be comfortable in their own home! And speaking of homes, why did they have to live at Lacey House at all? Or on the Marbury estates, for that matter?

He was feeling quite the rebel as he pulled out a chair next to where Honoria was already seated at one end of the long table. China and silver gleamed all around him, but James had eyes only for his wife. She wore a dark brown dress and her riotous hair had been wrestled into a tight bun. Honoria dressed for battle with her own passionate nature, he knew. His hands itched to slowly take off her clothes. Her spectacles were perched on her nose as she read a letter, and James noticed the large pile of correspondence on the table by her place setting.

She pointedly did not glance his way, and James contented himself with watching her until the food was brought and the servers discreetly withdrew from the room. When she put one letter aside and reached for another, he trapped her hand in his on top of the pile of paper. "Is that more important than entertaining your husband?"

"I am being dutiful," was her response. She finally looked at him, seeming to notice that he was nearby for the first time. "Your proper place is at the head of the table." She waved a hand toward the far end of the room. "It's down there somewhere."

"You are a difficult woman, Honoria Pyne."

"I merely strive for perfection," was her cool reply.

"And woe to anyone who gets in your way." He grinned, refusing to be provoked. "You're a perfect hedgehog, my prickly darling."

This time she grinned back, despite an obvious effort to remain stern. "Thank you. I will take that as a compliment, my lord."

He kissed her hand. "It was meant as one. Eat something." He released her hand so that she could pick up a fork. He leafed through the letters. "What's all this?"

"Begging letters from charities, mostly." She'd divided the correspondence into three separate piles on the pristine white linen tablecloth. "A letter from my father, and some letters of congratulations on our nuptials addressed to us both. Gifts have begun to arrive, as well." She picked up the third pile, which contained two envelopes. "These are for you."

Honoria went back to her own reading while James read the letter from his father. Then he broke the seal on the second letter. "This is from Reverend Menzies," he said with surprise after he read the salutation.

"I have one from him, as well," she answered. "Inviting me to visit his vicarage. Did he invite you under separate letter?" she asked curiously.

James ran his fingers through his hair. "He's acting as dear Derrick's second," he reluctantly told Honoria. She sat up very straight and her relaxed expression disappeared. It was like watching the sun disappear behind heavy clouds. He would have sworn that the temperature in the room went colder, as well.

"Oh?" Her tone was pure ice.

James ran a thumb along his jawline and tried to hide his jealousy and pain with a flippant, "Tell me, would you rather see Derrick or me come out of this alive?"

"I think you should both go to the devil, is what I think," she snapped out angrily. She blushed hotly, and looked as if she wanted to say much, much more. Instead, she glared furiously as James rose slowly to his feet.

"I need to leave for London right now if I am to be at the meeting place by dawn tomorrow," he said, as stiff as Honoria a few moments before. He knew what he wanted her to say, how he wanted her to act, but she wore the mask of a reserved Englishwoman right now. And he was in no mood to coax her out of it this time. "You should learn to give a little sometimes," he told her, as he rose to his feet.

It seemed like a very long way to the door, and the silence between them was as heavy and charged as the air before a storm. His hand was on the doorknob when she said, "Please don't do this."

He turned to find Honoria standing beside her chair. He'd hoped that she would come running into his arms. He sighed. "Honor requires it."

"We do not need more scandal." She applied logic and reason in a toneless, measured voice as hopeless anger built inside him. Her hands were clasped tightly together in front of her, the only sign that she felt anything. "Think of your family name, and of mine."

"I am."

"You have a responsibility to the Pyneham name and interests. My father wishes me to become a lady-in-waiting to the Queen. If my husband fights a duel, he will be disappointed in that wish. Dueling is against the law in England."

He nodded. "Yes. I know."

"You will be forced to leave the country." She remained perfectly still as she added, "Perhaps that is what you want."

"I will not be fighting in England," he answered her. He saw the fear of abandonment in her eyes and the slight quiver of her lower lip, but she still did not come to him. "My uncle at the Spanish Embassy has arranged the matter. 'Dear Derrick' and I will meet tomorrow morning on the grounds of the Embassy," he explained, before she could accuse him of running away to the continent so soon after fulfilling his vow to his father. "So, you see, no English law will be broken. Your queen will not be displeased. Your father will be happy. I'm going now." He opened the door.

"Why are you doing this?" she asked loudly, desperately, her voice cracking on the words. "What satisfaction can you possibly get from killing a bug like Derrick Russell? Why do you want to do it?"

He glanced back only long enough to see that she still had not come toward him. "I am not doing this for me. I am doing this for you."

The door closed.

Honoria was frozen in place, neither able to move forward nor to take her seat again. The world was upside down, out of focus—and

James was gone. She had let him go, doing nothing more than toss out a few words to try to stop him from this folly. She should have pleaded, begged him not to go, seduced him, even—she should have done *something!* He was gone to London, to a duel. He could be killed. She might never see him again.

You should learn to give a little sometimes.

The words haunted her; the truth of them hurt her. If only she had not come down to breakfast still stinging from the knowledge that he had sought her out from duty rather than undying passion. She had not thought herself a romantic, but apparently she was. So she had come down determined to be her normal, dutiful self—and had botched everything!

"I am a hopeless fool," she said to the empty room.

You should give sometimes.

"But every time I do, something awful happens."

Well, she hadn't given anything of herself this time, and he was gone anyway. James had given everything so far in this marriage: he'd courted her, arranged the wedding, seduced her, been gentle and humorous and understanding when she'd been moody and difficult. She'd shared only passion and the knowledge of old pain, afraid of feeling emotion, let alone expressing it. That was no way to begin a marriage; it was certainly no way to develop and sustain one.

Didn't she have a duty to be a good wife?

She almost smiled. Of course she did—especially to a man who compared her to warrior queens and legendary heroines. Especially to a man who rode to London to fight a duel for her honor.

A man like that didn't come along very often. What did it matter how and why they'd finally come together? Having James Marbury in her life was a gift from the gods. It would be hubris not to accept such a gift. She would take the gift, take the man. Honor him, cherish him, and love him for always. That was the least she could do in return for the joy he gave her—then, now, and hopefully for always.

Honoria felt as brave as Boudicaa, Zenobia, and Roxane rolled into one as she strode boldly out of the dining room and called to the butler in the hall, "Charles, have my coach readied—I need to go to Spain today."

Chapter 21

Joshua Menzies blamed his run of bad luck on the Honorable James Marbury. He could hardly wait until the man was dead, and one way or another, he *would* be dead soon. Menzies didn't put much faith in Captain Russell to do the job, even though he'd spent the last two days keeping Russell sober and assisting him with target practice. None of Russell's fellow officers or gambling cronies took any interest in acting as his second, so Menzies had become Russell's best friend and bosom companion in the hopes of destroying Marbury. For Menzies was certain there was no getting to the woman until her new husband was out of the way. Perhaps Marbury was sniffing around Honoria for the same reason Menzies was, to get his hands on the missing treasure, so Menzies was happy to see Marbury dead to get him out of the way as much as for revenge.

Menzies had discovered that Russell was good with a gun, but reckless. Right now the Royal Navy captain strode angrily through the damp grass in scuffed boots, heedless of the misting morning rain, still furious at the comment Marbury's father had made about Russell deserving an impersonal bullet rather than honorable steel to pay for his crimes of omission and commission.

"Omission and commission," Russell muttered now as he paced nervously back and forth in the walled orchard garden behind the Spanish Embassy. "What did that dried-up stick mean by that?"

Russell didn't bother lowering his voice, even though the viscount stood only a few yards away, talking quietly with an embassy official. A surgeon and his assistant from the embassy were also standing by. The Spanish diplomat resembled an older, darker version of James Marbury, so Menzies assumed he was the uncle who'd arranged for the field of honor to be on foreign soil. Pity. Menzies had had a nice, quiet spot in Smithfield picked out as a site for the duel. There, if Russell failed to kill Marbury, Menzies would have had an ambush of toughs ready to take Marbury out of the picture. Of course, the milords didn't bother taking a mere vicar's suggestion. But he had to admit that a foreign embassy was the ideal spot for dueling. The English government could not reach inside these walls, and the Spanish ambassador was happy to look the other way in an affair of honor.

"Honor," Menzies grumbled bitterly. Honor was for fools and the wealthy. It was Honoria he wanted. How amusing that it was Honoria the duelists fought over, when in the end it was Joshua Menzies who would have her—at least until he had the information he wanted from her. He rubbed his hands together in anticipation, then straightened alertly as James Marbury came striding into the garden.

Menzies's smile grew wider and wider as Marbury approached his relatives, though he hid his expression behind the prayer book he held up. The big man moved tiredly and didn't look as if he'd gotten any sleep, but he looked dangerous enough. Menzies supposed a hangover would be too much to ask for, but he added that wish to his prayers.

Russell moved beneath the shelter of a spreading oak and stared sullenly at the Marbury party. Menzies took the opportunity to move surreptitiously closer.

"Fine," he heard James Marbury say to the viscount in response to a worried question. "Is everything ready?" The viscount nodded, and produced a leather pistol case that he'd protected from the rain within the folds of his greatcoat.

The viscount touched his son on the arm,

then turned toward Menzies. "Reverend?"

Menzies straightened and stepped forward to fulfill his duties as second. He had a nice little speech prepared to humbly beg the combatants to reconsider in the name of God. It would be quite pretty, and hopefully completely ineffectual. He wanted to see some blood for all the trouble he'd been through!

"My lords," he began as the Viscount of Brislay clicked open the gun case for his inspection. "I—"

"Let's get on with it." Russell shoved him aside and snatched a pistol out of the case. He moved swiftly to stand toe to toe and eye to eye with James Marbury, then drew his lips back in an ugly sneer.

Marbury yawned, the back of his hand politely covering his mouth. "Yes," he said after he'd stared Russell down. He took the second pistol from the case. "Let us get this over with."

The Spanish diplomat came to stand between the men, placing them back to back after he made certain the single shot pistols were clean and loaded. Menzies, the attending physician, and the viscount moved back under the tree to witness the combat.

Honoria Pyne was the heir to a ducal title: hauteur, arrogance, and regal self-assurance were hers by birthright and training. She wouldn't even have bothered to knock, except the embassy door was locked. The icy formality of the man who opened the door did not halt her from coming inside. She did not wait just inside the door as requested when the butler went to fetch an official to speak with her. She barely took notice of the protesting attachés as she brazenly strode down the hall in search of a door to the rear garden.

Dawn was just now breaking. She had to hurry—to stop the fighting, or possibly grab a stick and beat both fools taking part in the duel senseless. She didn't know what she was going to do; she simply knew that nothing and no one was going to stop her from reaching James's side. She had quite a nice crowd of protesting Spaniards bustling around her by the time she found the garden door. She slammed the door on her small entourage as she stepped out into the misty gray day once more.

She threw the hood of her cloak back to take a better look around, holding her spectacles in her hand as wet lenses did not help her vision in the rain. Squinting, she made out a neat path through formally laid out flowers, and a dark blotch in the distance that had to be a row of trees. She hurried toward the little woods. As she drew closer she discerned the blurred forms of a group of people, two of them pacing away from each other. Honoria quickened her steps. One of the men was tall, dark-haired, broad-shouldered, and dearer than life to her. She didn't need her spectacles to know every detail of beloved face and form.

Then the duelists stopped and turned, arms raised.

Honoria hiked up her skirts and ran.

The sound of the double gunshots was momentarily deafening, but James turned when he thought he heard his name cried out. For a moment acrid gunsmoke blew into his face and blinded him. Then, through the gray mist, a copper-haired vision in silver came rushing toward him.

"James!" she called again.

"Honoria!" He dropped the empty pistol and ran to meet her, scooping her up in his arms and into a hard, deep kiss. She clung to him as tightly as he held her, her mouth on his hot and eager, her lush body eagerly molded to his. Her gray cape swirled around them like a storm cloud as he whirled her in a delirious, delighted circle.

"You came!" His voice was an intense whisper, his lips very close to hers. "You came." He set her on the ground, and pushed her cape away to reveal the silvery gray dress underneath. He put his hands on her waist, the satin sleek and smooth beneath his fingers. "You wore your wedding gown."

Her eyes were shining as they gazed into his, but she blushed a little, her hands twisting in the rich fabric of her skirt. "I thought—to give something— That, perhaps, we could make a new beginning . . ."

James gently touched her face, her throat, traced his finger around her lips, memorizing her all over again. His gaze locked onto hers and he nodded seriously. "A new beginning." He'd never been happier in his life. "I would very much like that."

Her smile of joy was all the sunlight he needed. Her kiss, when she pulled his mouth to hers a moment later, was rich with the promise of endless passion. If his father had not put his hand firmly on his shoulder, and said his name sternly, James knew that what sparked between them would quickly turn into more than a kiss.

James gave his father an annoyed look. "Yes?"

Not only was his father standing at his side, but his uncle and the vicar were also gathered around them. The three men looked as grave and grim as though they were attending a funeral. It was only then that James remembered where he was and what he'd been doing. Keeping his arm around his wife's waist, he looked toward the physician tending the man on the ground. "Will he live?" James called in Spanish.

The surgeon's assistant came to his feet and nodded deferentially. "No doubt, my lord," he replied in the same language.

"You didn't kill him?" Honoria asked indignantly.

"That's what I love about you," he told her. "You can sound affronted in any circumstances." He touched the tip of her nose teasingly as he spoke, and she answered with a small smile.

The fine rain had stopped, so Honoria put her spectacles on. The group around her came into focus. "I'm glad you didn't kill him," she told her husband. "Derrick isn't worth having on your conscience."

"He isn't worth causing a diplomatic incident over," James replied. "A flesh wound at a fight at an embassy might be overlooked, but the Queen's government would make a fuss over losing one of their Navy captains—even a useless one."

Honoria felt no curiosity to glance toward where Derrick lay; had no sympathy to offer the man. Russell had made his own trouble and must live with the consequences like everyone else. She supposed she should feel some compassion for his condition, but all she cared about was that James was safe.

A pair of footmen arrived with a stretcher to carry Derrick away.

Then Reverend Menzies stepped closer to her and James. "This field of battle is no place for you, Lady Alexandra." He put a gentle, consoling hand on her arm. "You must find these events unnerving." He gazed deep into her eyes.

She had only met the vicar a few days before, yet every time she saw him she found something about him disturbingly familiar. He's a good man, she reminded herself. He meant well, and tried to do good work. He was trying to help fallen women and needed her help in this worthy endeavor.

"I am truly sorry for that young man," Menzies went on, with a glance toward Derrick as he was carried into the embassy. "I tried and tried to make him see the error of his ways in the last several days." He patted Honoria's arm. "I will be at his bedside when he awakens to pray with him. In the meantime," he went on, voice and gaze insistent, "I beg of you, my lady, to come to St. Ambrose's with me. I wish to hold a proper prayer service in Captain Russell's name. Also," he said, with a brief glance toward James, "to pray in thanksgiving for your beloved husband's safe deliverance from danger. And perhaps to bless your marriage one more time," he added with a kind smile, glancing over the silvery gray gown she wore.

Honoria looked at James with open love. "I prayed for your safety all the way from Lacey House," she told him.

He touched her cheek. "Then there's no need for another prayer right now, is there?"

Before she could answer, Edward Marbury

stepped in. "I think that is a splendid idea, Reverend Menzies," he said solemnly, and ran a serious gaze over her and James. "Don't you agree?" The tone was not so much a question as it was an order. "Your cause was just, son, but prayer and forgiveness for those who have wronged us is good for all our souls," he told James. "And it would not hurt you to reflect on your life and future in a house of God."

"And this will be an opportunity for you to acquaint yourself with my charity work, Lady Alexandra," Reverend Menzies chimed in. "You did promise to take a personal interest in my young ladies."

Honoria did not recall making any such promise, but supposed it would be the right thing to do. He had said that there was one particular young woman he wanted to talk to her about. She and James exchanged glances while the minister and James's father looked on expectantly. They were trapped by these two good men. They were going to church.

James leaned close and whispered in her ear. "One hour and one prayer, that's enough. I want to take you to bed."

Honoria didn't even have the grace to blush. "Agreed," she stated firmly. "Definitely."

James turned a concerned look on Honoria after looking out the carriage's window. He dropped the velvet curtain back in place. "We're heading deeper into the slums," he told his wife. "Where is this church?"

"Somewhere near the Tower docks, I'm told. St. Ambrose's is quite a poor parish." Honoria sighed. "I normally don't mind helping the poor, but I do object to Reverend Menzies's timing."

"It will be over with soon." James settled his arm more comfortably around her, and his heart swelled with love when she put her head trustingly on his shoulder. He gently stroked her shining hair. "My father's right, I suppose." Though he resented the interference in their lives. Their lives. He smiled at the thought of them going through life as a couple. He couldn't think of anything better. Still . . . "Speaking of fathers, yours will be pleased that I didn't spoil your chance to become a lady-in-waiting to the queen."

Honoria lifted her head as she said, "I don't want to be a lady-in-waiting to the queen."

The rebellious expression on her face mirrored the rebellion stirring in him. He stroked her cheek, and straightened the spectacles perched on her nose. "Tell me," he said at last. "What do you want? What do *we* want?" he added as she went still and thoughtful. "What do we want to do with our lives?"

They stared at each other while the carriage rolled on through the bumpy, narrow cobbled streets. The smell rising off the river began to permeate the air, thick and sour with sewage and fish.

James barely noticed it. He was more interested in the new notion that was forming in his head. He took his wife's hands. "What if," he began, "we do what we want to do rather than what our fathers want us to do?"

"But what?" Honoria asked. "What do you want to do with your life, James?"

The carriage came to a halt. "The important thing is that we do something that makes us happy." As James helped Honoria out of the coach in front of the tumbledown church, he said, "Let's get this over with then settle in for a long talk—inside the privacy of that lovely curtained bed of yours."

"Of ours," she corrected with a saucy toss of her head. There was a sauciness to her walk, as well, as she proceeded him toward where the Reverend Menzies stood waiting for them by the church door. James lingered a few steps behind her, enticed by her swaying hips even though she was modestly covered with her dark cape. He smiled, reminded of the allure of veiled women in the bazaars of Algiers.

"Welcome, welcome," Menzies greeted them at the church door. He stepped away from it and gestured them through a churchyard dotted with untended, leaning headstones. "Let us go to the vicarage," he told them as he led the way. "There is something I want to show you."

The man sounded nervous. Honoria exchanged a glance with James, then they followed the vicar's thin form.

Joshua Menzies didn't know where the ruffians he'd hired to do the dirty work had gotten to, but he had hopes the three men would show up at any moment. Why couldn't Marbury and the blasted woman have arrived late? Aristos were never supposed to be punctual. They were supposed to keep their inferiors waiting. Instead here they were, and he was without the assistance he'd counted on to get the job done. The woman he could deal with, but Marbury was *huge*—the man's shoulders alone nearly filled Menzies's small study.

Inside, Menzies's mind raced. This was a mistake. He should have taken them into the church and said some prayers over them first. What had he been thinking? This wasn't like him. He did not panic. He took a deep breath and forced himself to be calm—his helpers would be here at any moment. He walked toward his desk, confident that he could control the situation until help arrived. Besides, if worse came to worst, he had everything he needed secreted in the desk drawer.

"Please be seated," he said as his guests looked with distaste at the filthy room. "Yes," he agreed with their silent disapproval. "It is in quite a filthy state. My housekeeper . . ." He shrugged. "Well, the slattern ran off with a sailor last week. She'll wander back eventually. She always does." He was tempted to be even blunter, just to watch the shock on their features deepen. He noticed how they sat close together in the chairs before his desk, their hands clasped across the short distance. She'd thrown off her cape, and the shimmering dress spread like a rich ocean around her. That she wore a ballgown in the middle of the day was most unconventional—but then, everything about the woman seemed to be. "How many languages do you read, Lady Alexandra?" Menzies asked.

She looked surprised, but answered readily, "Eight."

"I am fluent in eleven," he told her. He sat behind the desk and slowly opened the drawer. He gestured toward the blue bottle on the edge of the desk. "Would you care for a drink? Have you ever tasted gin, Lady Alexandra?"

She lifted her head proudly. "Gin?"

Her reaction to his effrontery made him smile. "It is all I have to offer, my dear," he responded, sounding almost like the humble clergyman he'd been trained to be. "Have I mentioned my father to either of you?" He glanced between the pair. Marbury looked half ready to throttle him. "You're annoyed, my lord." Menzies held up a hand and continued to speak in his vicar's voice. "Please bear with me. There is a purpose to what I have to say." Where the devil were those men?

"Purpose?" Marbury asked, eyes narrowed dangerously. Menzies saw him looking around warily, alert to any peril.

"You said there was something you wished to show us?" the woman added.

Menzies took out the letter and put it on the table. "This took over a year to reach me," he told them. "It is from my father." He shook his head sadly. "He has fallen on hard times, I'm afraid." He sighed, and looked directly at James Marbury. "My father is named Abraham."

"Really," Marbury responded without interest.

Menzies nodded. "We are an old Devonshire family, though our roots are in Scotland. Devonshire men are the finest sailors in Britain, you know. My father went to sea to make his fortune, and made it he did. Lost it, as well. Now it is up to me to restore what was ours." He picked up the letter. "My father has told me how." He looked at the woman. "I need your help, Honoria." Damning the missing henchmen, he lifted a pistol from inside the drawer.

Marbury was on his feet, knocking over his chair in his haste. Honoria was up an instant later. Marbury's eyes were on the gun, hers were on Marbury. Menzies found her devotion charming. Perhaps threatening her husband was the incentive to getting her cooperation. Besides, shooting her husband would be fun.

"Abraham?" Honoria said to Marbury. "Ibrahim? It's the same name in Arabic."

James carefully did not look at his wife. If he was going to get her safely out of this situation, he had to focus all his attention on Menzies. "Of course—Ibrahim Rais. I always knew he was European, but I didn't know he was English. I didn't know anything about his family."

"So you are the Spaniard he spoke of." Menzies brought up a second pistol.

Two guns, one man. This gave James an idea, and he moved fractionally away from Honoria.

Menzies sneered at him. "You know my father better than I do. He even says he loved you like a son."

"Oh, he did," James responded to the hysteria underlying the man's hatred. "And I wouldn't wish a father like that on any man."

"He has the scars to prove it," Honoria chimed in, and moved a half step from him.

James hid a smile as he realized she'd read his mind. Of course she had: they were of one mind, and spirit. He silently damned Menzies, and Ibrahim Rais, terrified he would lose the woman he loved, now that he had finally found her once more.

"He's a good father!" Menzies's voice was shrill. The man didn't seem to notice that his hands were widening as they slowly separated. "And I'm a good son. He wants his treasure—

it's my legacy. I'm going to do what he wants."

"Why?" James asked reasonably. He shrugged, the movement masking another step. He was getting closer to the gin bottle on the edge of the desk. Another step. Two.

"How?" Honoria countered, bringing Menzies's attention to her.

"You, Honoria," Menzies informed her. "Father says you are the key. That you translated his coded letter to me." He swung his gaze back to James. "The letter that you stole!"

"I did steal it," James admitted.

"I didn't translate it, however," Honoria said.

Menzies focused on her. "What?"

"I never got a chance to read it."

"What?" he demanded, insane fury boiling from him. He was quivering with rage and nerves.

Honoria appeared quite calm as she answered, "I saw it, but then your father tried to kill us and the French attacked." She shrugged and reached behind her for her cloak. "What with one thing and another, I never got around to reading the letter. Sorry . . . now, James?"

"Now!"

Honoria swung her cape at Menzies, and James snatched up the gin bottle and threw it. The cape swept one pistol from his hand; the bottle smashed into his other wrist. James was on Menzies before the pistols hit the floor. One gun fired as it landed, filling the room with a thunderous roar and the stink of gunsmoke. Honoria snatched up the still loaded pistol and held it while James knocked Menzies unconscious.

When he stood up, James took the gun from her.

"Good." She breathed a sigh of relief as his arm went around her shoulders. "I haven't the faintest notion how to use that thing. I suppose I could have hit him over the head with it if he'd overpowered you."

James looked down at the slender man on the floor, then indignantly at his wife. "Please!" Then he saw that she was joking to cover a bad set of nerves. "Come along," he said, and hustled her outside.

There he called for the coachman and footmen who had accompanied them, and gave instructions on guarding Menzies and fetching constables. A crowd slowly began to gather; he supposed the sound of a gunshot had attracted them.

It had begun to rain again, and he took off his coat and draped it over Honoria's shoulders. Then he took his wife into the dry warmth of the carriage and kissed her for a good, long time. As they waited for the constables to arrive they snuggled close, happy to be alive and together.

Finally, Honoria sighed and said, "Fathers."

"Funny how all three of us had obedience to

our fathers in common," James agreed.

She looked at him solemnly. "I'm not sure I'd call it funny." She glanced back at the church. "Tragic, in that man's case. I wonder what happened to that letter?" she added curiously.

"I still have it," James told her.

Honoria disentangled herself from his embrace and sat up straight. "What?" She sounded as indignant as Menzies had a few minutes before. "What do you mean, you still have it?"

He found her outraged expression adorable. He found *her* adorable. "I took it with me when we left my house." He watched her temper slowly flare as he explained, "At first I thought I might find someone else to translate it. Then it occurred to me that it might not be the best thing to show my face anywhere near Algiers, so I put it in a box and kept it as a memento. I didn't exactly have a lock of your hair to remember you by," he added, toying with a loose strand of her bright curls.

Honoria opened her mouth, but no words came out. He watched as her indignation slowly settled into thoughtfulness. She began to tap a finger slowly on her chin.

"What's going on in that pretty head of yours?" he asked.

"What do you want to do with our lives?" she asked in turn. "I don't have to be a duchess yet." She took his hands. "You don't have to manage estates or sit in the House of Lords or run off to your clubs and horse races. We don't have to go to balls if we don't want."

"Or ride to the hunt?" He got into the spirit of the thing. "I hate house parties."

"I loathe the opera. Court is boring."

"I'd like to build a house someday."

"Have babies—someday."

"Me, too." He took her by the shoulders, and knew his eyes were as bright as hers when he said, "We could go to Algiers."

She nodded eagerly. "No one would suspect Lord James Pyne-Marbury—"

"Or Marbury-Pyne—"

"—Of being Diego Moresco. The treasure might still be where Ibrahim Rais hid it. We could have quite an adventure."

"Do you want to go treasure hunting?" he asked her.

"You do need to get your silver sword back." She grinned. "Then we could go see the Pyramids." She bounced on the carriage seat. "Do you want to go to Egypt, too? I've been learning to read hieroglyphics."

"Of course you have." He beamed proudly. "As for the rest of the treasure—" James waved a hand. "We could give it to the poor. The sword I'd keep as a memento."

Her smile was bright with excited delight. "To hang over the mantel of the house we're going to build?"

"I'll hang it over the bed," he declared with a wicked laugh.

"Would that be wise, my love?" She kissed him gently, then with growing passion, until she had him panting with desire.

"You're right," he agreed, bending her backward on the carriage seat. His hands stroked her lovely breasts until she moaned and arched passionately against him. "The way we fight, having a sword over the bed might not be such a good idea."

Coming next month

Two terrific historical romances

By

Two unforgettable writers

Only from Avon Romance

The de Montefortes are back! . . .

Danelle Harmon's de Monteforte men are some of the most sinfully sexy heroes you've met in a long, long time. Now meet Lord Andrew de Monteforte, *THE DEFIANT ONE*, who meets his match in the sassy Lady Celsie Blake.

And don't miss Gayle Callen's latest . . . *MY LADY'S GUARDIAN*. Beautiful and rich, Lady Margery is a prize for any man—but the king has decreed she must choose a husband quickly. So she asks Gareth Beaumont to pretend to be her suitor . . . never dreaming he wanted her in his arms—for real!

Dear Reader,

Next month is June, and romance—and weddings!—are in the air. So if you've enjoyed the Avon romance you've just finished, then you won't want to miss any of next month's delicious Avon love stories, guaranteed to fulfill all of your most romantic dreams.

Love and romance in the old west is the theme of Susan Kay Law's sensuous, spectacular Treasure *THE MOST WANTED BACHELOR*. The richest man in town knows he has to take a bride, but he'll be darned if he'll marry someone who's just after his money! Then a pert young gal catches his eye—could it be that the most eligible man in town is about to marry?

Every now and then you can't help but wonder what it would be like to marry a millionaire. In Elizabeth Bevarly's contemporary *HOW TO TRAP A TYCOON*, Dorsey MacGuinness has written a bestseller that's become a handbook for single gals across the nation. But sexy Adam Darien isn't about to succumb to some gold-digging female . . .

Historical fans will be thrilled—Danelle Harmon's de Monteforte men are back! This time, *THE DEFIANT ONE*, Lord Andrew de Monteforte, meets his match in sexy Lady Celsie Blake, and when they're caught in a compromising position wedding bells ring . . .

Lady Margery Welles has the uncommon privilege of choosing her own husband, but she's in no hurry to wed. So she selects dashing knight Gareth Beaumont to pose as her suitor in Gayle Callen's *MY LADY'S GUARDIAN*.

Yes, June is the month for weddings—and none are more romantic, more beautiful, more sensuous than the ones you'll find here at Avon Romance.

Enjoy!

Lucia Macro

Lucia Macro
Senior Editor